Readers love the Belladonna Arms series by JOHN INMAN

Serenading Stanley

"I have such respect for this author. He uses both humor and drama to deliver a brilliant love story that never panders but is always intelligent and just pure fun."

—Gay Book Reviews

Work in Progress

"It's official… I'm head over heels with the Belladonna Arms."

—Sinfully Gay Romance Book Reviews

Coming Back

"I loved the witty writing style, the fully realized characters, the emotional storyline, the vivid setting. I loved everything about it and I hope this is not the last we will see of the Belladonna Arms and its tenants."

—Prism Book Alliance

Ben and Shiloh

"Author John Inman has built a family, beginning with a fairy godfather in Arthur, and has just continued to add to the group with one fascinating person after another."

—The Novel Approach

By JOHN INMAN

Published by DREAMSPINNER PRESS
www.dreamspinnerpress.com

Ginger Snaps

JOHN INMAN

Published by

DREAMSPINNER PRESS

5032 Capital Circle SW, Suite 2, PMB# 279, Tallahassee, FL 32305-7886 USA
www.dreamspinnerpress.com

Ginger Snaps
© 2018 John Inman.

Cover Art
© 2018 Aaron Anderson.
aaronbydesign55@gmail.com
Cover content is for illustrative purposes only and any person depicted on the cover is a model.

Trade Paperback ISBN: 978-1-64080-030-4
Digital ISBN: 978-1-64080-031-1
Library of Congress Control Number: 2017915079
Trade Paperback published April 2018
v. 1.0

Printed in the United States of America
∞
This paper meets the requirements of
ANSI/NISO Z39.48-1992 (Permanence of Paper).

Chapter 1

GIDEON CHASE stood on the corner of Broadway and Sixteenth Street and gazed up to the crest of the hill where an old six-story apartment building loomed. From a distance, the place didn't look too bad, standing there against a backdrop of cloudless, azure sky. It was framed by a couple of eucalyptus trees soaring high at either side like bookends. The building could use a paint job, of course. And the stucco was crumbling in spots. The wooden window frames appeared to have been gnawed on by rats, or more likely, rotted to mush by the relentless California sun beating down on them for God knows how many decades.

Well, okay, let's be honest, Gideon thought, *the building looks like crap. Still, it's a place to live. Maybe.*

On this humid summer afternoon, curtains hung limp through screenless windows like so many dog tongues panting in the heat, praying desperately for a cool breeze to come along and relieve them of their misery. Without screens on all those windows, Gideon couldn't help wondering how the tenants kept bugs, pigeons, and the odd cat burglar out, as if any respectable cat burglar would burgle a dump like the Belladonna Arms, which is what the building called itself. Gideon knew this by the rattletrap sign leaning precariously atop the roof of the structure. In daylight the sign read Belladonna Arms in tortured, rusted steel. At night, he knew, the rusty letters were replaced by flickering orange neon, tattooing its message onto the San Diego skyline like a beacon to mediocrity.

Standing motionless, staring up the hill with the blazing hot sun blasting down on his head, Gideon heaved a sigh. He patted his wallet to make sure it was still safely tucked in his back pocket. Everything he owned was in there. All the cash anyway. All the rest of his belongings were gone, of course. For that, he had his ex-lover to thank. Manny. Manny the fucktard. Manny the conniving little asshole who broke Gideon's heart and not being content with simply breaking his heart, also tossed everything Gideon owned into a Salvation Army collection bin while Gideon was at work. Books, TV, CDs, clothes—the whole kit and caboodle.

What kind of person does that sort of thing?

The only possessions Gideon could still claim as his own were his car, which had most certainly seen better days, and his laptop, which, thank God, had been stowed in the trunk of the car where Manny couldn't get his hands on it, or he would have thrown that away too.

A desperate mental recap of what he jokingly referred to as his "financial situation" caused the weight of the world to bear down once again upon Gideon's shoulders, and when it did, it squeezed out a couple of tears from his cornflower-blue eyes. The tears slid a familiar path down his ruddy, freckled cheeks until he gathered up the gumption to brush them away. They weren't the first tears he had brushed away this day. And they wouldn't be the last. Just realizing that fact made him heave another sigh and tear up all over again.

Gideon turned his head and studied his reflection in a storefront window. Under that merciless, pounding sun, his shock of red hair looked like someone had set a blowtorch to it, igniting it into a crown of glorious flames. His freckled face glowed pink in the heat too, and even his eyes were red from all the crying he'd done. He stuck his tongue out at his reflection, which of course made the whole portrait even redder. He still wore his Office Depot work clothes—black pants, red shirt with the little red name tag reading Gideon Chase pinned to his chest. Thanks to Manny, everything else he owned was currently being sorted, pawed over, and priced under a dollar at a Salvation Army warehouse somewhere, which was probably more than most of it was worth.

Sigh.

That last sigh was so pathetic, Gideon actually had to bite back a derisive chuckle while he averted his gaze from his sorryass reflection in the storefront window.

The chuckle died a quick death when the sidewalk beneath his feet gave a lurch. As if his life wasn't unsteady enough, San Diego had also been experiencing a flurry of minor, and not so minor, earthquakes over the past few days, sparking rumors of the Big One being about to hit. It was a rumor that surfaced in San Diego periodically, although with the number of tremors hitting lately, Gideon couldn't be sure this time still qualified as mere rumor.

Like he cared. Gideon already had enough to worry about. The Big One would just have to work a little harder to grab his undivided attention.

And so it did.

Staring once again up the hill while grabbing a parking meter to maintain his balance as the earth continued to jiggle beneath him, Gideon's jaw fell open as he watched an adobe roofing tile slide off the top of the Belladonna Arms and crash to the ground next to a parked car. When the tile shattered, the ensuing racket set off the car's alarm and startled the hell out of a really heavy lady in a flowery muumuu who was carrying a bag of groceries up the sidewalk. As if the flowery muumuu wasn't gaudy enough, she also wore a huge hibiscus blossom stuck in her hair. The exploding roofing tile caused the woman to spin around so fast the hibiscus blossom flew off in one direction and the bag of groceries sailed off in another, disgorging what looked like a spray of oranges, which filled the air around her. She was funny enough to look at *before* she jumped three feet into the air, dislodging her cargo and bellowing a less than feminine roar of terror that Gideon could hear half a block away. *During* the jump, she was even funnier. Poor dear.

Gideon guiltily wiped the smirk from his face, reached around to pat his wallet again to make sure it was still there, and waited for the earth to stop shaking. It was then that a hand came down on his shoulder, and it was Gideon's turn to jump straight up into the air and look like a fool, proving once again that payback is indeed a bitch.

He whirled to find his acquaintance Shiloh Smart standing there in a kilt and all the Celtic accoutrements that went along with it—tartan shoulder wrap, billowy white shirt with puffy sleeves, knee-high socks, the traditional sporran covering his crotch. The kilt ensemble seemed to fit the guy, although Gideon knew Shiloh was about as Scottish as a bowl of knishes, what with him really being Jewish and all. Shiloh was only dressed like a highlander because he was on his way home from work at the Scottish restaurant up the street. In fact, that's where the two had met. Shiloh served Gideon his very first order of cock-a-leekie soup and rollmops not two months prior. They'd been quasi-friends ever since, although today was the first time they had ever actually met outside the restaurant.

Gideon patted his chest as if calming his startled heart. He had been expecting Shiloh to join him, but that unanticipated tap on the shoulder during a jostle 4 on the Richter scale had clearly frazzled his already frazzled nerves. It wasn't his fault the total collapse of his private life, not to mention a shitload of earthquakes, had made him jittery.

"You came," Gideon said, tacking the words onto the tail end of a gasp.

Shiloh scooped him into his arms and gave him a robust hug. "I told you I would." He eased Gideon to arm's length to get a better view of the overall package. Apparently, the view wasn't all that promising. He offered a consoling pout. "You all right, Gid? How are you holding up? You look stressed."

A little sympathy was all it took to get a new burst of waterworks flowing. Tears blurred Gideon's vision yet again. He had cried so much the last two days he was starting to feel dehydrated, like his self-esteem had been tossed in a juicer and had every ounce of joy leached away, leaving nothing behind but a smear of desiccated pulp and a few quivering nerve endings.

Gideon ran his fingers through his hair and then regretted it. With his flaming red mane—which in truth wasn't that much redder than Shiloh's—standing on end, he must at long last look *truly* insane. He blinked away that last upsurge of tears, expelled another great, long, put-upon sigh, and stared at Shiloh in disbelief.

"Stressed? *Stressed?* Why *wouldn't* I be stressed? I'm sleeping in my car. I haven't showered in two days. I've got nothing!" As soon as he spat the words out, he deflated like an old balloon. He dropped his forehead to Shiloh's shoulder, embarrassed to let the guy see him spill yet another tear. Soaking up Shiloh's sympathy and drawing strength from it, he asked wearily, "Did you talk to Ben?"

Ben was Shiloh's lover. They lived together under the same roof. And that roof had a big neon sign sitting on it. The sign read Belladonna Arms. Yep. The building up the hill.

Shiloh offered a promising wink. "I talked to Ben, and Ben talked to his uncle Arthur. He's expecting you, and everything is set. Arthur understands your predicament, and he's going to give you a break on the rent for a while until you get on your feet."

Gideon's eyes popped open wide. "He is? Why would any landlord on the planet be nice enough to do a thing like that for a total stranger?"

"Because it's Arthur," Shiloh said with a patient smile. "Once you get to know him, you'll understand."

"Doesn't he have any business sense at all?"

"Not much."

"Is he crazy?"

Shiloh scrunched his mouth to the side, clearly trying to waylay a grin. "Let's not go there. We don't have time."

Gideon frowned, looking more confused than ever. "Umm. Okay."

Shiloh gave him a reassuring boop on the chin with a friendly fist, took a moment to straighten Gideon's shirt collar, and took a swipe at Gideon's hair, which was still standing on end. He frowned, as if realizing he had made no improvement at all, and said, "Fuck it. It doesn't matter what you look like. With your red hair, Arthur's going to love you. He has a thing for redheaded young men."

"Gay, huh?"

Shiloh rolled his eyes up into his head and coughed up a snorfling chortle. "You might say that."

Gideon gazed shyly down at his feet, then lifted his eyes to Shiloh's face. "I don't know what I would have done without you and Ben coming to the rescue." He blinked, trying to head off another spate of tears. "Thank you again for helping me out."

A very attractive blush rose to Shiloh's cheeks. He gave Gideon another gentle boop on the chin. "Don't be stupid. What are friends for?" He stepped back to stare up and down the city street. "Think that latest earthquake is over?"

They both stood silent for a minute. Gideon tried to gauge the relative stability of the earth's crust beneath their feet. It seemed steady enough. He cocked his head and listened to the city cranking back to life around them: the roar of San Diego traffic, the occasional toot of a car horn two or three blocks away, the raucous call of a seagull sweeping low over their heads, clearly out of his element among the pigeons and high-rises as if maybe the most recent spate of seismic activity had somehow jammed the bird's internal GPS and left him rudderless in unfamiliar territory.

The car alarm up the hill was silent now too. The city was back to normal, at least until the next tremor.

"That must be the twentieth shake-up in three days," Gideon said. "I hope a tree fell on Manny's head. Or a sinkhole opened up and swallowed his cheating ass." Now that was a cheerful thought. "Think I could be that lucky?"

Shiloh shrugged. He smiled and his dimples popped into view. "A man can hope." He glanced up the hill toward the Belladonna Arms. "Oh look! There's Arthur now!"

Gideon trailed his gaze up the hill to see what Shiloh was staring at, but all he could make out was the lady in the muumuu crawling around the sidewalk gathering up her spilled groceries. From this distance he couldn't be sure, but she now appeared to have the hibiscus blossom clamped in her teeth like a flamenco dancer. Gideon didn't see a landlord or anyone who looked like an Arthur anywhere.

He was about to say so, when Shiloh grabbed him by the shirttail and said, "Come on. Let's introduce you. Where's your car?"

"In the only free space I could find."

Gideon pointed down the street to where his battered Toyota was parked a block up Broadway on an overpass that spanned a freeway. A sudden rush of freeway traffic and the hum of a semi or two barreling along the interstate down below cast a pall of white noise over the sun-drenched air so that Gideon and Shiloh had to raise their voices to speak above it. An air horn bellowed somewhere off in the distance, causing Gideon to jump again. He really was a nervous wreck.

"Don't worry," Shiloh said, his eyes kind. "It's just a truck."

Embarrassed to be such an emotional twit, Gideon tried to straighten his shoulders and smile. He coughed into his hand to clear his throat, shooting for butch but no doubt achieving far less. "So. Do you really think this Arthur friend of yours will rent me an apartment?"

Shiloh gave him a good-natured bump with his hip. "Don't worry. You're already in. Arthur can't wait to meet you. There's been a vacancy since Ben and I moved in together. Arthur's been aching to fill it. You'll be two floors up from us. Neighbor."

"I'm still not sure I can afford to pay first and last month's rent plus a deposit and a—"

"I told you. It's taken care of. Arthur understands. He really does."

"I hate being a charity case."

Shiloh eyed him sadly. "You're not a charity case. You're a friend who needs a little help. That's all."

"I'm not Arthur's friend."

"No, but you're mine, and with Arthur, friendships expand exponentially. If I say you're a friend, then Arthur accepts you as one too."

Gideon dipped his eyelashes. "Am I really your friend?"

Shiloh stepped forward and scooped him into another embrace. "Yes, you are. You don't think I'm doing all this because of the lousy buck and a half you always tip me at the restaurant, do you? Now stop beating yourself up. Think of today as your first step on the way to a fresh start."

"I only tip you a buck and a half because that's all I can afford."

"I know. I was being a facetious bitch."

"Oh. Well, you did it really well."

Shiloh grinned. "Thanks."

Gideon sniffed and eased himself from Shiloh's arms. He tugged at his clothes, trying to pull himself together. Seeking something mundane to say so he wouldn't be such an endlessly depressing drama queen, he ventured, "It's been a long time since I've lived on my own."

Shiloh grinned. "Has it? Well, I wouldn't worry about that either. People who move into the Arms don't live alone very long."

"What's that supposed to mean?"

"You'll find out. Here we go. Let me introduce you to Arthur."

By this time they had scaled the hill and were standing behind the large woman wearing the flowery muumuu. She was still down on her hands and knees, scuttling about, gathering up all the oranges that had rolled to hell and back when the earthquake hit. The hibiscus blossom was no longer between her teeth but once again anchored over her ear where it belonged. Her back was to them—well, her ass actually, and a bountiful specimen it was too. Broad, deep, and quivering with indignation.

Gideon looked up and down the street and still didn't see an Arthur anywhere. At least he didn't until the muumuu-clad woman grunted her way to her feet and turned around.

Only then did the woman spot the two young men lurking behind her not three feet away. "Holy shit!" she yelped in a deep, tubalike voice, clearly startled by their sudden approach.

"Holy shit!" Gideon yelped right back before he could stop himself. He was startled too, but for a different reason.

That reason being this—the muumuu-clad woman wasn't a muumuu-clad woman at all. It was a muumuu-clad man in drag. And the worst drag ever. Aside from the floral ensemble, he might have been a truck driver. Big, brawny, and about as feminine as a fire hydrant. He wore a towering red wig, piled high with curls and with a couple of flowers stuck in here and there like afterthoughts. As if the flowers in his hair and the flowers on the muumuu and the hibiscus blossom tucked over his ear weren't enough, he also wore a lei of plastic orchids draped around his big, beefy neck, a miniature lei of tinier orchids wrapped around each massive wrist, and bigass dangling earrings in the shape of hydrangea blooms that bobbed around on either side of his watermelon-sized head like tennis balls. As if in counterpoint to all the decorative foliage, the drag queen clearly hadn't shaved in days. Anywhere. His face was hairy. His arms were hairy. His cleavage was hairy. Even his chubby shins, which were visible under the muumuu's knee-length hem, were hairy. As if all the body hair wasn't disconcerting enough, there was also a half-smoked cigar stuck up under the edge of the wig by his left ear for storage, and he was sweating buckets. His eyes had that desperately horrified stare that drug addicts acquire when they are about thirty-six hours late for a fix.

Or maybe he just needed plant food.

Gideon chuckled at that thought, then stopped chuckling when the earth gave another nudge beneath their feet. Apparently, tectonic plates were *still* shifting. And nerves were still rattling. The drag queen slapped a meaty hand to his chest with enough force to kill a cow while the other hand slammed the bag of oranges to his heaving bosom. His eyes, framed in the longest fake eyelashes Gideon had ever seen in his life, opened wide enough to look like two paper plates someone had hastily glued to the front of the drag queen's sweaty, unshaven, panic-addled face.

The old queen gritted his teeth and emitted a long-drawn-out squeal like a frightened Tilt-a-Whirl rider being spun to hell and back immediately after eating three chili dogs and a pound of onion rings, and trying not to barf it all up while praying for the ride to fucking *end already*.

When the jostling did finally stop and the earth quit jiggling beneath their feet, the drag queen blinked a couple of times, sucked in enough air to fill a hot-air balloon, and pounded his massive bosom with another cow-crushing blow, inadvertently juicing a couple of oranges while he was at it. Gideon and the other two stood on the street corner staring at each other, tense as statues, waiting for another tremor. When it didn't come, knotted muscles gradually relaxed, and Gideon breathed a sigh of relief, as did Shiloh. The drag queen, however, still looked ready to jump out of his panties at the slightest provocation.

"Arthur?" Shiloh ventured, flapping a hand in front of the drag queen's face. "You okay?" Gideon stared. *This* was Arthur, His prospective landlord!

Arthur took a moment, as if to blink away any residual panic. He slowly focused, first on Shiloh's face, then on Gideon's. His bloodred lips pooched into a big, kissy, inquisitive blob. Scrolling down from Gideon's head, his saucerlike eyes traveled south to Gideon's crotch, then down to his feet, back up to his crotch (where they lingered longer than they really should have) before finally climbing the rest of the way north to finish the journey back where they started, at Gideon's startled face.

"You must be him!" Arthur bawled, causing Gideon to jump. Tears sprouted in Arthur's eyes, the earthquake clearly forgotten—at least for the moment. "You're the poor boy who's come for help from your loving Auntie Arthur." He spread his arms wide, causing another orange to fly out of the bag and disappear into a hedge some six feet away. "Oh, honey, welcome home!"

Gideon forced himself to stand his ground when Arthur thrust the bag of remaining oranges at Shiloh and hurled himself forward. He dragged Gideon into a bone-snapping embrace, making him grunt, while Shiloh looked on, clearly amused at the horrified expression on Gideon's face.

"You poor sweet thing!" Arthur cooed down at Gideon, who stood a head shorter and a good hundred and fifty pounds lighter and who must have looked no bigger than a minute wrapped in Arthur's massive, hairy arms with his teeny tiny head buried between Arthur's gargantuan tits. "You poor, poor shattered dear! You heartbroken homeless waif!"

"I'm not *that* heartbroken," Gideon mumbled into a mouthful of muumuu.

"And brave too!" Arthur wailed all the louder. "So crushed and lost and cute and ginger and wounded and *brave*! Oh lordy, honey, you're just the most precious thing *ever*!" Arthur thrust Gideon to arm's length, thereby whiplashing Gideon's head and causing his teeth to rattle, then let his eyes range over Gideon yet again like he was inspecting a side of beef in a butcher-shop window. Seeming to like what he saw, he yanked Gideon into another spleen-bruising hug. By now Gideon was limp as a ragdoll, so pummeled he could barely fight back. Arthur absorbed him into his bosom like an Ebola virus gobbling up a white blood cell.

Clearly not content with smashing one young man in his arms, Arthur reached out and dragged Shiloh into the hug as well. While the armload of redheads flapped in his embrace like a mess of freshly landed salmon, Arthur cooed and crooned and purred to them until Gideon reached a state of utter humiliation, to say nothing of breathlessness. Shiloh too was gasping for air. Arthur must finally have caught on, and taking pity at last, he propped them on their feet and stepped back to study them one more time, his face beaming, his wig askew, and one great breast missing entirely since it had been squeezed around to the back where it dangled over Arthur's shoulder blade like a dowager's hump. With a shake of the shoulders, he swung it back into place, calm as you please, as if his tits were prone to migrate twenty times a day and it didn't really bother him anymore.

Gideon's ears burned, but a smile spread across his face nonetheless. For some reason, he felt safe with this big, outrageous person on his side, and Arthur had made it crystal clear that was exactly where he stood. On Gideon's side.

Now that his tits were realigned, Arthur took a moment to straighten his muumuu, readjust his wig, and reclaim his bag of oranges from Shiloh's arms. With a wink, he took a fistful of Gideon's shirt and dragged him up the steps toward the front door of the Belladonna Arms, while Shiloh tagged along in their wake.

"You're going to love it here, honey," Arthur said. He released Gideon's shirt and rested his hand on Gideon's ass instead, still propelling him forward. "The vacancy is on the sixth floor. We'll have to walk up, I'm afraid. The elevator's been out of order since I'm not sure when."

"Since 1962," Shiloh mumbled under his breath.

Arthur flapped a hand in Shiloh's direction. "Oh hush. I'll get it fixed one of these days. I swear I will."

Behind him, Shiloh cleared his throat. When Gideon peeked back at him, Shiloh mouthed the words "Never going to happen," causing Gideon to grin.

Arthur must not have noticed because he was still jabbering away like a magpie and patting Gideon's ass. "But don't worry, son," Arthur rattled on. "You're young and spry and cute as a button. A few stairs shouldn't bother the likes of *you*."

Apparently because he was neither young nor spry himself, Arthur grumbled something obscene under his breath as he propped the bag of oranges against the newel post and started the long slog up the shadowy staircase at the back of the building's lobby. Judging by the furnishings, Gideon figured that lobby hadn't been refurbished since about the time the elevator broke down. A rusty bank of mailboxes was screwed into one wall. A dusty plastic ficus tree stood in the corner behind a couple of wingback chairs that were spilling stuffing onto the floor, which was dirty enough already. A horrendously filthy mirror stretched from floor to ceiling on another back wall. Still trapped in the crook of Arthur's arm with Arthur's hand still parked on his ass (it seemed to have found a home there), Gideon dutifully allowed himself to be dragged along as the still-chattering landlord led his merry troop skyward up the stairs, leaving the seedy lobby behind.

Half a flight up, Arthur muttered a curse, pulled off his high heels, and flung them back down the stairs behind him. Still unsatisfied, he hauled off the wig and set it carefully on the second newel post, after which he wiped the sweat from his forehead, then dipped his hands down his bodice to pull out two large bags, both rustling mysteriously like sacksful of teeny pissed-off snakes, which he clearly used to fill out his bustline.

"Quinoa," he said, nodding at Gideon's confused expression. "I used to use chickpeas, but they rattled too much. Couldn't hear myself think. Quinoa might taste like crap when it's cooked, but *uncooked* it's a drag queen's best friend. The tits just *flow*, darling. They *move*. Mansfieldesque, if you know what I mean."

"Uh, sure," Gideon mumbled, chewing on his own tongue, trying not to laugh at the sincere expression on Arthur's face. He couldn't fail to notice that even *without* his quinoa tits, Arthur was fairly well-endowed. Still, perhaps his God-given tits simply didn't *flow* properly on their own.

Snort.

At that moment, a black cat came sailing down the stairs and shot between their legs, followed immediately by two more. Gideon spun to see where they'd gone, while Shiloh commented wryly, "That was Pancho, Yolanda, and Jesus, in case anyone's interested."

"Cute," Gideon said, as the patter of cat feet faded in the distance.

Arthur appeared not to have noticed the cats at all. Instead, now shed of all unnecessary *accoutrements*, he breathed a sigh of relief. "Ah. That's better," he said, sucking in a great gulp of unfettered air and resting his hand once again on Gideon's butt, as if just to be polite. He set off again, and less than half a flight up was once again cussing and bitching and whining under his breath because apparently Arthur *really* hated those stairs, especially in hot weather. Probably to take his mind off the climb, he started blathering on about this and that while the three of them trudged doggedly upward.

"Two redheads in one day, boys. I think that's a record. Before today the only redhead we had was Charlie the klepto on 3, who is nobody's idea of a hottie. Don't tell him I said so. Oh, and sweet Stanley on 5—he's sort of a redhead. Oh yes, and Harlie on 2." He hooked a thumb over his shoulder, aiming it at Shiloh, trailing along behind. "Then your friend, the Scottish rabbi here, who most certainly *is* a hottie, moves in." He leaned in close and spoke in Gideon's ear in a stage whisper that would have carried ten or twelve blocks on a clear day, "He's really Jewish, you know. Anyway, he falls in love with my nephew, so now he's family. What was I talking about? Oh yes. Redheads. Would you believe another young redhead signed a lease just this morning? It's true. And now along comes *you*, Gideon, *another* darling ginger to decorate the august halls of the Belladonna Arms. Am I blessed or what?"

"Who signed a lease this morning?" Shiloh asked, sounding faintly offended. "The Arms's rumor mill is clearly not doing its job. Usually everybody knows everything that happens to everybody in the building before anything really happens to *anybody*."

Gideon gave his head a shake, trying to dislodge that last horrible sentence from his memory banks before it could do irreparable damage to his thought processes.

"Reed Kelly, his name is," Arthur chirped, still speaking to Gideon and ignoring Shiloh completely. "A lovely young man. Butch as all get-out. A welder at the shipyards, I believe. Tall as an oak and built like a brick shitho—ahem. Let me rephrase myself. Tall as an oak and lovely. Just lovely. Shoulders like the Arc de Triomphe, hands as big as skillets, and a bulge in his pants that—ahem. Let me rephrase myself *again*. Oh hell, never mind. Let the bulge stand." With that he slapped his hand over his mouth and giggled like a schoolgirl. "And wouldn't we all love to see *that*? Tee-hee."

"Why haven't I heard about him?" Shiloh asked again. "What floor is he on?"

"Six. Right next door to young Gideon here just as soon as he signs the lease. Gideon, I mean. The other one signed a lease this morning. Did I mention he was butch?"

Fawnlike, he flapped his lashes in Gideon's direction. "Not that you're not, honey." He reached out to pinch his cheek, which startled Gideon so that he almost tumbled backward down the stairs. Arthur snagged him by the arm to keep him upright. "And don't worry. You'll sign. This apartment is simply *made* for you! Especially after you've seen your new neighbor. He's in 6A. You'll be in 6B. How cozy is that? I did mention he was butch, right?"

Arthur clammed up long enough to stare balefully up the next flight of stairs. He was evidently running out of breath from all the climbing now, so his commentary was a little more clipped due to oxygen deprivation. He dragged Gideon under his wing like a mother bird. "Perhaps you and Reed will become friends, honey." While still panting for air, he waggled an obscene eyebrow and readjusted the hibiscus blossom in his ear. Groucho Marx meets Queen Liliuokalani. "Maybe you and Reed will become even *more* than friends."

Gideon blushed and scrunched his forehead in a scowl at the same time. "The last thing I want is a boyfriend, sir. Ma'am. Whatever. My last boyfriend turned out to be the dick of life, so I think he cured me for a while. I'd rather be on my own for now. Besides, I'm not attracted to redheads."

Shiloh gave Gideon a sympathetic pat on the shoulder.

Arthur, on the other hand, didn't look convinced at all. In fact, he appeared downright skeptical. "Yeah, right. That's what redheads always say. And nobody ever wants another boyfriend after they've just broken up with their *last* boyfriend. Then they land in the Belladonna Arms and the pollen starts falling. All those young men who never want to fall in love again start swooning and pining, and their hormones start fizzing, and the next thing you know, my two separate tenants who never wanted another boyfriend fall madly in love with each other and decide to move in together, and poor Arthur is left with one rent coming in instead of two, but the tenants are happy, and poor Arthur is such a romantic slob that he's happy too, and the *next* thing you know a *new* tenant moves in and *another* romance springs out of the ether, and the whole merry round begins *again*." Arthur expelled a long-suffering sigh. His face softened as he turned to first Gideon, then Shiloh. "And you know what, boys? I wouldn't have it any other way."

Gideon cast an uneasy glance in Shiloh's direction, wondering what the hell he was getting himself into here. The higher they climbed and the longer Gideon listened to the clearly insane drag queen orating on romance, the more confused he became. "Excuse me, Arthur, ma'am, did you say 'love pollen'? What the heck is love pollen?"

It was Shiloh's turn to jump into the conversation. "I didn't believe in it either, but it's true. There's something about this building. Somewhere mixed in among the mouse turds in the baseboards and the dry rot in the walls, there's a little spore of romance that continually seeps through the ceiling and drops on people's heads when they aren't looking. We call it love pollen. It'll hit you too. Don't think it won't."

"Love pollen." Gideon couldn't have made his voice more dubiously unimpressed if he'd tried, but neither Arthur nor Shiloh seemed to mind.

"Just wait," they said in unison, eyeballing each other wisely. "You'll see." Then Arthur gave a happy bark, pointing at the numeral 6 painted on the landing wall. "Thank God! We're here. The penthouse. And lookee, Gideon," Arthur exclaimed merrily, clapping his hands and all but quivering in delight. He pointed down a hallway painted a venomous pea-green, with water stains on the ceiling and faded, battered linoleum on the floor, to the first door on the left. By his ecstatic expression, one would think Nirvana awaited just inside. "There's your new apartment, honey. 6B! Home sweet home. Are you thrilled, or what?"

"Agog," Gideon droned, still wondering what he'd gotten himself into.

When another cat flew past, Gideon didn't even bother to jump. This one was black-and-white with a rather disconcerting Hitler mustache decorating its upper lip. Gideon sent it on its way with a jaunty little Nazi salute.

Arthur was preoccupied fiddling with a gigantic ring of keys he had pulled from his cleavage. While he was trying to find the right key to open the apartment door, Gideon whispered in Shiloh's ear, "I want you to know I appreciate your help and all, but….." Here he sucked in a deep breath of air and finished up in a desperate hiss, "I don't think I want to live in this dump!"

Shiloh whispered back. "Nobody does until they're in. Then they never want to leave."

"It's a little rundown."

"You prefer sleeping in your car?"

"Well, no. But there are cats everywhere!"

"You don't like cats?"

Gideon blinked. "No. I love cats."

Shiloh grinned. "So what's the problem?"

Gideon eyeballed Shiloh; then he eyeballed Arthur. He reached a conclusion. "Oh, I get it. You're crazy too. I should have spotted it in the restaurant back when you handed me my first plate of haggis and tatties. I was clearly bamboozled by your sexy kilt and furry knees."

Shiloh giggled. "Wouldn't Ben love to hear you say that."

Ben, Shiloh's lover, stood six four, was all muscle, and Gideon knew it. "Now, now. Let's not be hasty. It was merely a whimsical jest. No need to notify the towering, macho, jealous-as-hell boyfriend."

Shiloh's snicker was cut short by the sound of the apartment door squeaking open. To the thunder of bare, flapping feet, Arthur barged inside, disappeared for a moment, then stuck his head back through the door to beckon them in.

Torn somewhere between trepidation and flat-out terror, Gideon peered around the doorjamb. Arthur scurried off to cuss and grunt and groan about the heat while jimmying open a few of the windows, nearly half of which were painted shut. Since the air in the closed-up apartment was hot enough to roast a goose, Gideon breathed a sigh of relief when Arthur finally managed to wangle enough windows open to allow a breeze to stir through the rooms, replacing the dead, still air.

Gideon peered around, to be polite more than anything else since he was bound and determined he would never stoop to living in this sweltering shithole. He begrudgingly noticed the apartment was indeed furnished. Nothing matched, of course, and certainly nothing was new, but it appeared functional in a threadbare, utilitarian, third-world-cesspool sort of way. Living room, kitchen, bedroom, bath. It was clean, at least, and Gideon didn't see any sign of rats, probably due to all the cats scurrying about the building.

He gravitated toward the living room window and was immediately struck dumb by the heart-stopping view. From this vantage point, which was not only six floors up but had the added benefit of being situated atop a *hill*, Gideon could see all of downtown San Diego laid out before him. At night, with the city's lights blazing below, the view must be incredible. Off to the left as he rested his hands on the sill, leaned through the screenless window, and peered along the side of the building, he caught sight of the grand Pacific Ocean, as flat as glass, spreading out to the distant horizon. The ocean breeze wafting over him not only cooled his heated brow and dried the sweat on his shirt, but it stirred up a smile as well.

Shiloh squeezed into the window beside him, and Gideon scooted over to give him room. Shiloh took in the panorama below. "Wow. Your view is even better than ours. Of course, you're two floors higher."

Gideon barely managed a whisper. "It's amazing."

"Told you," Shiloh answered, with just a hint of smugness. He stood there with Gideon, elbows on the sill, shoulders brushing, as Gideon stared out at the world through spellbound eyes.

Close to hand, a toilet flushed. Then came the watery hiss of a shower running. Then the *beep, beep, beep* of a microwave oven kicking into gear. Arthur was testing out the amenities.

"Yep," Arthur announced from another room, probably assuring himself more than anyone else. "Everything works." Then his thudding footsteps announced his approach to where Gideon still stood with Shiloh, soaking up the view.

"So what do you think?" Arthur asked in a smug tone that indicated he already knew what the answer would be.

"I'll take it," Gideon sang out, whirling around, happy for the first time in days.

The bliss lasted about three seconds. Then, with a sinking feeling, he coasted back to earth. "I mean, if I can afford it, that is."

Arthur delicately cleared his throat. "Shiloh, dear, would you mind vacating the premises for just a moment while Gideon and I talk a little business?"

"Sure," Shiloh said, and after giving Gideon a bracing pat on the back, he made himself scarce.

When they were alone, Arthur stepped close and scooped Gideon into an embrace. This embrace wasn't bone-crushing. It was gentle and kind and all-encompassing.

"Honey," Arthur whispered in Gideon's ear. "I know you're worried about finding a place to live so Auntie Arthur's going to help you with that. I also know you never want to fall in love again. Well, I'm sorry sweetie, but Auntie Arthur's going to help you with that too, whether you want her to or not. Anyway, I just know you'll be happy in this apartment. I have a sixth sense about things like that. So let's talk numbers. Tell me what you can afford."

Gideon swallowed the ball of emotion that had suddenly lodged in his throat. Five minutes ago he didn't want the apartment. Now he was terrified he would lose it before he ever got in. Still, his finances were what they were. No sense lying about it. Rising on tiptoe, he hissed the first figure that came into his head. It was the amount he had paid for his share of Manny's apartment.

Arthur listened politely, and when Gideon was finished, he repositioned the lad in his arms, smooshing Gideon's face against his chest again, patting the back of his head and rocking him back and forth like he might a dyspeptic infant.

"See?" Arthur cooed. "That wasn't so hard."

Gideon gently pried himself loose and gazed up into Arthur's eyes. "You mean you'll take the offer?"

Arthur smiled down at Gideon's upturned face. "Honey, I would have taken even less."

Gideon blinked and tried to swallow. The ball of emotion was back, clogging up his throat. "B-but why? Why are you being so nice to me?"

Arthur pinched one of Gideon's blushing cheeks, then with a dainty movement one would not expect from someone of Arthur's heft and girth, he deftly and oh so carefully brushed away a tear from Gideon's eyelash before it slid into freefall.

"It's what we do at the Belladonna Arms. We take care of each other."

"But you don't know me."

"Honey, over the years I've known a hundred yous. You're sweet and lost and maybe a little damaged. You think nobody loves you. You think you're alone. Well, let me be the first to tell you that under my roof, nobody is alone. All right? Will you trust me on this?"

Gideon reached out and laid a feathery touch to Arthur's massive forearm with his fingertips. "Shiloh said you were nice, Arthur. He told me not to be afraid."

Arthur's cherry-red lips spread into a satisfied smile. There was a lipstick smear on his front tooth, which didn't detract from the smile at all. "So are you? Not afraid, I mean?"

Gideon smiled back while his eyes filled with fresh tears. "No, Arthur. I'm not afraid. But I still don't want to fall in love again."

With that, Arthur offered up a kindly but exasperated sigh. "Oh, well now you're just talking out of your ass. But we'll let that go for now. Let's get you moved in first. Then we'll tackle your love life."

Before Gideon could protest, Arthur clutched him by the shoulders and lifted him straight up into the air so he could plant a big smudgy kiss on his forehead. "There!" he announced, lowering Gideon back to the floor. "The deal is made, the contract signed, your first rent payment is due at the beginning of the month, some three weeks hence."

"Really? Not until then?"

"Yes. Shiloh told me you've lost everything. The three weeks' grace period will help you stock up on groceries and things you need. I might even coerce a few fellow tenants to donate an object or two to make you more comfortable in the meantime."

"I don't want to be any trouble."

"Oh lordy, Gideon. Shut the hell up." Arthur stepped back and waved his arms around like one of the models on *The Price is Right* pointing out the prizes in the big showcase. "So what do you think? Don't you love it? Are you ready to move in?"

Gideon's eyes widened of their own accord. He was only now catching up on everything that had happened. "So I have a home? Just like that?"

"Yes, honey. You have a home. Just like that." Arthur smiled. "So when can you move in?"

Gideon looked down at his empty arms. "This is me," he said. "With everything I own. I guess I'm moved in already."

Arthur frowned, clearly appalled. "Well, that won't do. You mean you have *nothing*?"

Gideon pouted right back, but he tried to be brave about it. "Well, I have a laptop and two shirts that I used to use for rags crammed in the floorboard of my car. But yeah. Other than that this is pretty much it."

Arthur frowned again and stomped his size thirteen foot, causing the building to shake, or was that Gideon's imagination? "Well, I won't have it. Come this time tomorrow, you'll have everything you need."

"B-but how?"

"Never you mind how. Just don't worry. All right? Now give me a smile, son. Show me those choppers."

Gideon couldn't smile. Speechless, he could only stare at the mountainous muumuued man standing in front of him. "Th-th-th...." he stuttered, but the "thank you" wouldn't come either. "Crap," he sniffed, ashamed and embarrassed. "Now I'm gonna cry *again*!"

Arthur patted the side of his own head as if intending to check his wig out of nervous habit, but looked momentarily confused when his fingers touched bare scalp. He'd clearly forgotten having parked his wig on the newel post down on the second-floor landing.

Arthur hiccupped, sniffed, and made a kissy noise of commiseration before dragging Gideon into one more embrace. "Oh hell. Cry away, son. Who am I to judge?" With that, he threw his head back and started wailing too.

When Shiloh returned moments later, Gideon was still squished in Arthur's arms, breathless, mouth open, drooling and blubbering while Arthur sobbed over him with such operatic abandon, the mascara was dripping off his chin and dribbling down Gideon's back. He peered helplessly at Shiloh over Arthur's massive shoulder.

Shiloh gave his head a weary shake. He checked his watch and flicked a speck of lint off his pant leg. Obviously no stranger to Arthur's volatile emotions, he appeared bored but resigned to waiting for the waterworks to stop.

As a matter of fact, Arthur's waterworks stopped on a dime at the very moment when the earth gave another tiny wobble beneath their feet. Arthur released Gideon, shrieked, "Earthquake!" and took off running through the apartment, arms flailing, muumuu billowing, wailing like an ambulance. Alarmed, Gideon followed him to make sure he didn't stumble and hurt himself as he raced into the bathroom and threw himself into the tub, causing the building to lurch more than the earthquake had. Cowering there on his hands and knees, Arthur took a death grip on the spigot, pulled the muumuu over his head—thereby exposing his broad hairy back and bra straps—and waited for the end. Satisfied that Arthur was safe for the time being, if only from himself, Gideon returned to

Shiloh in the living room, wiped away the last of his tears, and said calmly, "So Arthur is always like this, then."

Shiloh replied around a yawn, "Pretty much."

With that, Gideon finally found his smile. He couldn't believe it. He was now a bona fide resident of the Belladonna Arms. His landlord was clearly insane, but what the hell. He'd never have to sleep in his car again!

Chapter 2

BLINKING BACK sweat, Reed Kelly tipped the face mask of his welding helmet to the top of his head and sucked in enough oxygen to keep himself from passing out. It was hotter than hell in the hold of this ship, where he had been toiling away for the past two weeks. The powers-that-be at the Navy shipyard where he worked had him retrofitting an old Navy LPD, and while he didn't mind the labor, he did have issues with the heat. Working with seams of fuming molten metal six inches in front of your face and squatting in a sweltering cast-iron box while wearing fireproof attire that didn't exactly *breathe* didn't help much either.

The *USS Dulmouth*, an Amphibious Platform Dock, did all sorts of weird shit when out at sea. With a displacement of 10,000 tons and a flat keel that allowed a close approach to the shore, it was capable of lowering its rear end into the water, dropping a tailgate, and pooping out a long string of boxy, troop-laden boats, laying them in the surf like chicken eggs. It utilized a flight deck topside to receive and disperse helicopters, which could also be stuffed with troops at a moment's notice. It had a massive cargo hold one deck below topside where it could store a dozen helicopters and park thirty landing craft until they were needed. Boasting a crew of 400, it could also house and transport a thousand more troops to any war zone, battle site, fracas, skirmish, hotspot, or snit locale the old farts in Washington could stir up in a misguided effort to make themselves feel tough and maybe augment their penis size while they were at it.

Currently, however, the *Dulmouth* wasn't *at* sea. She was sitting up on massive blocks in a dry dock in San Diego Harbor looking properly chastened and humiliated, what with her carbuncles and screws exposed, receiving a facelift and major overhaul. Inside and out.

Being a welder, it was the "inside" part Reed Kelly was most concerned with at the moment. That and trying not to die of a heat stroke six decks down in the behemoth's forward compartment, where he was currently, and had been for the last two weeks, attaching rebar to the inside of the bow to make the ship more collision-ready.

It was a hot, stifling job for which he was paid very well. It was also work that Reed was so skilled at, he could almost do it with his eyes closed. That freed his mind up for the contemplation of more pressing matters.

Like life. His own, in particular. Which, truth be told, had just taken a hell of a spin sideways.

A few months back while approaching his twenty-sixth birthday, Reed had suffered an epiphany. Well, not *suffered* exactly. Suffered would imply it was a bad thing. This epiphany wasn't a bad thing at all. In fact, it was the best and most *honest* thing that had ever happened to him.

Not that his wife had seen it that way.

Reed sighed now, remembering when he had actually taken action on that epiphany. It wasn't that far back. Just a couple of weeks. Amazing. It seemed like a lifetime ago.

It was a Sunday afternoon. He was barbecuing in the backyard. Salmon steaks. With golden ears of sweet corn wrapped in foil and steaming on the grill beside them.

Reed often wondered if Carol had suspected what was about to happen. She should have seen it coming, of course. She should have known what it meant to lie all those many nights in their massive king-size bed, staring at Reed's back as he pretended to sleep. Lonely as she watched him grow more distant with every passing month. Hurt that he never touched her anymore. Confused that his eyes avoided her face where before they had dutifully lingered. Maybe it was only Carol's fledgling catering business that kept her sane at all. She had been trying to get the business off the ground for months, and whether Carol admitted it or not, she was using it to fill the gap Reed had left in her life.

Somehow, on that day two weeks earlier in the midst of the salmon sizzling and the buttery corn steaming deliciously on the grill, making his mouth water even while his heart was shattering to pieces, the emotion, the truth, the *duplicity* of his life had flooded in on him all at once.

Carol was setting the picnic table Reed had built with his own two hands, glad to leave the cooking to Reed for a change. She looked cool and pretty standing there, barefoot in the grass, wearing a pale green sundress. The dress had straps that rose up from the bodice to tie at the back of her neck, exposing her pale shoulders. Humming softly under her breath, she arranged silverware and glasses of iced tea on the hand-tooled planks of the tabletop Reed had so lovingly constructed from nothing but a pile of mismatched lumber. In the shade of the sprawling pepper tree that dominated one corner of the backyard—one of the main reasons they had bought the house to begin with—Carol's short hair shifted in the breeze, and the folds of the dress stirred prettily about her knees when the wind caught it just right.

Somehow, at that moment, Reed had known it was time.

With trembling hands, he scooped their dinner onto plates— spatula for the salmon, tongs for the corn—then turned off the gas grill and carried the food to the table.

Carol looked up when Reed emptied his hands and turned to her. Her smile widened when he dropped to his knees before her and wrapped his arms around her hips, pulling her close. When he clutched her tight and buried his face in her belly, she stroked cool fingertips through his hair, but as he began to sob, her fingers stilled.

"So it's true, then," she said softly. There was no rancor in her words. Just weary acceptance.

He tilted his head back, his eyes awash with tears. "I'm sorry."

There was hurt in her eyes now. Hurt, but a fateful understanding too.

"Please don't hate me," Reed whispered. A faint, sardonic smile twisted her mouth. A tear slid free and washed down across her cheek. Her fingers began moving in his hair again. "Never," she said.

"I didn't mean for any of this to happen. I hope you know that."

"I know," she said.

But did she? Did she really? She would have the rest of her life to ponder the question. And Reed would have the rest of his life to either regret his decision or happily live the life of a gay man, which he had finally decided he truly was. He hoped she knew his decision was not brought on by anything she did or didn't do. It was a natural progression of truth. Truth inside himself. Still, it must hurt her. She loved him, after all. Or at least she *had*.

"The house is yours, Carol. The bank accounts too. I'll not contest anything."

Her pale throat worked. She tilted her head back momentarily as if to ward off more tears, staring into the pepper tree above. Reed followed her gaze, listening to a bird hidden somewhere in the branches trilling out a song. A sparrow maybe. Or a house finch. They had a lot of house finches, with their delicate tangerine-tinted breasts, fluttering about the property. It was another reason they loved the house so much.

"I'm sorry," he said again.

For a moment it seemed she might say she forgave him. In the end, though, she merely glanced down at the dinner cooling on the table, flies buzzing over it already, and eased backward out of his arms. Her eyes were empty. Not shocked, not pained, just empty. With a final tender caress of his cheek with cool fingers, she turned and walked slowly toward the house. She stepped inside and closed the back door silently behind her.

Leaving Reed alone, still kneeling in the grass, the summer breeze drying the tears on his cheeks. And, God forgive him, feeling for the first time in years—*relieved*.

REED STOWED his work gear in the padlocked storage box in the bed of his pickup. Helmet, gloves, tool belt, the sweltering, sweat-stiffened welding jacket he wore to ward off sparks. The truck, his tools, and a haversack of mundane items like clothes and a toothbrush, along with a goodly amount of guilt, were all he took from his four-year marriage to Carol.

They had filed divorce papers the day before. The house, a fully renovated and totally paid-for fixer-upper on the poor side of town, he had immediately signed over to her in front of a lawyer, ceding all rights. And although the divorce would not be finalized for six months in accordance with California law, he went to the bank and had his name removed from their checking and their joint savings account, leaving both balances solely in her name. It wasn't much. A few thousand. But it would give Carol a cushion until she got her feet on the ground. The lawyer thought he was crazy, of course. Even Carol hadn't seemed to expect such generosity. She accepted with grace and even held his hand in the lawyer's office when emotions began to get the better of him.

Later, in the hallway, she had briefly hugged him.

"I'm glad now there were no children," she said. Looking up from the embrace, she asked through rising tears of her own, "You did love me once, didn't you?"

"I *still* love you," he said. "But not the way you deserve." He studied her face, his eyes kind. "You'll be all right. I know you will. Now you can concentrate on your catering business. Get that going and you'll be so busy you won't even know I'm gone. Honest."

"What you don't know about women is a lot."

Reed gave a self-deprecating shrug. He glanced away, embarrassed. But she was right. "I can't very well deny that, can I?"

She offered him a distracted smile. The sort of smile that doleful memories inspire. Fleeting. Less than kind. Maybe a little disappointed that the memories weren't grander, did not touch more deeply, hold more truth. "We had fun for a while at least."

Reed laid his hand to her cheek and said with forced cheer, "We did indeed."

She stepped back then, away from his touch. Looking down at herself, she straightened her skirt with an efficient little flick of her fingers, touched the gold loops in her ears to make sure they were securely attached. Without making eye contact again, she trailed a hand down the sleeve of his shirt and said softly, "Be happy, Reed," before turning away.

He stood motionless as the staccato clack of her high heels receded down the hall and disappeared inside the elevator. With a *ding*, the elevator door closed and she was gone. Just like that.

Standing alone in the empty hall, Reed listened to the silence around him, all the while wondering if he would ever know love again.

And now, cranking up the pickup, gunning it a minute because it needed a tune-up and was a little sluggish on the get-go, he dropped the dusty Ford F-150 into gear and drove toward the shipyard gates, heading toward his new home. His new life. And wishing Carol happiness in hers.

Again he wondered if he would ever be loved again.

Was the fact that he had taken his first apartment as a gay man inside the less-than-hallowed walls of the Belladonna Arms—aka Love

Pollen Central, or so the drag queen landlord had informed him with considerable pride—Reed's first clue as to how that question would turn out? He might have been willing to believe it if the drag queen, Arthur, hadn't been so ridiculous looking as to pretty much call into question every statement he made.

Ridiculous and sweet actually, Reed thought as he steered his pickup through the streets of downtown, his tools rattling in the back at every bump. Weaving through traffic, he aimed for the Belladonna Arms, which he could see in the distance, perched atop the only hill in the city.

He had worked a later shift today, and with the sun sinking in his rearview mirror and the sky slowly darkening above his head, he watched the neon lights over his new home spring to life for the very first time. One of the *L*s was flashing as if about to go out, but still the sign was legible. The Belladonna Arms! it beamed out proudly, sort of like a homeless person standing in rags, shivering in the cold but boasting of his own poverty. For in truth, there was very little for the Belladonna Arms to boast of. Still, the Arms was home now, and excitement rushed through Reed's veins. His new and honest life had finally begun.

Reed wasn't proud to be gay—not yet—but he was excited to have finally found the courage to accept it. Truthfully, he was not well versed in the practices of gay love. He had engaged in a few anxious liaisons with men he had met in bars—trysts that usually left him consumed with guilt and terrified that Carol would find out—but those sticky, hurried episodes might somehow prove to be the key to his eventual happiness.

He felt more real in the arms of the few men he had bedded than he had ever felt in Carol's embrace. If he hadn't buried his true feelings when he was younger, he would have accepted himself for who he was sooner. He would have known not to drag Carol into his life at all. But he had been afraid then. Ashamed. Maybe even a little blind to his own needs. It was only later, when he was approaching his midtwenties, after he and Carol had been together a while, that his blindness lifted and the urges became stronger than the fears. Far stronger.

Was he bisexual? He didn't know. What he did know was that the gay side of him was far more demanding of his emotions than the straight. And he would never have a moment's happiness until he let that gayness breathe. Freedom would be out of reach until he became the man he was born to be. He was tired of the hiding and the guilt and the hurt he inflicted on Carol. She deserved better, and so did he.

So now the wheels had been set in motion. Who the hell knew where they would carry him? Wherever his journey led, Reed would at least have the satisfaction of knowing he had boarded the right train to get there.

With a jolt, he parked his pickup on the incline leading up to the apartments, climbed from the cab, dusted some of the day's filth from his clothes, and headed home.

Home.

The smile that suddenly sprang to his face when he considered that tiny one-syllable word caught him by surprise. The ache in his heart that had followed him all day as he bled sweat in the bowels of that bloody ship suddenly relinquished its grip, leaving a hopeful, expectant breathlessness behind. He stopped in his tracks to stare up at the dilapidated old building. Dump or not, this truly was his new home. Given half a chance, he might even be happy here, if he gave himself enough leeway to try.

Did he miss his fixer-upper house in the slummy part of town he had worked on so diligently? Yes. Did he miss Carol? Yes, surprisingly, he did. More than he was willing to admit, in fact. But what he did not miss was the pressure of being someone he wasn't. Of living in someone else's skin, under the umbrella of someone else's expectations. The shedding of that aspect of his old life—the posturing, the lies, the purposeful stunting of his true needs and desires—left him resoundingly at peace with himself for the first time in years.

His long-legged stride almost jaunty now, Reed kicked himself into gear and climbed the front steps. Overhead the whine of an airliner swooping low across the city on its approach to Lindbergh Field cut through the air. Among the Belladonna Arms's many other faults, it was directly beneath the flight path. Scores of flights roared past daily. But at that moment, Reed couldn't find it in himself to care.

As he crossed the Arms's front porch, his footsteps echoed hollowly on the weathered boards. It was a homey sound he rather enjoyed. The air was redolent with the scent of honeysuckle, which blossomed along the porch railing. Reed pulled up short when a movement caught his eye off to the right. It was Arthur, his new landlord, standing in the vast side yard past the edge of the porch. Decked out in a pink chenille housecoat and with bunny slippers on his feet, he was hanging white petticoats on a clothesline. The bunny slippers were rather rundown—the ears limp and drooping, flopping around when he moved.

Arthur spotted Reed at the Arms's front door and sang out, "Whoo-hoo!" around a mouthful of clothespins. He spat out the clothespins, gave a helpless shrug as if he knew how ridiculous he looked, and bellowed loud enough to be heard six blocks away, "A woman's work is never done!"

Reed coughed up a laugh and waved back. Before he could get roped into a long-drawn-out conversation with the oddest landlord in Christendom, he ducked into the lobby out of sight.

He stood just inside the front door and took a deep, calming breath. Here it was, what he had wanted. Why he'd uprooted his entire existence. Why he gave away a house, dissolved a marriage, broke a woman's heart, and set out on his own. For a gay life. Pure and simple.

Well, now he had one. And if his new landlord was any sort of yardstick, it was turning out to be a gayer life than he *ever* could have imagined.

He grinned and headed for the stairs. A cat sat on the bottom step, a black-and-white beast with a little black mustache like Hitler. Reed bent and twiddled Hitler's ears in greeting. The cat said hello in return and followed him all the way up the stairs to 6. When Reed unlocked his front door and swung it open, the animal ran in before him like he owned the place.

Chuckling to himself, Reed followed the cat inside.

DRIPPING FROM the shower, Reed wiped the steam from the mirror over the bathroom sink and studied his reflection while he dried off. His strawberry hair was too long. He'd have to get it cut one of these days. The freckles he had hated in childhood had faded with puberty, thank God, except for a few still scattered across his shoulders. Still, his skin was pale, like most redheads. The strawberry pelt of hair on his chest and belly had been there since high school. His legs were long and coated with pale blond hair, and his hips were lean. He was lean all over really. About two missed meals away from being scrawny, in fact, or so Carol used to tell him.

He paused long enough with the towel at his back to wonder what Carol was doing at that precise moment, but he quickly pushed the thought away. That part of his life was over now, and she was better off without him. She was a strong woman. She would be all right. Hell, the only time she'd ever shown weakness or bad judgment at all was when she fell in love with *him*. She was probably pretty much agreeing with him on that point about now too.

All clean and dry and smelling of Ivory soap, Reed went to hang up his towel when the damn towel rod fell off the wall and landed at his feet with a clang, narrowly missing his toes. He set the rod aside until he could bring his tool belt up from the truck. After shaving at the sink, he had to wait forever for the water to drain. He'd have to fix that too. Still naked, he stepped out of the bathroom and gazed around. There were a lot of things that needed work. As a matter of fact, good old 6A was a bit of a mess.

A floor-length mirror leaning against the bedroom wall needed to be hung. The windows throughout would hardly open at all, having been painted shut at some time or other. There were a few loose boards in the living room floor that squeaked when he crossed them, and he suspected a good fumigation wouldn't hurt the joint either. He hadn't seen a cockroach yet, but it wasn't hard to imagine a battalion of them hiding in some crevice or other, watching and waiting for the new tenant to leave a cheeseburger lying around so they could swoop out and carry it away in a feverish fit of good fortune. He also needed to fix the security lock on the front door. The chain was barely attached. A sneeze from out in the hall would probably blow it right off the wall. Maybe he'd even install a burglar alarm. The Belladonna Arms didn't exactly inspire confidence as to what sort of other tenants might be found roaming the halls.

Well, he was handy. He'd just have to fix the place up. Heck, it might even be fun.

A wailing from the other room sent him running to see what was going on. He found Hitler scratching at the front door, tail all puffed out, growling to be let out. Opening the door just wide enough to let the cat squeeze through, Reed stuck his head out into the hall and watched the beast make a beeline for the stairs without so much as a "See ya later."

"Asshole," Reed muttered under his breath. He left his head in the hall long enough to once again check out the water-stained ceiling, the ragged linoleum on the floor, the battered pea-green baseboards. Jesus, the Belladonna Arms really was a dump of the first magnitude, he thought, as he pulled his head back inside like a startled turtle and locked the door behind him.

Still naked and pondering all he could do to renovate the apartment, he plucked a beer from the refrigerator (which needed a new light and quite possibly a new gasket around the freezer door). He leaned through the one living room window that could be opened all the way. Bending over and propping his elbows on the sill, he stared out at the city lights, which were starting to flicker on one by one as the earth spun and the dusk receded and darkness began to settle over the California coast. The stars were out already. The air was balmy and smelled of the sea. Night birds were just waking up in the eucalyptus tree outside his living room window.

Reed sipped at his beer while the cool evening breeze caressed his bare skin. It felt so heavenly it was all he could do not to purr like a cat. Well, maybe not Hitler. But a *normal* cat.

"Hi," a voice said. "Looks like we had the same idea."

Startled, Reed jerked around, and there, not more than six feet away, protruded the head and shoulders of another redheaded young man staring out at the city lights. Or at least he had been. Actually, now the redhead was staring at *him*.

Reed was suddenly very aware he was naked. He glanced down to make sure all his dangly parts were hidden below the sill. They were, so he let his eyes travel back to the stranger beside him.

"You must be the new neighbor," Reed said. "I thought I heard somebody moving around over there."

"Yep. That was me."

The guy, who looked to be about Reed's age, only a little shorter, and with far redder hair, tipped him a friendly salute. He had a beer bottle in his hand too. He was wearing a red shirt. And probably pants, which was more than Reed could say, not that it bothered him much, being naked. It wasn't like his balls were hanging through the window, flapping in the wind.

Reed grinned, hoisting his own beer. "Two minds with a single thought. I'm Reed."

When the young man smiled, Reed caught a glimpse of snowy teeth in a freckled face. *Poor guy. His freckles haven't faded at all. He probably looks now like he did at nine. Only taller.*

"I'm Gideon," the freckled guy said. "Nice to meet you."

Each man leaned farther out the window and tried to clink their bottles together, but they couldn't quite reach. The one called Gideon said, "Clink, clink" instead, and they laughed.

"So just moved in, huh? How do you like the Arms? Gideon, was it?"

"Yeah. Gideon." He aimed his freckled face out at the city. His smile had disappeared. One second it was there; the next second it was gone. "Well," Gideon practically mumbled so Reed had to lean a little farther out of the window to hear. "Nothing much works. The spigot in my tub barely dribbles, and my showerhead doesn't work at all. You need a monkey wrench to turn the faucet in the kitchen sink, and there's no clothes rod in my bedroom closet."

"I could give you a hand fixing some of that," Reed offered, catching himself by surprise. But why the hell not? Everybody wasn't as handy as he was. And he suspected the work orders got misplaced on a regular basis around here. From the looks of Arthur, they were probably forgotten the moment they were turned in. The landlord clearly had far more important things to worry about. Such as what earrings to wear. The snag in his pantyhose. Keeping his tits adjusted.

"Really?" Gideon asked, snapping Reed out of his reverie. "You'd do that? That would be great. I'd really appreciate it. I don't even own a hammer."

Reed gave him a thumbs-up. "Don't worry. I do. And it's no problem. I'm naked at the moment, but maybe this weekend would be okay."

Gideon took on a worldly air of exaggerated disinterest. "This weekend would be great. And just so you know, I have no problem with naked handymen. Not a lick." A smirk came, plumping up his cheeks and causing two dimples to spring to life among the freckles. "Well, *maybe* a lick. You know. Just to be polite."

Reed no longer had to wonder if the guy was gay. Since he had no problem with naked handymen and he lived in this building, how much more proof did he need? He also wondered if all gay men were as upfront about their sexual proclivities as his new neighbor. Reed had a lot to learn about this new life he had embraced. It was daunting in a way. Exciting as hell in another. Too exciting, maybe.

To hide his embarrassment, Reed laughed a phony laugh and hoped the guy wouldn't notice the blood rushing to his cheeks. "Uh, thanks. I'll keep that in mind." Then out of nowhere, a surge of desire rushed through him, surprising him so that he almost toppled through the window. Where the hell had *that* come from? Suddenly he was really glad his dick was hiding behind the window sill. Much more chitchat like this and it would be filling up with blood like a water balloon and banging its little head against the wall.

Before he realized what he was saying, Reed added, "I'm not much into redheads. Sorry." The surprising thing was it was true.

Gideon gave an exaggerated shrug. "Don't be sorry. I'm not into redheads either."

Reed didn't know if he was relieved or what. "Well, I guess we know where we stand on *that* subject."

"Guess we do."

"Sort of eases the pressure."

"Sort of does. What was your name again?"

"Reed."

"Oh yeah. Met any of the other tenants yet?"

"Not yet. You?"

Gideon took a pull from his beer before answering. "I know Shiloh and his lover, Ben, who live down on 4. Ben is Arthur's nephew. I don't know anyone else really. I've only been in the building about—" He glanced down at the watch on his wrist. "—three hours."

"There seem to be a lot of couples in the building," Reed commented. Somehow that simple sentence saddened him a little.

Gideon laughed. "According to Shiloh, this place is a matchmaker's paradise. *Everybody* ends up spliced. How about you, Reed? You looking for a lover?"

Reed shrugged his bare shoulders. He gazed out at the city lights as if the matter meant very little to him, which he suspected was a lie of the first magnitude. "Whatever happens, happens, I guess. Why? Are you?"

Gideon didn't hesitate at all. "No. I've had my fill of lovers for a while."

Reed leaned a little farther out the window to study the young man next to him. He saw both sadness and anger in the eyes peering out from above those freckled cheeks. What could have happened to turn the guy so emphatically against lovers? His last one was a jerk, maybe? There was a broken heart lurking behind that innocent face, Reed figured, and for that he was sorry. Gideon seemed like a nice guy. A little damaged, but nice. And what can you really think about a man who doesn't even own a hammer?

For the first time, he took note of the name tag on Gideon's chest. "You work at Office Depot?"

"Yeah. Downtown." Gideon poked a finger at the city skyline like he could almost touch it. "Right over there, as a matter of fact. At the foot of Broadway. Down by where the cruise ships park."

Reed grunted. "Then I'll probably see you one of these days. I need a new computer. Lost my last one in the div—" Divorce, he was about to say, but that would raise a whole lot of questions he didn't feel like answering. "Well, I just lost it." Actually, he had given his computer to Carol, along with everything else inside the house except his tools and clothes. But this guy didn't need to know that.

"Sure," Gideon said. "Macs are on sale right now. You can't beat a Mac. I might even be able to wangle you an extra discount if you sign up for our credit card."

"Really? That would be great."

After that, the conversation sort of fizzled out. Both men's beers were almost empty, and Reed was beginning to feel a little silly standing there naked for so long.

He was about to excuse himself when the earth gave another one of its little jolts. The tremor was over almost before it began. This one not much more than a three on the Richter scale, but unnerving nevertheless, coming as it did on the heels of so many others.

Before Reed could comment on the tremor, Gideon cocked his head, freezing in place, and said, "Shh. Wait for it."

Reed had just enough time to say, "Huh?" when he heard a horrendous wail of terror coming from somewhere far below. As soon as the wail of terror receded, a string of falsetto curses pierced the night.

Gideon grinned. "Our intrepid landlord. The shake-up must have jarred his eyelashes loose. I hate it when that happens too."

Reed laughed. "Poor guy. He seems a little high-strung."

"Gee, you think?"

They both laughed again. It was *nice* to laugh. Reed hadn't done it much lately.

"Well…." He stared down at his empty beer bottle before shyly excusing himself. "Best go fix myself some dinner. Have a nice evening, Gideon. It was good meeting you. I'll stop by on the weekend—fully dressed, mind you, ha-ha—and we'll see if we can make some of those repairs."

"That would be great, Reed. Thank you. And it was good meeting you too. Honest."

They locked eyes for a second, then as if on cue, Reed pivoted away from the window and stepped back into his own little world, safely entrenching himself inside his brand-new apartment walls. He still felt out of place in this ramshackle old building, but it would get better. After all, it sort of had to, didn't it? This was his haven now. This was where he would press the Reset button on his life.

He stood there, listening to the silence. Since Reed didn't have a television, or much of anything else for that matter, the silence was profound. But it was reassuring in a way too. He didn't mind it. He ate a quiet dinner, trying to ignore his own loneliness, slightly bewildered by the empty rooms around him. Later, in the silent darkness of a deepening night, Reed lay sleepless in his unfamiliar bed, reading, trying to convince himself he was actually home.

Shortly after midnight, a sound intruded into the silence. He set his book aside and stared at the wall beside the bed. It was muted weeping, coming from next door. Gideon was crying.

Poor guy. Reed lay ramrod straight, his fists clenched at his sides. *He must be missing his lover. The one who broke his heart.*

Hours later, just as dawn crept into the room, Reed's own tears fell. But they fell from the depths of a dream.

Reed would not remember them when he woke.

Chapter 3

ON HIS first morning in the Belladonna Arms, Gideon Chase opened his eyes feeling like he'd been pummeled with bowling balls for the last eight hours. Horrified, he remembered back to the night before, tossing and turning on that goddamn bare mattress without so much as a sheet to cover himself or a pillow to stuff beneath his head. Had he really cried himself to sleep? Good lord. What was he? Five?

Groaning, he worked his legs over the side of the bed and tried to sit up straight, all the while digging the sleep boogers out of his eyes and staring down morosely at his morning hard-on as if he'd never seen it before in his life. Said hard-on was staring back at him with its one little rheumy eye, clearly as appalled by what it was seeing as he was. Great. Even his dick was finding fault this morning.

The day before, Gideon had lugged his belongings up the six flights of stairs to his new home. His belongings consisted of a laptop, a couple of dirty shirts that had been lying in the trunk of his car for the last six months, and his backpack. That was it. Everything he owned.

He stumbled through the apartment with his dick still bobbing around, stiff as a post. After a quick pee, during which he had to awkwardly tilt his pecker downward to hit the toilet, he dragged himself into the kitchen for breakfast. Like that was even empirically possible. A stove and a microwave came with the apartment, but they were pretty much useless without anything to cook. He couldn't even nuke a cup of instant coffee. For one thing, he didn't have any coffee. For another thing, he didn't have a cup. Or even a spoon.

Jesus.

He trudged back into the living room, hooked his backpack off the lumpy old couch, and lugged it into the kitchen. His dick had gone down by now, so he plopped his naked ass on a straight-backed chair and scooted up close to the kitchen table. Digging around in his backpack, he finally exclaimed, "Aha!" and pulled out a Snickers bar he had purchased a couple of weeks back and then proceeded to forget about.

Breakfast.

While he gnawed on the candy bar, he gazed around the kitchen. He wondered idly what sort of nuclear cleaning agent would erase the fossilized grease stains from the wall behind the stove. Or should he even try? Not today of course, but maybe in a couple of years. The old Kenmore refrigerator parked in the corner had a big dent in the door, as if rather than being delivered to the premises on the back of a dolly in the standard caring fashion (probably around the close of the Spanish-American War), it had instead been simply tipped off the back of a careening truck as the driver sped past the Arms's front door.

Gideon swiveled his head around, examining the premises further. There were chips and cracks in the kitchen linoleum. There were chips and cracks in the kitchen sink. There were even chips and cracks in the Snickers bar, since it had been rolling around inside his backpack for the last two weeks.

He sighed.

As if the gods weren't finished messing with his head this morning, there came a furious rapping at his front door. Very businesslike. Very insistent. Gideon stiffened in his chair. His first thought was it must be Manny, come to plead for his return. Yeah, right. His second thought was no matter who it was, maybe he would sit here and not make a peep until they went away because frankly all that pounding on his front door sounded like bad news to him. His third thought was to grow some gonads, throw on some pants, and answer the stupid door.

The third option was the one he chose.

He knew, of course, it couldn't be Arthur, because Arthur didn't look the type to crawl out of bed at the crack of dawn. And even if he did, he probably wouldn't set one high-heeled foot outside his apartment until he had spent three hours applying makeup and fluffing his wig and picking the right gown. It also couldn't be Shiloh, since Shiloh didn't get up early either, working nights at the restaurant and all. The only other person Gideon knew in the building was the redheaded guy next door with the freckled shoulders. Reed, was it? And Reed said he would swing by to help Gideon with a few repairs *on the weekend*, not before.

Almost curious now to see who it was, Gideon wrestled himself into the same pants he'd been wearing for the last three days—thanks to dickhead Manny and his asshole gesture of donating everything Gideon owned to the Salvation Army. Still shirtless and tugging up his zipper, Gideon swung the door open, expecting anything.

Aside from one small niggling error in his calculations, he was right. It wasn't any of those three previously named people. The one niggling error was that it *was* indeed another redhead. This redhead was tall, gangly, and had a humongous zit on the end of his nose that looked like it was about to explode at any moment. His carroty red hair, which was hell and gone redder than Gideon's own, stuck straight up off the top of his head in a too-long flattop that looked remarkably like a scraggly pencil eraser. In fact, the man bore a remarkable resemblance to that squeaky little Muppet guy, Beaker.

Standing next to Beaker was Beaker's Muppet buddy, Bunsen Honeydew, or a close human facsimile, since he was chubby, cherub-faced, and about two heads shorter than his friend. Instead of a lab coat like Bunsen, he was wearing a ten-gallon cowboy hat, complementing brand-new skintight blue jeans, the legs of which looked as stiff as stovepipes. He had Tony Lama boots on his feet and a western shirt with fake pearl snaps that was doing everything it could to hold in the guy's belly, which could have used a comprehensive regimen of sit-ups and planks and maybe a touch of liposuction to mold it back into the shape God had surely intended it to have. A bolo tie with a chunk of turquoise big enough to choke a moose dangled down the guy's chest like a stethoscope.

The redhead, on the other hand, was dressed in an ill-fitting brown UPS uniform, with scuffed shoes and his shirt only half tucked in. He was wrestling with a big brown cardboard box with UPS labels stuck all over it, balancing the box in his arms while at the same time working a finger up his nose like he was digging for gold. As soon as Gideon showed his face, the guy had the decency to pluck his finger out of his nose with an almost audible *pop*! and try to look normal, although as far as Gideon was concerned, it was already too late for that.

Still juggling the box around in his arms, Beaker stuck the same hand out in front of him, boogery finger and all, and offered to shake.

Gideon decided on the spot that he would rather set himself on fire than shake that hand. He also decided on the spot that this couldn't be an actual UPS delivery since the box had already been opened, and none too neatly either. Then it had been taped shut again and all the ragged flaps brought together with what looked like about thirty feet of masking tape. He thought he heard a teeny scuffling sound coming from inside the box, but that must have been his imagination.

Gideon dragged his eyes from both the hand *and* the box and tried to make his face politely inquisitive. "Can I help you guys?"

His two visitors let their eyes meander over Gideon's bare torso, where they lingered far longer than they should have at the spot where Gideon's zipper had been closed but the pants had yet to be buttoned. Gideon stood there with all the forbearance he could muster, arms folded across his chest, waiting for the two perverts to let their gazes wander back up to his face, which they eventually did. As soon as he knew they weren't gawking at his crotch anymore, Gideon raised his eyebrows high to reemphasize his original question. "Let's try that again. Can I *help* you guys?"

The sarcasm dripping off Gideon's words appeared to jolt the UPS guy back to reality. "Uh, hi! I'm your neighbor down on 3. Charlie's my name." He hooked a thumb at his partner. "This is my husband, Bruce. He lives on 3 too."

Gideon still wouldn't shake hands but he did try to act friendly, although he didn't much feel like it. "Makes sense you'd both live on 3, being married and all." He waited for a chuckle from either one of them—after all he'd been making a wee joke—but the two just stood there at his doorstep mindlessly staring back. Gideon sighed. Fine, then, no more jokes. "Nice to meet you. I'm Gideon. What's up?"

Charlie looked down at the box he was clutching as if he suddenly remembered it was there. Without preamble, he thrust it at Gideon. Too surprised to resist, Gideon took it.

Before he could ask for an explanation, Charlie lobbed the explanation straight at him like a football. "Arthur said you didn't have anything, and Bruce and I, well, we have lots of crap lying around, so here's some stuff maybe you can use. Sorry your lover donated all your stuff to the Salvation Army. Boy, was *that* a dick thing to do. Arthur told us. It wasn't a secret, was it? Well, actually it doesn't matter if it was a secret or not. I've already told about six people. Bruce probably told more than that. Besides, there are no secrets in the Belladonna Arms no matter how hard you try to keep them. I seem to be rattling on so I think I'll shut up now." Without further explanation or apology, he clapped his mouth shut like a suitcase and did exactly that.

While he was shutting up, his partner, Bruce, lifted his arms up over his head, being careful not to dislodge his hat, and with pinkies high, delicately touched his two index fingers together. Rising on tiptoe with his heels turned in, he bent his knees in a plié, then rose back up on tiptoe and slowly and gracefully lowered his arms. When he was finished, he gazed blandly about like a cow idly wondering which part of the south forty to start grazing on next.

Charlie eyed his lover fondly, then looked back at Gideon. "Bruce is taking an internet course in ballet," he explained. "He practices constantly."

Gideon blinked a couple of times. *An internet course in ballet?* He stared at Charlie, then at Bruce, then back at Charlie. As a change of pace, he stared down at the box in his arms, then finally back at Charlie one more time. Meanwhile, Bruce was performing a nelly little pirouette with his arms up over his head again, still being careful not to dislodge his ten-gallon hat. With gracefully bent knees, which made his stiffass blue jeans crackle like aluminum foil, he hopped up and down the hall while his bulging belly flopped around in front of him. He was clearly bored with the conversation and had decided to work on his form instead. *Margot Fonteyn meets Dale Evans meets Slim Pickens.*

Gideon decided he'd try not to laugh. It was an uphill battle. "I'm speechless," he finally said. And it was true. He was.

For the first time, Charlie twisted his mug into a smile that almost made him handsome. "That's funny," he said. "You're speechless and I don't know when to shut up. It's the medication, you know. Makes me blabber."

"Blabber," Bruce agreed with a grunt while bending to touch his toes, all ten of which seemed a little out of reach. When he straightened back up, Gideon was almost sure he heard a tendon snap.

As if to prove his point about blabbering, Charlie started talking again, blatting out words like a rogue machine gun. "Have you met Sylvia? She'll probably be up to welcome you into the building. Watch out for her kid. Don't stand within puking distance. The kid can projectile vomit with precision aim. Nailed Bruce the other day. Blew his hat clean off his head."

"Oy," Bruce said, still spinning. "And what comes out of his other end is even worse. Peels the wallpaper right off the wall."

"Are you guys on speed?" Gideon asked. It seemed a reasonable question to him.

It barely broke Charlie's concentration. "No," he blandly replied, before steamrolling onward with more blathering chatter. "Oh, and if Sylvia brings you cookies, no problem. She makes great cookies. But if she brings you anything else, drive out into the desert somewhere and bury it. Deep. Especially if it's meat loaf. The military just designated Sylvia's meat loaf a weapon of mass destruction. Trust me. It sucks."

"Sucks," Bruce agreed, arms straight out to either side, hands flapping, like he was trying to lift off. "Even flies won't eat it."

Gideon blinked. Again. While he was sort of curious now to see what was in the box, he couldn't find an opening in this bizarre conversation that offered an opportunity. Meanwhile, Bruce had one hand on the hallway wall and one leg sticking straight out behind him in arabesque. Gideon had to work at it to drag his gaze back to the other whack job standing in front of his door. "Huh? I mean, oh. I'm sorry, Charlie. Are you sick?"

Charlie looked honestly surprised by that. Surprised and concerned. "Why? Do I *look* sick?"

"No," Gideon quickly responded. *Aside from that horrendous pimple.* "But before you started blabbering about something else, you said you were taking medication. I simply assumed…."

Charlie barked out a laugh and started to poke his finger back up his nose again. At the last moment, he apparently thought better of it, much to Gideon's relief. "Oh no! Ha-ha. I take medication for my kleptomania. Bruce takes it too. We met in a counseling group for thieves. Isn't that romantic?"

Gideon was getting tired of blinking. His eyelids were cramping up. "Here I go again being speechless," he said, somewhere between bewildered and amused. *A counseling group for thieves?*

"Nice jeté," Charlie said, watching Bruce with a critical eye.

Gideon was no expert on ballet, but even he knew the jeté was crap. Still, the guy was trying. He had to give him credit for that.

The box gave a lurch in Gideon's arms, startling him so that he almost dropped it. It gave another jiggle, startling him *again*. "Say, I think there's something alive in he—"

Charlie glanced at his watch. "Oops. Gotta run. Almost time for work. Listen, Gid, if you need anything in particular, let me know. I work at UPS, and stuff falls off the truck or gets lost in the warehouse or simply finds its way into our apartment all the time. It's kind of amazing really. Like spontaneous migration. Anyway, don't be shy. Just shout out. Well, nice meeting you. See ya. Bye-bye. Auf Wiedersehen. Toodles."

And before Gideon could say goodbye back, Charlie bustled off down the hall with Bruce hopping gracefully along behind him like a pet kangaroo, jeté-ing all over the place.

The box was going crazy now, lurching in Gideon's grasp, tilting first one way then the other, like maybe there was a basketball bouncing around inside. Gideon wrestled it into his apartment, dropped it on the floor, and kicked his front door shut behind him.

He stood there for the longest moment staring at the box. Then he nudged it with his toe.

"Meow," said a voice from within.

"Huh?" Gideon dropped to his knees, grabbed a flap of masking tape at the edge of the box lid, and gave a tug. The lid popped open and out flew a tiny kitten, not much bigger than a hamster. The kitten gave its head a shake, gazed around for a second like a bus passenger disembarking at the wrong stop and wondering where the hell he was, then stalked directly toward Gideon, tail high, and started climbing up his leg, purring like a Volkswagen.

Gideon peeled it off his pant leg and held it at eye level. The kitten was a female. At least it looked like one. She was an orange tabby with white boots and white tips on her ears and an attractive white bib of fur decorating her throat. She couldn't have been more than six weeks old.

"Hi," Gideon said, charmed in spite of himself.

At that, the kitten's motor shifted into high gear and her purr filled the apartment like the hum of machinery gearing up on a factory floor. It was a really big purr for a cat that didn't weigh more than eight ounces, and while the purr went on and on, the beast's big golden eyes, sweetly innocent, studied Gideon's face.

"Meow?" it said again.

Smiling, Gideon tucked the kitten up under his chin and peered down into the box. There was other stuff in there. Cool stuff. Stuff he might actually be able to use.

Sitting cross-legged on the floor like Geronimo at a powwow and still holding the kitten tucked under his chin, Gideon started emptying the box with his free hand, laying things out around him. A set of brand-new sheets, still packaged in plastic. *Those* he could use. A skillet, also sparkling new. A humongous ladle like a witch might use to stir a pot of potion before laying a hex on a neighboring village. He wasn't sure what he'd do with that. A box of peanut brittle—ooh, more breakfast. A bottle of Windex. A bottle of mouthwash. A brand-new soccer ball. Hmm. A Westinghouse three-speed mixer, which he sat there staring at for the longest time because, while he didn't have any cake mix in the house, maybe he could use the damn thing to chip the rust stains off the tub. Or not. Lastly, he pulled a five-pound bag of kitten food out of the box.

"Oh wow!"

Gideon immediately poured a mound of cat food into the skillet and set the kitten in front of it. Apparently not one to stand on ceremony, the kitten dug right in. And while the kitten dug in, Gideon tore open the box of peanut brittle, and he dug in too.

Except for the crunching and the humming (sometimes Gideon hummed while he ate) and the continued purring from the cat, they ate in companionable silence. The peanut brittle was pretty good. Apparently so was the cat food.

"I think I'll call you Punkin," Gideon said, assuming the mantle of cat ownership without so much as a whiff of angst. Punkin didn't seem to mind either, since at the sound of his voice, she turned from the skillet of cat food and climbed up into Gideon's lap once more. Pushing her face into Gideon's bare belly, the kitten immediately fell asleep, purring like a log truck chugging up a hill. Gideon slid his fingers through the kitten's fur, and the rumble of that strident purr traveled straight up his fingertips into his heart.

For the first time that morning—for the first time in *days*—Gideon truly smiled.

"You're safe now," he whispered. "Maybe we both are." And then he smiled again. His smile stayed in place until another knock came at the door.

He and Punkin looked toward the sound together. Why did Gideon get the impression this was going to be a hell of a day?

IT TURNED out to be one of the oddest mornings Gideon had ever spent.

First came a gorgeous, green-eyed, buzz-cut hunk of manhood named Roger Something-or-other with his cute little lover, Stanley, who apparently was an archaeologist, of all things. Roger and Stanley dropped off a bag of canned goods. Food. Actual food. Beans, corn, canned tamales (no time to be picky), corned beef hash, a jar of pickles, *another* jar of pickles, a loaf of bread, a stack of paper plates, a jar of pickled pigs' feet—which Gideon knew he'd never eat as long as he lived—and a half-eaten bag of corn chips—which he knew he *would*.

"Sorry about the corn chips," Roger said. "We got hungry when we were packing things up."

Gideon was all but speechless with gratitude. He'd be even more speechless if he actually owned a can opener. "You shouldn't have done this," he said. "All this stuff probably came right out of your own pantry."

"What are friends for?" Stanley asked, adjusting his glasses and snuggling closer to Roger as they stood in the doorway. "Plus we still don't know why we bought the pigs' feet. They've been lurking in our cupboard for over a year. Eyeing us every time we open the cupboard door. Mocking us. Calling to us when we sleep."

"Don't get carried away," Roger whispered, making Stanley blush.

They all had a good laugh over that, even Stanley, then Roger leaned in and stroked Punkin's chin. "See you got a cat already."

"Yeah. From Charlie and Bruce."

"In that case, it's probably the only thing they brought you that wasn't stolen."

Stanley bumped his lover with his hip. "Now, now. It's the thought that counts."

Roger buried a kiss in Stanley's strawberry blond hair. "It is indeed," he cooed. "Sorry."

Gideon felt a pang of jealousy watching the easy, loving way Roger and Stanley interacted. A moment later he remembered what a jerk Manny had been, and the pang of jealousy ratchetted up a notch.

After Roger and Stanley came Milan and Harlie. Milan was a towering hunk of Mediterranean manhood, and Harlie was his far shorter, but just as handsome, lover. Both men looked embarrassed by their own act of kindness in handing over a bag of still-warm bakery goodies. A loaf of french bread. A dozen croissants. Enough sourdough biscuits to pave a small boulevard, and a big gooey apple cobbler still hot to the touch.

"I'm a baker," Milan explained.

"I'm his assistant," said Harlie.

"He's also a writer," Milan added, causing Harlie to blush.

"Cool," Gideon said. He smiled his thanks before taking a moment to breathe in the smells. If someone would come along now with a gallon of ice cream and a pound of butter—and a can opener—Gideon would never ask for anything else as long as he lived.

Gideon was suddenly stricken with emotion. His eyes started to mist over. Standing there with his arms full of bakery bags, his belly full of peanut brittle, and his vision full of Milan (God, the guy was dreamy), Gideon felt humbled for one of the few times in his life. He was truly stunned by this latest act of kindness from his fellow residents at the Belladonna Arms. It might be argued that Arthur was simply using good business sense by giving him a break on the rent, since he'd be making it up on future rents. But the other tenants had nothing to gain by their generosity. They were simply being kind.

Because he couldn't bear not to, and because his arms were too full to offer an actual hug by way of a thank-you, Gideon stepped closer to each man and gave them a gentle nudge, forehead to chest. First Milan, then Harlie.

"Thank you," he said, sincerely.

Flushed with pleasure at Gideon's response, Milan and Harlie awkwardly excused themselves, promising a dinner date later on to get to know each other better, which Gideon gratefully accepted. After that, Gideon watched them go, hand in hand. They turned and waved a last goodbye before pattering down the stairs side by side.

(Later Gideon would learn they lived on 2 and that Milan was actually Arthur's lover's son. Gideon would have to make up a spreadsheet to keep everybody straight.)

Gideon carted his loot into the kitchen, being careful where he put his feet so he wouldn't step on Punkin, who seemed to be everywhere at once as she explored her new domain. He set the bags on the counter and quickly hustled off to pull on his work shirt. At least that way if any more tenants came to the door bearing gifts, he wouldn't meet them half-naked.

When after five minutes no one else came knocking, Gideon turned right around, tore off his clothes, and stepped into the shower to begin his day. Remembering his showerhead didn't work, he took a tub bath instead, toweling off afterward with one of the dirty shirts he had dug out of his trunk the day before. He had two days off from work, and he would need those two days to get settled and to purchase a few things he needed, the most important of which was clothing. He couldn't live in the same work shirt, the two rags he'd brought in from the trunk of his car, and the same pair of pants for the rest of his life. Hell, he was feeling funky already. His socks were starting to squish when he walked. Punkin looked so sad seeing Gideon headed for the front door once he was dressed, he did an about-face and curled up on the couch with the kitten in his arms, reassuring her he'd be right back. While Punkin's eyes slowly closed and her little paws ceased kneading Gideon's chest as she tumbled into pussycat dreamland, there came another knock on his apartment door.

Leaving the kitten nestled asleep on the cushions, he answered the door, making sure to plant a friendly smile on his face before he did. After all, the tenants were stopping by out of the goodness of their hearts. The least he could do was let them know he wasn't a jerk.

Knowing Arthur and the Belladonna Arms as he did, the tenants he found on his doorstep this time were a bit of a surprise. The trio consisted of a man, a woman, and a child, which in the Belladonna Arms was akin to finding three lug wrenches in a box of feather boas. In other words, heterosexuals were a rarity around these parts.

Remembering what Charlie had said about projectile vomiting, Gideon took a step back as he stared at the baby strapped to the father's chest. The kid was facing forward and kicking his legs like an outboard motor, banging his poor dad in the nuts every few seconds. Just as the poor man was beginning to turn green, and before any greeting could be expressed, the mother reached over and captured the kid's ankles in a death grip.

The woman was a good two heads shorter than her husband and flat-out beautiful. She had her bobbed brown hair pulled back in a simple ponytail, and her face was untouched by makeup except for a gentle brush of lipstick that pinked her lips. She held on to the flailing kid like it was old hat, the easy smile of greeting never once leaving her face.

The father was tall and thin, had big ears, and was rather cute in a geeky kind of way. He breathed a grateful sigh of relief to have his balls out of danger and cheerfully stuck his hand out to shake hello.

"Hi," he announced. "I'm Pete. This is my wife Sylvia, and the wriggling ball of misery strapped to my chest is Artie, our progeny, God help us all."

Sylvia laughed and slapped his arm. To slap it she had to release the kid's ankles, and the moment she did, little Artie cried, "Goo-goo!" and kicked his daddy in the nuts again. Pete's eyes crossed, and Gideon cringed.

Sylvia expelled a long, deep sigh, and after unstrapping the kid like a parachute, she set him on the ground, still kicking. Since his legs were in motion already, as soon as his feet hit the floor he took off running straight into Gideon's apartment. His fat little legs bowed and unsteady, his tiny hands flapping around all over the place, he made a beeline across the living room floor and plowed into the wall on the opposite side of the room with a horrendous crash. The minute he hit the wall, he collapsed onto his diapered ass and sat there shaking his head, sort of like Bugs Bunny after being whacked in the face with a frying pan.

It was Pete's turn to sigh. "He hasn't mastered turning yet."

"So I see," Gideon said. "Excuse me for asking, but is he—"

"Normal?" Sylvia asked. Two very attractive dimples appeared in her cheeks. "We'll let you know when we figure it out."

As all three of them stood in the doorway peering in, Punkin lifted her head from the couch where she had been sleeping and, finding herself alone, gave a plaintive meow.

Little Artie whipped his head around, spotted the kitten on the couch, and with a couple of grunts and what sounded remarkably like either a fart or an oboe hitting C minor, he pulled himself to his unsteady feet and took off running straight for the cat.

Without reducing his speed even one iota, he plowed into the couch like he'd plowed into the wall, knocking himself on his ass *again.*

"He hasn't mastered deceleration or stopping either," Pete said. "We're so proud."

Sylvia laughed.

Artie farted again.

Punkin meowed.

"Come on in," Gideon said, leery of their deciding to take off and move to Europe, leaving the kid in his care, for which he wouldn't blame them one little bit. Well, yes he would. Hey, he already had a cat. That was plenty.

As Gideon ushered them inside, he noticed the shopping bag in Sylvia's hand. When she saw him glance at it, she handed it over.

"Housewarming gift," she said, reaching up to tuck a strand of hair behind her ear.

"Cookies?" Gideon asked hopefully.

"Meat loaf."

"Oh."

Gideon accepted the bag with all the enthusiasm of a man being handed a roadside bomb. He peeled "Thank you" off his tongue with considerable difficulty and, holding the bag at arm's length, carried it into the kitchen.

He rejoined Pete and Sylvia in the living room. Sylvia was petting Punkin on the head, and Pete was strapping the kid back into the harness on his chest. As soon as he was in, he kicked Pete in the nuts to show his appreciation. Shortly after that, they left. Pete was limping.

At least the kid hadn't puked.

After Sylvia and Pete, came Lester and Dan.

Lester and Dan seemed to have been spit out by the same photocopier. They each wore bow ties knotted neatly at their throats. They both wore geeky black glasses. They both had their crisp short-sleeve shirts neatly tucked into freshly ironed khaki pants. They both had too much hair product slicking their hair straight back off their foreheads like they'd just climbed down off a motorcycle going a hundred miles an hour through a bowl of Jell-O. And they both wore perfectly polished wingtip shoes. Not only did they look like twins, they were also *physically* connected since they were holding hands. Somehow Gideon got the impression they were *always* holding hands. Like Tweedledee and Tweedledum. Or the creepy twin girls in *The Shining*.

"Lester and Dan!" they chirped in unison when Gideon opened the door. "We're librarians!"

Gideon wasn't quite sure what to say to that, so he jokingly asked, "Are my books overdue?"

The joke was lost on Lester and Dan. Their smiles faded, and little worry lines striped their foreheads. "We certainly hope not. When did you check them out?"

Gideon sighed. "I was kidding."

Neither Lester nor Dan cracked a smile. "We see." They shot furtive glances at each other as if wondering what sort of person would joke about a thing like that.

After a pause, the one on the left (Gideon had yet to decipher who was Lester and who was Dan) said, "Hope we're not imposing. We brought you a present to welcome you to the Belladonna Arms." Hooking a thumb toward his partner, he added, "By the way, I'm Lester and he's Dan."

So that much was cleared up.

"That's sweet of you," Gideon said, although he didn't see any evidence of gifts. They were still just standing at his door holding hands. "So," Gideon ventured when the silence began to grate, "are you two lovers, then?"

This time Dan took the floor. "Oh yes. We just moved in together. We met out back in the toolshed when we were hunting for buried treasure a few months back."

"Buried treasure," Gideon echoed, trying desperately not to gawp.

Dan didn't seem to mind the interruption. *Or* the gawp. "Yes. Buried treasure. Then we got sprayed by a family of skunks and had to strip off our clothes while we waited for someone to bring us something to wear that wasn't soaked with skunk juice, and while we were naked and waiting down in that toolshed, we discovered we were mutually attracted to each other, stinking or not."

"Skunks," Gideon said. He wasn't sure but he thought he was developing a tic in his left eye.

"Yes. Skunks. Try to keep up. By the way, have you met Sylvia? Isn't he pretty?"

Gideon cocked his head. "Did you say *he*?"

Lester took over. "Well, he used to be a he. After the sex change operation, he became a she. Him, I mean her, and Pete are really married, though."

"What about the baby?"

Dan giggled. "Stinky little rascal, isn't he?"

Gideon ignored the interruption. "No, I mean, how did they have a baby if she was a he?"

"Kid's adopted," Dan explained. "They should have shopped around for one that smelled better."

They both laughed while Gideon stood there staring at them. His tic had stopped, but now he was pretty sure he was getting a headache. Or maybe a brain tumor. "You said something about a present?"

"Oh yeah!" Lester plucked his hand out of Dan's and fished around in his back pocket for a minute, eventually pulling out a slip of plastic that looked like a credit card.

"Holy shit," Gideon said, staring at it. "You're giving me a Visa card?"

Lester and Dan both looked at the card. It *was* a Visa card, and it had Lester's name on it.

"Oops," Lester said. "Wrong card."

Dan offered Gideon an embarrassed smirk while they both waited for Lester to fish around in his back pocket again.

"Ah! Here it is," Lester said and held up another slip of plastic. He passed it to Gideon, who hesitantly plucked it from his fingers.

This time it wasn't a Visa card. It was a library card. And it had Gideon's name on it.

"We checked the files at the library," Dan explained, "and found out there was no library card registered in your name, so we got you one. It has no expiration date, you'll notice. It's good until you die. Free books for life. Hope you're a reader."

Oddly enough, Gideon was thrilled. He *loved* to read. Beaming, he said, "Thanks, guys!"

Lester reached out and tapped the card with a fingertip. "It's not just a library card. We also included a $20.00 gift certificate for the library coffee shop. I assume you know the library is only a few blocks from here."

"Yeah," Gideon said, even happier with the gift. "It's close to the Office Depot where I work."

"Well, isn't that fortuitous!" Lester exclaimed, just shy of tittering.

Gideon flapped the card in front of his nose as if breathing in its bouquet. "This is great, guys. Thank you so much. I'll see you both at the library one of these days."

"You bet," Dan said, and glancing at his watch, he cried, "Oops, we have to run. We're working today. See ya, Gideon. Welcome to the Arms."

They were halfway down the hall, headed for the stairs, when Gideon called out behind them, "Say! Did you ever find that treasure?"

They stopped and whirled around, still holding hands. "Yes," Lester called back. "There was even some money involved," he said, throwing the line away like it meant very little to him. Then both Lester and Dan pointed a finger at each other. The motion looked well-rehearsed, like maybe they dragged it out at the occasional cocktail party after they'd had a few. "Although the real treasure was *him*!" they sang out, beaming.

"So never badmouth a skunk," Dan said, suddenly glowering and wagging a finger like a disgruntled schoolmarm. That line sounded rehearsed as well, but Gideon didn't mind. It sounded sweet too.

"Thank you, guys." Gideon waved his library card in the air. "Have a great day."

"You too!" they called back, already disappearing down the stairs. And just before Gideon stepped back through his door, Lester called out from two floors down, "See you at the library!"

Dan chimed in with, "Happy reading and don't dog-ear the pages! Librarians *hate* that!"

Gideon laughed and closed the door behind him, proudly eying his brand-new library card.

Chapter 4

REED'S FIRST face-to-face meeting with the redhead next door was far more enjoyable than he expected it to be.

It was Saturday morning, not too early because he didn't want to appear eager. He had spent the last two evenings after work repairing some of the defects in his own apartment, banging around with his trusty hammer, making horrible whining noises with his industrial-sized electric drill, and probably annoying half the building's tenants while he did it. He thought he would donate a few hours of his time now to see what he could do to help out his new neighbor and in the process maybe annoy the rest of the tenants with the racket he could make. Not that they seemed very prone to being annoyed.

Actually, Reed had never seen a friendlier bunch of people than the residents of the Belladonna Arms. He had never seen an odder bunch of people either, starting with Arthur, who pretty much sent the needle on the odd-o-meter straight into the red zone. Not that it mattered. Reed wasn't exactly a picture of mental health himself.

He donned a pair of old gray sweat shorts, threw a T-shirt he had sawed the sleeves off of ages ago over his head, and slipped his sockless feet into a grungy pair of tennis shoes. No sense dressing up just to get dirty. He gathered up his tool belt, which weighed about a ton and a half, and strapped it around his waist, taking a moment to adjust it a little better so it wouldn't drag his shorts down around his ankles. He then grabbed two beers from the fridge and headed next door.

Gideon answered on the first knock.

"Hi," Reed said, thrusting one of the beers in Gideon's face. "Ready to get to work?"

Gideon stood there, a head shorter, his hair a shade redder, all decked out in a brand-new pair of khaki shorts that were still creased with store wrinkles and had a price tag dangling off the leg. Topside he wore a red polo shirt with Office Depot stenciled on the chest. He was barefoot, and his legs were just as fuzzy as Reed's—and much to Reed's surprise, sexy as hell. In fact, once he saw them, it took considerable effort for Reed to drag his eyes back to Gideon's face. When he did, he felt a definite uptick in his heart rate, which he attributed to the fact that he was simply horny. That little problem would be remedied later, since tonight was going to be the first night of his newly single life when he would hit a gay bar or two to see if he could dredge up a trick. He hated to admit it, but the prospect scared him half to death. He wasn't quite sure why.

But all that was forgotten for the moment as he stared at his freckled neighbor standing in front of him looking innocent and sweet and (for a redhead) pretty darn scrumptious. He was apparently thirsty as well, for the moment Reed offered the beer, Gideon swept it out of his hand and screwed off the cap, which he tossed over his shoulder to send it clattering across his living room linoleum, tilted the beer bottle back, and poured half of it down his throat before he stopped with a satisfied, lip-smacking, "Ahh."

Then he added a guilty grin to the equation. "Hi yourself."

Reed laughed. "Drink much?" Only then did Reed notice a slightly maniacal gleam in Gideon's eyes.

It was quickly explained when Gideon flung his arms wide to encompass the apartment behind him, "Nothing works in this place! I asked Arthur to fix my shower, and he told me to take a sponge bath until he could arrange a plumber, sometime in October. That's *three months away*. I told him the oven didn't work—he told me to eat salad. I told him the windows would barely open, and he rattled off the EPA's smog numbers for San Diego County and told me I was better off holding my breath anyway. The only time I got a rise out of Arthur was when I told him the mantilla he was wearing with his flamenco dancer's outfit made him look old. He fixed that right away, don't think he didn't. Tore that sucker right off his head."

Reed offered what he hoped was a sympathetic clucking sound. Not quite knowing what to say, he took a slug from his beer instead, eyes wide, staring at Gideon's face. And his legs. And his basket. And then his face again. Sort of mesmerized, he continued to stand in Gideon's doorway, nodding his head, *tsk*ing, clucking, sipping at his beer and readjusting the tool belt at his waist since it seemed bound and determined to drag his shorts right off his ass. The thought of where that might lead was almost mind-boggling.

He finally breathed a sigh of relief when Gideon's face softened and he smiled around the tip of the beer bottle pressed to his lips.

"Sorry about the rant," Gideon said as the blood rushed up to redden his ears. "And thanks for the beer. God knows I needed it." He stepped back and gave an exaggerated salami-salami-baloney bow, waving Reed inside. As Reed strolled past, Gideon mumbled under his breath, "Wow."

Reed turned to catch Gideon staring at his ass. "What?"

"Oh, nothing," Gideon hastily stammered, taking another sip of his beer while trying to look innocent. "That's just one handy-dandy tool belt."

It was Reed's turn to blush. "Oh. Well, thanks. And you don't have to suck up, you know. I wasn't going to charge you for the work anyway."

Gideon gave him an embarrassed glance. Somewhere down in the depths of it, Reed spotted a glimmer of guilt, as if they both knew it wasn't Reed's tool belt he'd been staring at.

"Thanks," Gideon said, suddenly shy. Or self-conscious. Or both.

Being struck off guard by apparently shaming Gideon when he didn't really mean to, Reed shuffled from one foot to the other, giving a manly rattle to the tools at his waist. He gazed around like maybe he would spot a repair job waiting to be tackled and he could just light right into it. When he didn't see anything blatantly amiss, like maybe a broken sewer line dribbling crap through a living room wall, he stuck out his hand and said, "We meet at last."

Gideon dredged up a smile that was warmer now, but still a little tenuous around the edges. "I guess we do. Umm, good to meet you, Reed."

They shook hands, and Reed savored the icy feel of Gideon's beer-bottle-cold fingers buried in his great paw. His eyes skidded over Gideon's clean jawline, blurred only slightly by a brush of unshaven beard, which was barely enough to spot at all unless the sun hit it just right from behind, limning his cheeks in a halo of golden light. The dimples were still in place from the unsteady smile he continued to offer, and when the tip of Gideon's tongue slipped out to moisten his lips and his eyebrows climbed higher as he waited for a response, Reed felt his fingers tightening around the man's hand as if with a will of their own.

Embarrassed, he quickly slipped his hand free. Remembering his manners only at the last moment, he echoed, "Nice to meet you too."

Gideon stepped back, and with a little distance between them now, Reed watched Gideon's eyes glide over him yet again, not overtly, but clearly appreciative nevertheless. There was no point in denying Reed enjoyed being the recipient of that look. He enjoyed it a lot.

"Redheads," he mumbled, trying to find a little humor in the situation. When Gideon looked confused, Reed pointed a finger back and forth between the two of them, first aiming at Gideon, then at himself. "Us, I mean. Redheads."

At that, Gideon laughed. "We are indeed."

"I'm not into redheads," Reed said, taking himself by surprise. *What a stupid thing to say, and at this particular moment, what a fucking lie.*

"I know. Neither am I," Gideon stammered. "But I think we covered that the other night while we were hanging out our windows chatting."

"Oh yeah. I forgot."

Gideon winked. "At least now we know for sure, since it's been stated twice in no uncertain terms. We don't like redheads. So there. Ha!"

They shared a forced chuckle. At least it was forced on Reed's end.

He swallowed. *I'm acting like a twit. Why am I so turned on?* Coughing up a phony laugh, he chucked Gideon on the arm like the biggest, butchest asshole in the world. "Yep, now we know for sure, big guy."

"Yep, we got that out of the way."

"Sure did. No redheads for either one of us. Nosiree." Reed slapped himself silly inside his own head. *Shut up. Shut up now.*

A rustling sound started up behind him, and grateful for an excuse to stop this string of insipid conversation dead in its tracks, Reed whirled around to see a soccer ball come rolling across the floor in his direction. Directly behind the soccer ball came a tiny prancing kitten, trying to catch it.

"That's Punkin," Gideon said proudly. "Another redhead. She's a new tenant too. I need to get her some smaller toys."

Reed tapped the soccer ball with his toe to send it back the kitten's way and managed to roll it right over the little cat, knocking it on its keister. Not being bothered in the least, the kitten scrambled back onto all fours and chased off after the ball in the opposite direction.

"Oops," Reed said, biting back a laugh. "Didn't mean to mow the little guy down."

Gideon shrugged, still eying the kitten. "Girl. And don't worry. I've done it about ten times already myself. Strangely, she doesn't seem to mind. At least she keeps getting up."

"Well, that's good. I came over to help you out, not murder your cat."

Reed and Gideon turned to face each other, and Reed found himself echoing Gideon's smile. He didn't feel so much like a twit anymore. Or did he?

"So…," he said, embarrassed yet again, still a little bit unsteadied by those gorgeous blue eyes taking him in.

"So…," Gideon repeated, then fluttered his lashes as if blinking himself back to the moment. "Still feel up to doing some work?"

GIDEON STARED at Reed's broad back and bare arms as he stood in the tub, working on the showerhead. Gideon had parked himself on the edge of the tub at eye level with Reed's ass and thought, *Well now, this is the best seat in the house.*

He would have given three Office Depot paychecks to be able to reach out and stroke the back of those strong, fuzzy legs poking through the leg holes of the ratty old shorts Reed was wearing. Red hair aside, Reed was just the sort of man Gideon found most attractive. Tall, neatly muscled, rangy, and masculine. Not a nelly bone in his body. And he knew how to do things. Just look at him wield that wrench!

Gideon couldn't help wondering what other things Reed might know how to do.

"Did you just break up with a lover too?" Gideon asked. Then he thought he should backtrack a little so he wouldn't sound so nosy. "I mean, everybody in the Arms seems to have moved in after suddenly finding themselves newly single and heartbroken and desperate to find accommodations. I mean, why else would anybody move into this dump? So are you newly single and heartbroken too? Just wondering."

With his arms held high, Reed ducked his head and peered through the hair in his armpit, eyeballing Gideon as if wondering why his new nosy neighbor was sitting there behind him snooping into his love life. Gideon flushed but stood, or rather sat, his ground.

"Well, I'm newly single," Reed said, clearly being evasive but sounding a little amused as well. "How about you?"

Gideon shrugged, not so happy that the question had been thrown back in his face. "Well, I'm single, God knows, and I was certainly desperate enough for accommodations." He flung his arms wide to encompass the place he now called home in case he needed more proof. "But heartbroken? Not so much. My heartbreak morphed into pure unadulterated hatred about four days back. Trust me, the hatred's more fun."

He waited until Reed had turned back to the showerhead and recommenced gnawing at the rusty fucker with the jaws of his wrench. Figuring he couldn't get much snoopier than he had already, Gideon decided to dig a little more. "So did your lover dump you, or did you dump him?"

Reed lowered the wrench and turned to stare. Since they were facing each other now, Gideon couldn't help but notice that his head was at the perfect level. If Reed took one step forward, his crotch would bump Gideon's nose. And wasn't *that* a titillating observation.

Before he could fantasize any more, Reed stooped and twisted the spigot down below enough to make a tiny stream of water run free. He dipped his fingers in it and splashed the water over his face, playfully flicked another splash in Gideon's direction, making him jump, then reached back down to turn off the tap.

"Why are you asking me all these questions?" Reed asked. He didn't look mad; he looked curious.

Having the question posed so forthrightly, Gideon had to admit the truth. "I don't know. I guess I just want to know about you."

"Why?" Again Reed didn't seem annoyed.

So Gideon decided to tell him. He had already made an ass of himself. Why worry about making it worse? Still perched on the edge of the tub, he leaned back against the shower wall, propped his knee up to rest his chin on it, and studied Reed standing before him. The bulging calf muscles, the trim hairy knees, the golden skin tone of his long fuzzy legs. And higher up, the broad shoulders, the strong capable hand gripping the wrench, the tool belt dragging his shorts down enough to open a gap between the top of the shorts and the bottom of the shirt, displaying a brush of red hair around a tidy little belly button that Gideon found most alluring. It took more willpower than he had used in three years to drag his eyes back up to Reed's face.

"Well," he said, "looking the way you do, I can't imagine anybody dumping *you*, so I figure you must be the one who did the dumping. Am I right?"

Reed frowned, but there was a smidgeon of reluctant intrigue in the frown. And the faintest trace of a smile as well. "Maybe," he said.

"You broke your lover's heart, I'll bet. The little glimmer of sadness that's currently burning there in your eyes tells me it still bothers you that you did."

Reed was clearly surprised that Gideon would say such a thing. "I guess you imagine yourself being psychic, huh? Dabble in ESP, do you? Read Tarot cards? Hold séances? Bend spoons?"

Gideon laughed, brushing off the remark. "You don't like to talk about yourself, but you're lonely too, so our talking right now, no matter how aggravating I am, doesn't bother you too much. At least doing this pro bono work for a needy neighbor got you out of your empty apartment. You figure that's better than nothing."

"Now you're talking out of your ass." Reed smiled, but the smile was still friendly. Sort of.

Never one to know when to shut up, Gideon asked, "How long were you with your lover?"

This time when Reed frowned, it had more heart to it. The tiny smile inside it was gone. When he answered, his words were clipped. Cool. "If you must know, I didn't have a lover."

Gideon blinked. "Sorry. You lost me."

Reed studied the wrench in his hand as if he were considering bonking Gideon in the head with it. When he turned back to Gideon, his eyes were no longer amused. They weren't angry exactly, just sort of uneasy. "I said I didn't have a lover. I had a wife. And yes, I broke her heart."

Gideon's jaw dropped. Not at the words, but at the pain on Reed's face. Forgetting what he had wished he had the courage to do earlier, he simply did it now without thinking. Stretching an arm out, he laid his hand over Reed's knee, stroking the skin there with his thumb in what he considered to be a comforting gesture. Nothing more.

Reed stared down at the hand, then back to Gideon's face. "Anything else you want to know?" he asked.

Gideon's thumb continued to move through the hair on Reed's knee, across the bony hardness and satin heat. He detected the faintest tremor beneath his touch, or at least he imagined he did. Gideon had never felt more ashamed in his life.

"I'm sorry," he said, pulling his hand away. "Suddenly a little good-natured prying doesn't seem so much fun anymore. I-I didn't know you were straight."

"I'm not," Reed said. And with that, he turned to reconcentrate his attention on the showerhead, presenting Gideon with his broad back as if enough words had passed between them and now it was time to get back to work.

Gideon dropped his hand to his lap, his nerve endings still buzzing as he remembered the feel of Reed's knee beneath his fingertips.

Unfolding himself from the edge of the tub, he dredged up a smile he didn't feel and said softly, "I'll get us another beer."

REED HAD to admit it. Gideon's apartment was in far worse shape than his own. He also had to admit he didn't mind helping Gideon make it a little more livable. After the rocky start, what with Gideon's relentless prying, Reed began to enjoy the conversation, even when it continued to turn a probing eye on himself. The beer helped. They'd gone through five apiece by now. It was afternoon already. They'd been together for three hours and were about half-drunk. Oddly, Gideon's endless interrogation didn't affect Reed's ability to wield tools and fix stuff. At which Gideon seemed truly impressed. He had developed a slight slur in his words about thirty minutes back, which Reed found pretty cute.

"So is there anything you *can't* do?" Gideon asked. He was currently lying facedown on the kitchen linoleum with his nose in Punkin's belly while Reed lay flat on his back next to him with his head under the sink, trying to remove the gooseneck so he could clear the crap from the trap and get the sink to drain again. With them both stretched out side by side on the floor, and considering the beers they'd consumed, it was perhaps understandable that Reed was entertaining some rather amorous imaginings. They were quickly forgotten when he banged his finger with the wrench.

"Yow shit fuck damn crap!"

Reed stuck his filthy injured finger in his mouth at the same moment that Gideon reached out and laid his hand on Reed's bare thigh in commiseration.

"You okay?"

Reed lifted his head, his finger still in his mouth, and gazed down the length of himself to see Gideon lying there beside him with his hand still resting on Reed's thigh, his fingers not more than six inches away from his balls. Gideon, still on his belly with the kitten tucked under his chin, was currently staring along the same expanse of Reed's long frame, his eyes wide and clearly concerned. When Gideon's fingers shifted slightly over the tender skin on his thigh, Reed jumped.

In a voice a little creakier than usual, not from pain but from a sudden infusion of hormones, Reed said, "Can you pass me that screwdriver?"

Gideon's eyes were so centered on Reed's face, heat rushed to his own.

"Uh-huh," Gideon grunted, and removing his hand, he sat up and cast around, looking for the screwdriver Reed wanted. While he did that, Punkin took off across the floor to climb Mt. Reed, walking across the summit of his chest and booping her nose against Reed's chin. Reed laughed and patted her tiny head in response. Her motor kicked in.

"I like your cat," Reed said.

"Me too," Gideon said, handing him the screwdriver. "Here."

"Thanks."

"Your finger all right?"

"I'll live."

"You're really butch. I'd be calling an ambulance. EMTs. Dr. Phil. The six o'clock news."

Reed laughed. Setting the kitten carefully aside, he squirmed a little deeper under the sink and lifted his arms to go back to work. Gideon still sat beside him, watching. The silence was not uncomfortable. It also didn't last long.

"Why did you leave her?" Gideon asked. His voice was as warm and smooth as hot chocolate. With the pleasant buzz of five beers coursing through his system, Reed thought he could probably listen to it all day and it wouldn't bother him much. Even the prying questions weren't as annoying as they had been about four beers back.

Reed sighed deep. Without pausing in his work, he spoke quietly. It was almost as if he were talking to himself. "I was a late bloomer. Not because I didn't know the truth about myself, but because the truth wasn't something I wanted to accept. We married so young, you see. I didn't know myself then. I managed to carry off the deception with Carol for a couple of years, but soon I began to change. Carol probably thought I'd simply lost interest in her. But it wasn't that. I just discovered new interests rising up inside myself."

"Men," Gideon said, his voice hushed.

Reed nodded. "Men. I couldn't live the lie anymore. It wasn't fair to her. It wasn't fair to me. No one was happy. No one could ever *be* happy until I righted the wrongs and accepted myself for who and what I was. And the only way I could do that was to pull back from Carol and set us both free."

Again, Gideon laid his hand on Reed's leg. On his shin this time. It was a comforting touch. Reed enjoyed it. He stopped what he was doing and once again stared down the length of himself to study Gideon's hand on his skin.

"You're a toucher," he said softly.

"Does it bother you?" Gideon asked, not moving his hand.

"No," Reed said. "It doesn't bother me."

Their eyes shifted toward each other, connecting for a long, silent moment. "Did she ever forgive you?" Gideon asked. "Your wife? Will she be all right?"

Reed laid the wrench on his chest and pushed his hair up off his face with a dirty hand. "I hope so. I never meant to hurt her."

Gideon's fingers moved through the hair on Reed's leg. Just slightly. Enough to be noticeable. "I'm sure she knows that."

"Thanks," Reed said, every molecule in his body centered on the heat of Gideon's hand resting on his leg. His cock moved inside his shorts. It startled him so, he banged his head on the sink.

"Ouch!" he exclaimed.

"Ooh!" Gideon winced.

With his face on fire, not from banging his head but from the embarrassment of having his dick suddenly threaten to spring to life, Reed wormed his way out from under the sink, jarring Gideon's hand loose in the process. Grunting his way to his feet, he stood at the sink with his back to Gideon, twisting the spigot to On to get the water running, and as soon as he did that, he ducked his head back under the sink and checked for leaks. Nothing.

"I think I got it," he said. It was true. The sink was fixed. Happily, his dick had gone back to sleep as well. *Jesus, that was close.*

He turned to Gideon, who still sat on the floor at his feet gazing up.

"Can I fix you a sandwich?" Gideon asked, his dimples in full view as if maybe he knew a little bit about everything that had just happened as well as Reed did.

Much to Reed's surprise, he heard himself say, "No. I'm not hungry."

"Oh," Gideon said. "Okay."

Reed offered a hand to hoist Gideon off the floor, and once he was on his feet, they were face-to-face for what seemed like about an hour and a half but couldn't have been more than two seconds. The heat that rose in Reed's face was echoed by Gideon's blush.

"Th-thank you," Gideon stammered, glancing at his newly functional kitchen sink, each and every freckle on his face ablaze. "That sink was really pissing me off."

"I'm sure it was," Reed said. "And you're welcome." He bent down to gather up his tools, inwardly kicking himself for saying no to a sandwich.

"Maybe I can do something for you sometime," Gideon said.

The words were so sweetly stated, with clearly no double entendres implied, Reed stopped what he was doing and offered Gideon a smile.

"Is there anything you *can* do?" Reed asked, joking.

At that, a wicked light entered Gideon's eyes. No doubt fueled by five beers, he grinned, exposing his dimples yet again. "Not to brag, but I have several talents you know nothing about."

Reed swallowed when a sudden burst of understanding burrowed its way inside his head. His mouth curled up in a suggestive grin he couldn't contain. "I'm sure you do."

Before Gideon could respond, Reed straightened his tool belt and said almost reluctantly, "If there's nothing else for me to do…."

"Actually, a *few* things come to mind, but I think I'd have to know you better for those. In the meantime, how about fixing the lock on my front door? And helping me get my windows open?" He took Reed's hand and led him through the kitchen to the living room.

"Only if you have more beer," Reed said, enjoying having his hand wrapped up in Gideon's. And enjoying a lot of other things too.

"IT NEEDS oil," Reed said after a cursory examination of the front door lock. "That's why the key sticks."

Gideon stood to the side, sipping at his sixth beer. He was having more fun than he'd had in months. To his practiced eye, Reed didn't seem too miserable either. "Oil, huh? Do you have any?" Gideon asked. At which Reed shot him a look of pure devilment. "Are you kidding? Lubricant is my middle name."

Now it was Gideon's turn to swallow with a damn near audible gulp. It coincided with a rush of pure hunger that rampaged through his lower colon at the exact same moment. He hadn't felt one of those in a while. "Golly, Reed. That's awfully good to know."

Reed took a pull on his sixth beer, clearly amused by Gideon's reaction.

Gideon caught the look and returned it with one of his own. "You're having fun, aren't you?" he asked.

Reed didn't bother denying it. "Yeah. You?"

"Indubitably."

Reed's eyebrows shot up as he pulled a long chisel from his tool belt. "Then maybe it's time we put *this* sucker to good use."

Gideon stared at the chisel like it was a cast-iron dildo. He flapped his hand in front of his face as if he were having a hot flash. He did it jokingly, of course. Didn't he? "Umm, not quite sure what you intend to do with *that*."

Reed glanced at the chisel, then back at Gideon. "As soon as I squirt some oil in your keyhole, I thought I'd scrape the paint off your window frames so you can open your windows all the way and get some fresh air in here. What did you think I was going to do with it?"

"You don't want to know."

Gideon enjoyed the view of snow-white teeth glimmering behind Reed's grin. The grin was quickly replaced by a far broader smile, a really handsome one. Gideon was caught off guard by the sudden intensity of Reed's gaze. He stared, mesmerized, as Reed lifted his arm to prop himself against the door frame, exposing the smooth underside of his not inconsiderable bicep and the forest of red armpit hair that carpeted the flesh beneath it.

"You're a tease," Reed said, as if the truth had suddenly slapped him upside the head. He didn't seem to find that truth particularly appalling. In fact, he looked pretty darned tickled by the whole thing.

Gideon tore his gaze from Reed's armpit and managed to refocus on his face, although it wasn't easy. *But I don't like redheads*, a voice screamed inside his head while another voice screamed, *Oh, shut up*.

"I think maybe you're a tease too," Gideon finally said. Truthfully, it was the first thing that popped into his head, but after he said it, he realized it was probably true.

"Maybe we shouldn't drink so much this early in the day," Reed said.

"Or maybe we should drink more," Gideon countered.

Both men laughed at that, and just as quickly, a spate of silence settled around them.

Reed glanced at the chisel in his hand. "Best get to the windows, then."

"I guess so," Gideon answered, sucking in a calming breath of air. What the hell had just happened? Why were his nerve endings sizzling?

To Gideon's surprise, Reed slipped the chisel back into his tool belt and pulled out a spray can of Klean-Strip paint remover. "Gotta lube it up first," he explained. "Then the chiseling will be easier."

"Oh. Sort of like the keyhole."

"Exactly."

Gideon chose to ignore the fluttering of his heart while Reed went from window to window, spraying the inside of the window tracks. When he was finished, he said, "It'll only take a few minutes to soften the old paint."

"Oh, okay," Gideon said. He motioned to the couch. "Sit down and we'll take a break."

After everything they had talked about and after consuming a six-pack of beer each, Gideon suddenly felt shy. He wasn't sure why. They sat in silence for a couple of minutes. During that time, the humor gradually fell from Reed's face as he stared down at his big hands cradling his latest beer. He flexed his fingers around the bottle like maybe they hurt a little bit. Two of his knuckles were skinned.

Out of nowhere Reed said, "I never want to hurt anybody again like I hurt Carol."

Gideon twisted on the couch to study the man beside him. "Y-your wife?"

"Yeah." Reed sucked in a shuddering breath while his thumb slid tracks through the condensation on his beer bottle. "She didn't deserve what I did to her."

"I'm sure she understood," Gideon said. "She must know you had no choice but to be true to yourself."

"I hope so." Reed blinked as if intentionally shedding the sadness from his eyes before turning them to Gideon. "What about you? Did you deserve what your lover did to you?"

"Our cases are different," Gideon said. "You left your wife so you could be yourself. With Manny it was all about his dick, as usual. He left me because he wanted somebody else in his bed for a while."

"I can't imagine why," Reed softly said. Gideon lifted his gaze to the man beside him. Not knowing what else to say, he came back with a quiet "Thank you." He watched as Reed turned his eyes back to his beer bottle. Since he'd been given a compliment, Gideon expected a flash of teasing sarcasm to light up Reed's eyes, but it never came. Reed had meant what he said. When Gideon realized that, he slid his fingertips along the side of Reed's arm in silent appreciation for the kind words.

"You're easy to talk to," Gideon said, immediately pulling his fingers back into his own space, his voice low, barely ruffling the comfortable silence between them.

At that, Reed lifted his eyes to Gideon's face. "So are you. I think it was therapeutic, me telling you all this stuff. I think maybe being able to say the words helped clear some things up inside my head. Maybe it did for you too. Thank you, Gideon."

"Sure. Glad I could help. Although none of this really applies to me. I already had things cleared up inside my head. In a nutshell, Manny was a jerk, and I didn't deserve to be dumped on like I was or have everything I owned tossed into a Salvation Army collection bin to be distributed among the poor. Period. I was a saint. He was the devil incarnate. No room for confusion at all."

Reed smiled. This time there was a little sarcasm in it. "Gee, I wish I had your sense of self."

Gideon offered a worldly smirk. "Yeah, you should work on that."

They shared a mutual self-effacing glance. As if the sharing had suddenly become too intimate, Reed turned to the nearest window.

"Best to finish up the work. Besides, these paint thinner fumes are killing me."

"What are you doing later?" Gideon asked. The words had tumbled out of his mouth so unexpectedly, he wasn't quite sure of the motivation for them. Well, yes he was, but he wasn't ready to admit it to himself yet.

"I'm going out," Reed said, not exactly evasive, just determined. "I owe it to myself," he added before polishing off his beer. He glanced up. "You want to go?"

"Oh!" Gideon responded, taken off guard, knowing instantly he couldn't go out. He had like three dollars to his name. Maybe four if he gathered up his loose change. Hating himself for it, he said, "No. Thanks. You go on without me. I have things I should probably do here."

"Oh, okay," Reed said, casting a disconcerted glance first at Gideon, then out to the room, as if that clearly wasn't the answer he had expected. "I—uh—just thought I'd ask. Let me finish the windows, and I'll be out of your hair."

Helpless, Gideon watched as Reed hauled himself off the couch and walked on those long, beautiful legs to the nearest window.

"I've got two chisels, if you want to help," Reed offered, his eyes skirting back to Gideon for a second. Shy again. Uncomfortable. No longer teasing.

"Oh, sure. Lemme at it." Gideon reached for the chisel, trying to ignore the fact that it looked like it needed to be run through a carwash a couple of times. He was also trying to come up with a way to change his mind about going out, but there was no way. Asking for a loan or sitting around waiting for Reed to buy him drinks would have been too humiliating.

Reed's mouth finally molded itself into a smile again when he looked over to see Gideon with the chisel in his hand, since he had clearly never held one in his life.

"Anything I should know?" Gideon asked, staring at the chisel like maybe it would bite him if he didn't keep an eye on it.

"Just scrape the layers of old paint out of the window tracks. Try not to chip off a finger or fall through the window," Reed said.

"Gotcha," Gideon muttered. He ducked his head as a little rush of sadness stuttered through him. He *really* wanted to go out with Reed. Hit a few bars. Have a few laughs. See where the evening might lead.

With a sigh, he despondently poked his chisel at the window sill. A teeny tiny flake of old paint fluttered to the floor. He still had four windows to go.

Great.

THAT NIGHT, more out of a stubborn sense of duty than because he wanted to, Reed visited three gay bars and stood around uncomfortably consuming five beers, not really tasting any of them. Three of those beers were bought for him by others. He was propositioned nine times, told he was hunky six, had his dick ogled at the urinal twice, and would eventually go home alone. Oddly, while traipsing from one bar to the next on this Saturday night, single and unattached for the first time in ages, he couldn't enjoy himself. He had lost interest. No one he met measured up to what he wanted. No matter how good they looked or how sexy they were, they were clearly either too slutty for words, didn't know how to carry on a conversation, or were so drunk nobody with an ounce of self-respect would have crawled into bed with them.

The last nightclub he visited was called Numbers. It was a shitkicker bar not far from the San Diego Zoo, which, judging by the clientele, seemed more than apt. He stood there alone among a raucous crowd of desperately exuberant gay men, each and every one of them soused to the gills. Country music blasted in his ears while he leaned on the proverbial meat rack, feeling lonely and humiliated and totally out of place. Missing Carol. Wondering what she was doing. Wondering if by leaving her he had made the biggest mistake of his life. Aching inside for something he couldn't quite explain even to himself.

When even his beer buzz couldn't survive his mood and he found himself tumbling back into an unwelcome sobriety, he knew it was time to give up and go home.

He was walking tonight, since the last thing he needed was a DUI. Happily, there were several gay bars sprinkled around the city within walking distance of the Arms. *Unhappily*, for Reed anyway, not one of them had offered him anything close to what he thought he was seeking.

He dropped a dollar bill on the bar beside his last barely touched beer and squeezed his way through the manic, testosterone-reeking crowd to the front door and freedom. Once outside Numbers, sucking in a humongous gulp of balmy night air to clear his head and thanking God for the sudden silence, he set off walking down Park Boulevard, headed home. He could have hailed a cab, but he needed to stretch his legs. He needed peace and quiet. He needed to think.

It didn't surprise Reed at all that the first place his thoughts carried him was back to his afternoon with Gideon. He was pretty sure that destination had been hovering around inside his head all night. It had been kind of an eye-opener for Reed, the hours he had spent with his new neighbor. The easygoing way they had connected right off the bat. Unlike the putzes he had met in the bars tonight, Gideon had actually been fun to talk to. Gideon knew how to carry on a conversation. Gideon even knew how to laugh. At himself, at Reed, at everything. Reed sort of liked that. Nothing was sacred.

Gideon was also pretty good at digging up secrets. Reed had spilled his guts more with Gideon about everything he had been going through, what with the breakup with Carol and all, than he had shared with anybody, well, *ever*. And the odd thing was, Reed didn't regret it. It had been cathartic, speaking out loud about what was happening in his life. The mistakes he had made. How he was trying to set things right, sort things out. Gideon's sympathetic ear had been just what he needed.

As for the other thing, well....

Gideon wasn't Reed's type, of course, being a redhead and all, but still he was far from revolting to look at. Reed thought back to his first sight of Gideon's pale legs, bared from the thighs down in those godawful new cargo pants he had been wearing. The lovely coat of strawberry-blond hair that covered those legs, not unlike the hair on Reed's own. The crisp sharp line of Gideon's calf muscles. The gentle indentation of his quads above his knees. The way his red hair waved around on top of his head when he moved, gleaming in the sunlight shining through it from the window behind him as he opened his door to usher Reed inside. He pictured Gideon's hands, the way they flew all over the place when he talked, like his tongue was attached to his wrists or something. And the way Gideon continually reached out to touch, to pet, to offer a caring pat now and then when the moment suited.

Most of all Reed remembered Gideon's smile. And the easy way it sometimes came at you out of nowhere when you least expected it.

Reed's mouth twisted into a smile of its own as he strolled down the street recalling the time he had spent with Gideon. He wondered how Gideon's smile would taste. How would it feel to bend down and press his lips to Gideon's mouth? To inhale Gideon's warm spent breath and have Gideon's arms come up in response, clutching Reed's waist, pulling him closer, offering more. Offering everything.

Reed stumbled to a stop by the rose garden across from Balboa Park, not much more than a mile from home. He closed his eyes, inhaled the scent of rose blossoms wafting on the night breeze. Realizing he was standing there in the moonlight sniffing flowers like an old lady, he gave his head a clearing shake and laughed at himself.

God, could he be any more pathetic? To prove to himself that maybe he was barking up the wrong tree anyway, mooning over Gideon the way he was, he recalled how Gideon had turned down his invitation to go out tonight. He had said no not more than three seconds after Reed had asked, so clearly Gideon wasn't any more interested in Reed than Reed was interested in him.

Reed might find himself fantasizing about kissing the guy and stuff, but that's as far as it went, right? Whoever heard of two redheads dating anyway? Redheads *never* liked other redheads. It was kind of a law. Wasn't it? Not that Reed knew so much about what gay people liked and didn't like. He hadn't been one long enough to find out.

It was during that quiet moment as Reed stood next to the bank of roses, their bright multicolored heads bobbing in the wind, that the earth beneath his feet gave another gentle nudge. It was hard to tell how strong a tremor it really was when you were standing outside in the dark with nothing to gauge the movement—-a swaying chandelier, maybe, or the rattle of dishes in a cupboard. But Reed was pretty sure it was enough to send poor Arthur screaming in panic back at the Belladonna Arms, his face probably slathered with night cream, his size thirteen feet encased in marabou-feathered house slippers, maybe a frizzy boa trailing down his back as he stomped from room to room, wailing like a banshee and desperately seeking a place to hide.

Reed chuckled to himself at the mental image. A moment later he cast a silent plea skyward that he would never end up as gay as Arthur. Because really, that was just *too* gay. Funny thing, though. For all his narcissistic eccentricities, for all his outrageous get-ups and the oceans of makeup he slathered all over himself, Arthur was still maybe the most generous and kindhearted person Reed had ever met. Sort of a dichotomy there. How could a person be so centered on himself and yet so caring of everyone else at the same time?

Reed's mouth softened in a lazy smile as he started walking. Remembering Arthur. Remembering Gideon.

Remembering Carol.

Stumbling to a halt again, he plucked his cellphone from his back pocket. He stared at it as it lit up in his hand. His thumb itched to hit number 2 on speed dial. Number 2 on speed dial was Carol's cellphone.

Reed stood there in the shadows—he was halfway between streetlights now, and the streetlights on Park Boulevard were pretty far apart—staring at the phone. When his thumb moved, it hit Photos instead of 2. Carol's picture popped up immediately. It was a snapshot Reed had taken at the beach a couple of years back. Carol, her eyes big and bright over the top of an ice cream cone, her feet coated with sand, the hem of her summer dress tied in a knot at her hip because she had been wading in the surf and didn't want to get it wet.

Reed sighed, staring at the photo. As he had done more than a hundred times in the last couple of days, he wondered what she was doing right now. Was she sleeping, still getting used to having no one beside her in the big brass bed they'd bought for twenty bucks at a yard sale during their first year of marriage? The deal of the century, they always called it. That was back when things still clicked. Back when Reed's true desires had been buried so deep inside his psyche he could still function the way he was supposed to function. Like a straight man. Like a husband. He could still make love to Carol then. It was never an earth-shattering experience, but he could do it. And he could pretend—to himself and to her—that he truly enjoyed it too.

Then his ability to pretend had somehow simply vanished. Lovemaking became an ordeal. And a terrifying one at that.

Sadness struck him when he recalled the last time he had tried—and failed. Almost a year ago. How later he and Carol had laughed about it. Happens to everybody, they'd said. No big deal. But when Reed never tried again, all the laughter pretty well stopped. From both sides of the bed.

Again Reed stared at the number 2 on his cellphone screen. Strangely, his thumb no longer itched to tap it. He clicked off the phone and tucked it back in his pocket—a little desperately, maybe, as if the urge to call Carol might rise up again and he would act on it before he could dredge up the willpower to stop himself.

He resumed his walk, plodding now, the spring in his step erased by a sudden emptiness inside. He just wanted to get home. He didn't want to think anymore. He didn't want to remember. He simply wanted to close his door behind him, lock and bolt it, barricade himself inside his crappy new apartment, crawl into bed, and fall asleep.

Maybe this gay life wasn't all it was cracked up to be after all.

And maybe, just maybe, he had made the worst mistake of his life in accepting it as his own.

Chapter 5

AFTER THAT one day when Gideon Chase and Reed Kelly spent a few hours together making Gideon's slummy apartment livable, their dawning friendship simply petered out for lack of trying on either one of their parts. That was how Gideon saw it anyway.

Gideon didn't know if he had said something that made Reed mad, or maybe (and he was still kicking himself over this one), maybe it was the way Gideon had refused Reed's invitation to go out that night with no explanation and no apology. Just a flat-out no.

How could Reed have known Gideon said no because he couldn't afford a night on the town? And why hadn't Gideon dredged up the *cajones* to just admit the truth right off the bat? He was broke. Period. Surely Reed would have understood. He was going through an upheaval in his own life. Reed couldn't have been exactly financially flush either if he had stooped to renting an apartment in the Belladonna Arms.

Here it was two weeks later and Gideon was still trying to rationalize the fact that they hadn't spoken once since that day. It was this rationalization that gave him hope that maybe he hadn't really shot himself in the foot as far as getting to know his new neighbor went. Reed was busy at work, after all. Down at the shipyards. (Damn, that was butch.) He had been working overtime for two weeks and was hardly seen around the apartment complex at all during the daylight hours. Gideon heard this through the building's grapevine, which he had quickly discovered to be an excellent source of news for anything to do with the inmates—scratch that, *tenants*—of the Belladonna Arms. Arthur was not only the grapevine's CEO and senior news anchor, gleefully spewing tidbits of gossip wherever he went and to whomever would listen. He was also its most diligent investigative reporter and avid contributor. As far as Arthur was concerned, the Belladonna Arms News Hour was a public service for everybody under his roof and consequently *always* on the air.

Everybody else did their bit to keep the news flowing too. Gideon had no idea what they were saying about *him*, and truthfully his life was in such a state of shambles, he didn't care. Whatever gossip they were digging up about the new guy in 6B couldn't be much worse than what the new guy in 6B was thinking about himself.

Still, his life tripped gaily forward. Not happily, mind you, just gaily.

Sometimes late at night, Gideon would hear Reed moving around inside his apartment next door. In fact, Gideon could pretty well deduce what Reed was doing at any given moment simply by standing on his bed, pressing his ear to his bedroom wall, and holding his breath while he listened. Talk about being nosy. If he put an inverted glass to his ear and stealthily pressed it to the wall, he could eavesdrop even better. As far as investigative reporting went, Arthur was an amateur compared to Gideon Chase.

Aside from what was going on—or *not* going on—with the hunky redhead next door, Gideon was at least beginning to get a handle on his own life. Arthur's kindness in giving him three weeks to make his first rent payment had been a lifesaver. The fact that he had been inundated with donations of household stuff from the other tenants had ceased being humiliating after about the tenth time he'd answered his door. Now he merely accepted what came his way with grace and what he hoped was just the right amount of humility.

Only that morning he had opened his apartment door to find an alarm clock resting in the bottom of a shopping bag draped around his doorknob, along with a little bag of sugar-sprinkled donut holes, which he loved. It was a gift from Arthur and Tom. Tom Burger was Arthur's lover. He was as tall and rangy as Arthur was rotund. A good-looking older guy who was just as normal as Arthur wasn't. He owned a deli and restaurant up the street in the heart of downtown (thus the donut holes), and was equally as kind, if not a little more subtle about it, as Arthur. They were a perfect pair and seemed to dote on each other, proving yet again that opposites do indeed attract. Making a mental note to thank them later for the clock, Gideon kissed Punkin goodbye and hurried out the door, headed for work. As he bustled down the puke-green hallway, he thought he heard Reed moving around inside his apartment. Getting ready for work down at the shipyards, he supposed. Or maybe fixing himself breakfast.

Gideon spared a few seconds to poke along in the hope that Reed would come barreling out of his apartment and plow into him in the hall, but that hope was lost by the time Gideon reached the stairs, so he headed on down, determined to get this day over with as quickly as possible.

Since the Office Depot where he worked was only ten blocks away, Gideon walked, just as he did every day of the week unless it was raining cats and dogs. And since he lived in beautiful, arid, deserty San Diego, California, deluges were few and far between. San Diegans were far more apt to be sweltering under a heat wave, or find themselves bouncing around in the throes of a teeth-rattling earthquake, the latest flurry of which hadn't lessened much of late. Happily, the tremors weren't bad enough to kill anybody yet. They might tip over a few knickknacks and frazzle a few nerves, but that was the extent of their damage so far.

Arthur had a differing opinion, of course. No matter how gently the tectonic plates shifted beneath his feet, he still didn't like it. In fact, he threw a hissy fit with every teeny jolt. Gideon walked along Broadway now, with the heat of the morning sun burning on the back of his neck, nibbling on a bear claw from Tom's deli, where he had stopped in to thank Tom for the clock and wish him a happy morning. During the rest of his stroll to work, Gideon chuckled to himself thinking of Arthur.

When Reed shunted Arthur aside and barged into Gideon's memory banks for the bajillionth time in the past two weeks, his chuckle died in his throat and was replaced by a dreamy faraway look (that Gideon probably didn't know was there.) He mooned along for the rest of his way to work, not watching where he was going, bumping into parking meters and other pedestrians, remembering things about Reed that he probably shouldn't be thinking about at all. The way Reed had looked standing in his tub, his golden arms stretched high, banging away at Gideon's piece of shit shower nozzle. His gloriously sexy legs. The fetching shape of his butt, outlined beneath those crappy gray shorts he'd been wearing. The teasing glimpse of his belly button. The way his tool belt barely clung to his lean hips. His strong, capable hands. That killer smile.

Memories of Reed were good while they lasted, but a little time at work killed even them. Two hours after clocking in, Gideon was already punch-drunk, reeling under an avalanche of printer complaints and gigabyte questions and a depressing interlude with one clearly overmedicated asshole who got in Gideon's face and raved on and on and on about needing *that one particular style of ink pen and nothing else would do, dammit*!

It was coming on to Gideon's lunch break, thank God, when Reed Kelly suddenly burst back into his thoughts, instantly dissolving all anticipation of lunch or anything else. That moment came when Gideon looked up from retrieving a stack of calendars some dumbass kid had pulled off the shelf and left lying in the middle of the aisle to see Reed standing there in front of him in full corporeal splendor, staring down with a really attractive smile spread across his face.

The first thing out of Gideon's mouth was "You know what I hate about working with the public?"

"No," Reed said, still grinning. "What?"

Gideon sighed. "The public."

Reed coughed up a commiserating grunt. "Poor guy." He proceeded to offer a second sympathetic grunt, then squatted down beside Gideon to help him gather up the scattered calendars.

When everything was neatly back on the shelf, they stood facing each other at eye level. Well, eye-to-chin level. Reed was half a head taller.

"Hi," Reed said, bringing his killer smile back into play. It was the same smile Gideon had been mooning about all day. "Hi back," Gideon said, trying to ignore the sudden infusion of heat in his cheeks. "It's-it's good to see you again."

"You too."

They stood like that a moment, each silently studying the other. Gideon barely avoided shuffling his feet, although he suspected Reed was on the verge of that as well. When Gideon spotted his boss eying him from across the store, he cleared his throat and struck a more professional note.

"Can I help you with something?"

"Well, yeah. Remember we talked about me needing a computer and you said you could get me a discount? Of course, if the sale's over, that's okay. I understand. But I still need a computer. I'm getting tired of staring at the walls in the evening."

"What happened to your old computer?"

"I left it to my ex."

"Don't you have a TV?"

"I left her that too. Besides, I hate TV."

"Oh. Well, okay, then. Let's show you what we've got."

"You work on commission?"

Gideon frowned. Unknowingly, Reed had hit on the one aspect of his job that annoyed Gideon most. "Uh, no, not a penny. Strictly slave wages. But we do get a coupon for a free turkey at Christmas. It's quite a boon. Truly."

Reed offered another of his patent sympathetic clucks. "Then fuck 'em. In that case I'll take the cheapest computer you've got."

Gideon smiled at that. He even gave his heart a fluttery little pat. "I get the impression there was a gesture of goodwill in there somewhere, and for that I thank you."

Reed didn't say anything, but he looked pleased. He picked up a ream of typing paper off a shelf, studied it for a minute like he'd never seen anything so fascinating in his life, then put it back and refocused his attention on Gideon, his expression inscrutable.

"Inscrutable," Gideon said.

"What is?" Reed asked.

"Your expression."

"Imagine that." A tiny smile lifted a corner of Reed's mouth, exposing one dimple. Just one.

Gideon thought that one dimple was sexy as hell. And here he didn't even *like* redheads. Well, he didn't *use* to. "The computers are this way," he said, shaking himself back to reality. He quickly turned away before he started salivating. It was in the *Office Depot Employees Manual*. Page 22. Do not drool on customers no matter how sexy they are.

Gideon, with Reed trailing obediently behind, wove his way past Telephones, Printers, Toners, Games, Game Cheat Manuals, *Used* Game Cheat Manuals, Office Furniture, and an extra acre or two of miscellaneous office crap before finally hitting the Computer aisle, where he stopped in front of one particular display unit. His favorite computer of all time.

"There it is," he said, as proud as if he had invented the thing himself. "The 21.5 inch iMac desktop. Latest model. Best computer on the market. Easiest to use, longest work life, elegant, light, no clunky tower to clutter up your desk, and so user-friendly it will do everything but make your coffee in the morning. Hell, it might even do that if I can figure out where to pour in the water."

"Purty," Reed said, apparently struck so dumb with admiration he had slipped into Appalachian mode. He glanced at the price tag, then back to Gideon. "Any chance I can get a discount if I open an Office Depot account like you said?"

"Uh, no. That promotion is over."

"Oh. And you get no commission whatsoever?"

"Not a sou."

Gideon watched as Reed took another glance at the price tag. He had already made up his mind, Gideon knew. Reed just hadn't realized it yet. Gideon had been selling computers for two years now. He could spot a done deal from fifty paces on a foggy day before the buyer even knew he was hooked.

Reed quickly proved him right. "Fine, then. I'll take it anyway."

Gideon shook his head. "No, you won't."

Reed looked so surprised, it was almost comical. "Why the hell not?" he asked, clearly on the brink of getting a wee bit snippy.

Gideon tried not to laugh.

He turned away long enough to rise up on tiptoe so he could see over all the surrounding shelves of merchandise and make sure no one was close enough to listen in. Still on tiptoe, he faced the other direction and peered around Reed's head after laying his hands on Reed's broad shoulders to balance himself so he could do it, which oddly enough made his dick twitch. Trying not to think about his twitching dick, he slowly swiveled his head 360 degrees like a NASA radar dish. His boss was over by the checkout counter, annoying the clerk. Both other sales people were piddling around miles away. One was selling a calculator to a guy who didn't look like he could add two and two together without it, and the other clerk was picking his nose way off in the corner by a rack of posters. He was really going at it too. Pretty soon he'd be hooking an optic nerve and pulling his eyeball out through his nostril.

Since no one was within earshot, Gideon lowered his voice and edged so close to Reed his nose was almost in the guy's shirt pocket.

"Listen very carefully," Gideon whispered. "I'm not selling this computer to you because Apple has it on sale for a week starting yesterday, and you can purchase it for three hundred dollars less than we offered it even when it *was* on sale. They even have printers on sale. We don't. Their warranty is better than ours too. And the clerks are cuter. Trust me. Go to the Apple store. Buy it there."

Reed eyed him with what might have been construed as a little extra respect. "I guess you really *don't* work on commission."

"Nope."

Reed gazed around the store, not unlike Gideon had done a minute earlier. "You won't get in trouble?"

"Not if you buy something else," Gideon said.

"I don't need anything else."

"Buy a candy bar on your way out the door. Or a pack of pencils. A buck nineteen. Ticonderoga #2. I always like those better."

Reed grinned. "I guess I could do that."

As if Gideon wasn't close enough standing there with his nose practically resting on Reed's chest, he suffered a hormonal rush when Reed decided to edge even closer. When he bent down to whisper in Gideon's ear, it was sexy as hell.

"I'll buy the computer from Apple, and I'll even buy your stupid candy and stupid pencils as I slink my way out the door so you won't get fired, on one condition."

Gideon's heart gave a tiny lurch. Or was it another earthquake? No, he was pretty sure it was his heart. "What condition is that?" he whispered back.

Reed's breath blew warm across his face. "Let me use the money I'll be saving to take you out to dinner, Gideon. Just dinner. Nothing untoward. Nothing pushy or emotionally stunting. Just a simple meal. We can eat out or eat in. Your choice. Saturday night. What do you say?"

"I like pizza," Gideon shyly admitted. On a less than shy note, he was enjoying the hell out of Reed's sweet breath stirring his eyelashes. He also enjoyed being close enough to watch Reed's Adam's apple bob up and down while he talked. It looked like he hadn't shaved that morning. There were little sproutings of baby red beard hairs all over his neck and chin. How macho was that? Gideon practically had to shove his hands in his pockets to keep from reaching up and stroking Reed's bristly jaw. *And oh dear me, wouldn't that piss off the boss.*

Reed smiled a warm smile, as if he had a pretty good idea what Gideon was thinking. "Good. Pizza it is. And we'll eat in. After dinner you can help me hook up my new computer."

Gideon gave him a gentle punch in the gut. There wasn't much give when he did it either. It was a nice firm belly. Yesiree. Gideon added a phony huff of exasperation, which was strictly for show. "I should have known free labor would come into it somewhere. Sneaky bastard."

"You bet," Reed said. "Anything that's worth having is worth being sneaky about."

"So I guess my computer expertise is worth having, huh?"

They were standing so close that Gideon could still feel Reed's warm breath brushing his skin. "That and a few other things," Reed said, his smile slipping away. He reached up as if to flick an imaginary speck of dust from Gideon's collar. His fingers lingered there, twiddling the fabric, while his voice hummed softly, like a long low note gently blown on a trombone. "I don't believe you about one thing, though."

"What's that?" Gideon asked, fully aware that his dick was twitching again.

Reed's smile returned as he gave a gentle tug to Gideon's collar, then dropped his hand to his side and stepped back. "The clerks at the Apple store can't possibly be any cuter than they are here."

"Oh," Gideon said. "Uh, thanks."

Reed grinned. "Any time." And without speaking another word, he spun on his heel and walked away, snatching up a pack of pencils, two Snickers bars, and a rattling box of Milk Duds, and dumping it all in front of the clerk at the door. Twenty seconds later Reed and his little bag of goodies were gone.

Gideon stood in the computer aisle all by himself, listening to the fizz of his hormones carbonating in his veins. He furtively adjusted his dick, which had gone from twitching semiconsciousness to full-fledged rampaging boner in about 3.2 seconds. A new record.

Jesus.

AS FAR as he knew, Gideon was still at work when Reed came home from the Fashion Valley Apple store three hours later with a brand-new iMac all boxed up and cradled in his arms. Gideon had been absolutely right about Reed saving a hunk of money, and he could add another hundred to the savings when he threw in the printer, which had been on sale as well. On the other hand, Gideon had been dead *wrong* when he said the clerks at the Apple store were cuter than the ones at Office Depot. To Reed's unpracticed eye, they didn't even come close. Gideon Chase had them all beat, hands down. Every single one of them.

And Reed didn't even *like* redheads.

He knew one thing, though. He should have been excited about the new computer, and he sort of was. But he was more excited about his dinner date scheduled for Saturday night. He was trying to figure out a better choice than pizza for dinner. Since Gideon had steered him toward saving so much money, he could spring for something a little classier. It seemed the least he could do was make their date as memorable as possible. And good lord, now that he thought about it, it really *was* a date, wasn't it? What else could you call it?

The words thundered suddenly through his head. *Holy moly, I've got a date.*

One little piece of trivia he didn't want to think about was the fact that he had been a wee bit duplicitous in his dealings with Gideon in *acquiring* that date. He knew perfectly well how to hook up his new computer. He told Gideon he didn't so he could spend more face time with the man. These days, for some inexplicable reason, face time with Gideon was what it was all about.

A surge of blood rushed up to his ears when he remembered how he had brazenly flirted with Gideon while they were standing in the computer aisle back at Office Depot. Reed had never flirted with a guy in his life. On the few occasions when it had been required, he had always let them do the flirting. Let them make the first move. What the hell had induced Reed to do such a thing *now*? As if he didn't know.

He stood on the front porch of the Belladonna Arms, feet nailed to the floor, awkwardass box in his arms, still blushing up a storm and trying to chew the guilty, exuberant grin off his mouth. God, he was a mess.

Silently laughing at himself, he swiveled the computer box through the Arms's front door and ran smack into Arthur standing in the middle of the lobby staring at his reflection in the big floor to ceiling mirror that graced one end of the room. Well, *graced* wasn't exactly the right word to use, since the mirror was just as crappy as the lobby. Dusty, chipped, mildewed in one corner, with splintered cobwebs of cracks exploding here and there on its dingy surface. It looked like it hadn't had personal contact with a rag and a bottle of Windex since Reed was in maybe the eighth grade. The FBI could have shipped it to Quantico and used it for Fingerprints 101, that's how many greasy hands had left their mark on it, not to mention a few lipstick-stained lips, and what clearly looked like a naked ass print about three feet off the floor on the left side. Reed didn't even want to think about how *that* got there.

But the mirror ran a pale second as far as touristy type attractions went. Arthur standing in front of it was the A ticket to *this* extravaganza. Actually, Reed couldn't be absolutely sure it was really Arthur standing there at all. It was hard to tell with all the white fabric billowing everywhere. Folds of it. Mountains of it. Great rolling *oceans* of it. Yards and yards of blindingly white satin or silk or tulle or brocade or chiffon, or maybe a mixture of all five for all Reed knew, trailed off in every direction. And an even longer train of it stretched out across the lobby to where it lay piled up against the baseboard like a snowdrift, too long to be splayed out *en masse* unless Arthur either knocked down a wall or dragged the dress out onto the street where he could shake it all out and let his train roll off down the hill behind him.

All Reed could see of the actual Arthur was his big round head poking through the top of those excruciatingly white satin waves, sort of hovering there, six feet off the ground, while down below his rotund body was sheathed in white all the way up to his multitudinous chins. He looked like a bowling trophy wrapped in a gigantic flour tortilla.

Reed couldn't quite believe what he was seeing. It defied understanding. He set the computer box down so he could dig his knuckles into his hips and stare a little harder while he tried to figure it out.

"Is that…? Is that a *wedding* dress?" he asked.

Arthur swiveled his head around to face him, his chubby cheeks glowing pink either from embarrassment or from blood deprivation. The bust line of the dress looked really tight. Arthur batted false eyelashes and pursed his bee-stung lips, which were painted a deep shimmering red. Aside from those lips, the bursting capillaries in Arthur's face supplied the only splash of color within thirty feet.

He purred coyly. "You noticed. Isn't it lovely?"

Reed dug a fingernail into the palm of his hand, hoping to draw blood and maybe slash a couple of nerves so he wouldn't laugh out loud. The undulating field of white surrounding Arthur stretched knee deep for yards and yards in every direction. Reed had never seen so much white in his life. "You look like the blizzard of '06," he said. "With ears."

If there was an insult in there, Arthur chose to ignore it. "Thank you, darling. Help me with my veil."

From the mountainous folds of snow-white tulle his head rested atop, seemingly hovering weightless six feet off the ground, Arthur extended a draping, flowing, endless appendage of gauzy white netting, which, until he moved it, had simply blended in with all the rest of the dress, sort of like one little cumulous cloud slipping away from a bank of thousands.

Reed blanched. "Who, me?" he asked in a small voice. "I'm a welder. I don't do veils."

"Oh pishposh," Arthur laughed. "Don't look so stricken. I'm not impugning your manhood, honey. I just need a little help. Now get over yourself and help me with this. It looks weightless, I know, but with all these rhinestones sewed on it weighs a ton. Help me strap it to my head."

Reed couldn't have been more appalled if Arthur had tried to hand him a dead possum. "Should I spot weld it to your skull or use a nail gun?"

Arthur's eyelashes dipped alarmingly. "Don't piss me off, darling. I'm not in the mood."

Somewhere about twelve feet back from where Arthur's head sat perched atop this mountain of white, Reed spotted something moving beneath the folds of fabric. A little rolling hill rose underneath the long train and glided across the lobby floor, buried beneath yards of shimmering satin—or whatever the hell it was—sort of like a big fat mink scurrying under a snowbank, pooching the snow up as it scampered along. Somewhere deep inside that tumbling upheaval of cottony, shimmering chiffon, Reed thought he could hear tiny footsteps and an occasional giggle.

"Take it, Reed!" Arthur demanded, holding out the gigantic ball of netted veil. "And don't step on little Artie when you hook it on."

"So that's what that is!" The rolling hump froze in place at the sound of its name. A moment later, it goo-gooed happily and started moving again, heading straight for Arthur. Reed knew Artie had reached his goal when Arthur jumped straight up into the air like he'd been goosed with a cattle prod. He slapped at the fabric hanging off his butt and cried, "You scamp! Your hands are *freezing.*"

"What are you wearing under there?" Reed asked, suddenly suspicious.

"Nothing, darling. I didn't want to add any bulk to my new trim figure. I've lost a pound and a half, you know. It took me nine months."

"A real woman could have had a baby by then."

"Imagine that," Arthur said, obviously unimpressed. He pounded his foot pettishly under the dress, causing the fake ficus in the corner of the lobby to quiver and shed a scattering of plastic leaves across the floor. "Fix my veil, dammit!" he cried. His little snit disappeared in an instant when he spotted the great big box sitting on the floor by the lobby door. Curiosity lit his face like a 300-watt bulb. "Ooh. What's that?"

"New computer," Reed said, trying to untangle himself from the mile-long strip of netting he'd had thrust into his arms, digging through it, looking for anything that might be used to attach it to a human head.

While he fought with that, he asked, conversationally enough under the circumstances, "So when's the wedding, Arthur?"

"Soon, love." Arthur hauled out a pair of rhinestone earrings, each of which looked equivalent in size to the ball they drop at Times Square on New Year's Eve. He hooked them on and patted them in place. "My wig isn't finished yet. I just want to see how the veil will look with the earrings and the dress."

At one end of the veil, Reed found a half-circle of some shiny hard substance that appeared to have been snipped from a sheet of aluminum siding. Since it was bendy and had some spring to it, he slapped it over Arthur's head, snapping it in place behind his ears. He stepped quickly back in case brain matter should start spilling out.

"Now straighten the veil," Arthur demanded. "Spread it out behind me. Gently now. We don't want any snags in the netting. Drape it all the way back to the far wall. Lay it out even. Don't step on Artie."

Artie giggled again at the sound of his name while Reed sighed, doing as he was ordered. "I feel like a Gloucester fisherman hauling in a load of shrimp," he groused, fighting with the endless netting while little Artie continued to giggle and chatter nonsensically somewhere beneath the cottony fabric tide.

"Oh hush," Arthur snorted. "Both of you." He patted his head, gave a tweak to the band of aluminum clamped to his skull, adjusted an earring, and gave his ass a wiggle as if that would settle everything in place. "So how does it look?"

"Big," Reed answered.

"Big!" Little Artie cried from somewhere down below.

Sylvia poked her head out from Arthur's apartment door, which was standing open by the stairs at the back of the lobby. She had a smudge of flour on her nose, and her hands were covered in what looked like cookie dough. "Did Artie say an actual word?"

"He said 'Big'," Arthur answered, clearly bored with any topic of conversation that had anything to do with anyone other than himself.

"Where is he?" Sylvia asked.

Reed pointed to the mounds of billowing white, first at one place then at another. It was hard to pinpoint the spot exactly because the kid kept moving around. "He's somewhere under there. Arthur's naked, you know."

"Well, that should further Artie's education," Sylvia mumbled before ducking her head back through the door and disappearing from sight.

Arthur stuck his fat hand out in front of him. On one sausagelike finger rested a teeny silver band with a teeny tiny white stone encircling one kielbasa-sized knuckle.

"Be honest, darling. Do you think this ring overpowers the dress? I don't want to appear gauche."

Reed suspected nothing short of a snowplow could overpower Arthur's dress, but he refrained from saying so. Life was fleeting. Why ask for trouble when you didn't have to?

Chapter 6

HITLER SAT on the kitchen counter, one leg held high, toes gracefully pointed skyward, claws extended. He was diligently (and audibly) cleaning his butt with his little pink tongue. The cat reminded Reed of Charlie's lover, Bruce, practicing his arabesque, only Bruce didn't ordinarily lick his ass while he did it. At least not in public.

A stack of pizza boxes sat cooling on the kitchen table. Since he hadn't known which kind Gideon preferred, he had made an executive decision and ordered three different flavors. He figured what wasn't eaten, they could split up later. It was probably a good thing Reed had a dinner date tonight. Here he had been residing in the Arms for more than three weeks, living the life of a single gay man, or so he kept telling himself, and not once in that time had he hooked up with anyone for sex. He had taken matters into his own hands a few times, of course, usually while fantasizing about Gideon next door, but thank God Gideon didn't know that. Reed was actually sort of sorry even *he* knew it. Knowing he had shot jism all over the bedroom on various occasions while thinking about the very same person who was coming to join him for dinner made Reed a little nervous. Either because he might have set himself up for disappointment later if they actually *did* end up in bed together, or because, if they *didn't* end up in bed, he would figure Gideon just wasn't interested in him, and what would that do for future episodes of fantasizing about the guy?

Or worse yet, what if they went to bed together and *Gideon* was the one disappointed? Although Reed seriously doubted Gideon had been fantasizing about *him*. In fact, that was so beyond the realm of possibility, Reed didn't even consider it. Not much anyway.

As nervous as he had ever been in his life, Reed tried on several different outfits before settling on the most casual thing he owned. Lounging pants and a V-necked T-shirt. He did make sure to wear a pair of snug briefs under the lounging pants. It might at least serve to impede the occasional hard-on from surfacing at inopportune times. Or if not impede it, at least restrict its movements and make it less noticeable. He didn't want to come off as a desperately horny pervert. Not today anyway.

Reed brushed his teeth for the umpteenth time, took another nervous pee, carefully washed his hands afterward, singing the birthday song twice while he did it like his mother always told him to do, and finally gave his hair a wee adjustment in the mirror. He gazed carefully up each nostril to make sure there was nothing unfortunate dangling inside, checked for eye boogers too, while he was at it, and just as he was thinking about brushing his teeth again, there came a knock at his front door.

He raced through the apartment and made such a horrible thumping clatter doing it that he scared the crap out of Hitler, who with his ass still moist, sailed through the kitchen window to anchor his claws in the eucalyptus tree outside. From there he would carefully work his way six floors down to the ground. It was the same way Hitler almost *always* gained access to Reed's apartment. Via tree.

Reed quickly forgot about the cat. He stood at his front door, sucked in a deep calming breath, molded a welcoming smile on his face that he hoped didn't look too insane, and reached out with a trembling hand to turn the knob.

Reed peeked around the edge of the door and found Gideon standing in the hallway, beaming back. He was wearing the same baggy khaki shorts he had worn the day Reed helped him with his apartment, only now they had been worn long enough that the store wrinkles had smoothed out and the price tag had either been removed or fallen off of its own accord. He was barefoot, as was Reed, and he was also wearing a T-shirt, only Gideon's shirt was newer and didn't have a V-neck. On the other hand, Reed's shirt didn't have a squirming bulge in the front and a tiny orange kitten head poking out of the neck like Gideon's.

Before acknowledging Gideon at all, Reed reached up and tickled the white bib under Punkin's chin, causing a purr to kick in that sounded remarkably like an outboard motor.

Gideon gave an exaggerated pout. "No welcome tickle for me?"

Reed laughed, hoping it didn't sound *too* fake—God, he was nervous—and reached up to give Gideon's nose a tweak. "There," he said, suddenly a little *less* nervous. "How's that?"

"Perfect," Gideon said, replacing his pout with a grin. "Ooh, and I smell pizza."

"You do indeed," Reed said proudly and grabbed a fistful of Gideon's shirt front to pull him through the door.

GIDEON HAD fretted over his dinner date with Reed all day. The moment Reed opened the door and Gideon saw that Reed looked just as nervous as he did, Gideon's worrying abated a bit. When they exchanged pleasant gibes culminating in Reed grabbing his shirt and dragging him bodily inside, Gideon stopped worrying altogether.

Reed pointed to the sofa, said to himself, "Beers," and immediately stalked off to the kitchen to fetch a couple. He brought them back, the bottles ice-cold and dripping with condensation, and handed one to Gideon without offering a glass. Gideon assumed that would set the tone for the evening—two buddies butching it up, swilling beers, telling raunchy jokes, and acting straight even though they both knew they weren't.

Gideon wasn't so sure he liked that agenda, so as soon as Reed handed him his beer, he rose from the couch, snagged Reed's shirt as Reed had snagged his at the door, and pulled him in for a quick peck on the cheek.

"Thanks," Gideon said, his lips still close to Reed's face. When he leaned back to gauge the reaction, he was delighted to see Reed's eyeballs had grown big and round in the middle of his handsome face. "I mean, for all the repairs you did on my apartment. It's actually livable now, thanks to your hard work."

"Oh. Well, uh, you're welcome," Reed said, and for a fleeting second, his free hand came up, the one that wasn't holding the beer, and slipped around to Gideon's back to pull him a wee bit closer.

Gideon could have sat down and written a thirty-page essay on how much he enjoyed that big broad capable hand resting in the small of his back. And also how much he enjoyed Reed's clean scent. Clearly, he had just stepped out of the shower, which sent a whole new series of imaginings stampeding through Gideon's head. He envisioned water sluicing off Reed's long body, down his lean flanks, puddling at his feet. Reed's fiery red pubes slathered with suds. Reed's dick, still a mystery at this point in Gideon's life since he hadn't been introduced to it yet— dammit—happily bobbing around in the lather and the shower spray, stiff as a post.

"You smell good," Gideon said.

And that, at last, seemed to spark a reaction. Reed's ears turned red. "So do you," he said softly.

Punkin, apparently feeling left out, said, "Meow," and both men smiled at the kitten as she squirmed down Gideon's belly under the shirt and dropped to the floor at their feet. She set off to explore, prompting Reed to comment, "She's grown since I saw her last."

Gideon plopped down on the couch and was gratified when Reed plopped down beside him rather than commandeering one of the other seats in the room.

"Kittens grow up fast," Gideon said. He glanced at the living room window. "I spotted a cat sneaking through your window the other day. Yours?"

Reed followed his glance to the empty window and smiled. "I guess you mean Hitler. No, he's not mine. Not entirely, at any rate. He's just a neighborhood cat burglar who stops in for tuna once in a while. He climbs the tree outside and jumps through my window when the mood strikes. I'm not sure if he's trying to adopt me or what."

"Don't get your hopes up," Gideon said with a quiet laugh. "I've heard about Hitler. He visits everybody in the building. Schmoozing all and claiming none. As soon as he's fed he'll drop you like a hot potato and move on to greener pastures. Just *like* a man, huh?"

Reed didn't smile; he merely shrugged. "Not all of them, I hope."

"No," Gideon said, his eyes appraising. "Hopefully not all." A momentary flash of panic crossed Reed's face, as if he were suddenly desperate for something to say. He turned to Gideon and asked, "So everything in your apartment still works? Shower still runs? Sink still drains?"

Gideon settled back on the couch and took a long pull from his beer before answering. "Everything works great." He pointed to the two big boxes stacked in the corner next to a battered secondhand desk that obviously came with the apartment. "Looks like you're ready for me to return the favor and hook up your computer and printer."

"Yeah," Reed said, "but later. Let's just talk and relax for a while. Unless you're hungry. If you are, we can eat. The pizzas are cold anyway. We'll just nuke the slices as we graze along."

"Later is fine," Gideon said. "Talking sounds good."

An odd silence claimed the room. Gideon took pity on Reed when he saw him again flailing around for something to say.

"So how are you liking the Belladonna Arms?" Gideon asked. "Settling in okay?" Relief washed across Reed's face before he ever opened his mouth. Clearly spontaneous conversation wasn't Reed's greatest talent.

"I love it," Reed said. "You?"

"Love it. And how are you getting along with Arthur?"

Reed didn't hesitate. "I love Arthur too."

"So do I."

"Have you seen his wedding dress?"

Gideon rolled his eyes. "I told him it needed to be bigger and a little poufier."

Their gazes gravitated toward each other, and the moment their eyes met, they laughed. As soon as the chuckling died down, Reed said, "I've never been to a gay wedding."

Gideon's smile was still bright on his face. He could feel it there, shining away. "Most gay people don't call it a gay wedding."

"They don't? What do they call it?"

Gideon's smile dimmed. Deadpan, he said, "A wedding."

"Oh. Yeah."

And they laughed again.

Their spate of good humor didn't survive Gideon's next question. "Have you seen your wife? Is she getting along all right?"

Reed shot an uneasy glance Gideon's way before heaving himself up from the couch. By the time he was on his feet, the residue of his smile had faded from his lips. After scooping his beer bottle off the coffee table, he strode to the window and gazed outside. It was dark, and the city lights were laid out from the foot of the hill the Arms was perched on to the faraway reaches westward. Off to the left, the color and light of the San Diego skyline neatly ended, as if snipped away by a gigantic pair of scissors. Beyond that, beyond the hemline between land and water that marked the California coast, only pitch-black remained as far as the eye could see. That was south, where the sprawling Pacific Ocean spilled out to the farthest reaches of night. Gideon could imagine it all from where he was sitting. After all, he enjoyed the same view from his own living room window.

"She hasn't called," Reed said, his voice flat. He sipped at his beer, keeping his back to the room. "I'm a little worried about her."

Gideon rose and crossed the room to join him. He squeezed in at Reed's side to claim his share of the view, standing close enough that their shoulders touched. Closing his eyes for a moment, he savored the cool night air blowing across his face.

When Gideon spoke, he aimed his words at the city lights outside, not at the man beside him. "I'm sorry," he said quietly. "I shouldn't have asked that."

He turned in time to see Reed give his head a tiny shake. "No, it's okay. I don't mind you asking. I just… well, I've never been divorced before. I'm not sure about the protocol of the whole thing. Should I call her and see if she's all right, or should I let her be? Will she think I don't care if I don't call, or will she think I'm prying if I do?"

Gideon considered the ramifications of each option. He also considered the look of pain that had so suddenly crossed Reed's face. He was sorry he'd been the cause of it. But he thought maybe Reed needed advice too, so he figured he might as well give him some, since there didn't seem to be a lot of friends hanging around for Reed to ask.

"I can only tell you what I'd think if I was in her position," Gideon said slowly. "I mean, if you want to know."

Reed turned to him with a look of quiet desperation. "Tell me," he said.

Gideon tore his eyes away and stared out at the city again. "I think I'd be hurt if you didn't call. I think I would feel even more abandoned than I felt when you left me. If you don't call her, Reed, she'll think you've forgotten her completely. Or worse, she'll think you don't care."

"I don't want to hurt her any more than I already have."

"Then call. Let her know she's still in your heart. She is, you know. I can see it in your eyes."

Reed blinked. "Can you?"

"Yeah." He reached up and brushed Reed's hair away from his eyes, surprising himself. Reed didn't seem to mind so Gideon left his fingers there a moment longer before pulling away. "Another benefit to calling," he said, "is once you've done it, you'll know. Either she'll bite your head off, or she won't. Either she'll thank you for phoning, or she'll tell you to go fuck yourself with a baseball bat."

"I don't have a baseball bat."

Gideon frowned. "Then you may have to buy one."

Slowly, a vague smile began to light Reed's face. His eyes stayed on Gideon for a while, then casually turned back to peer through the window again. Silence reigned while they each took a nip from their beers. The leaves of the eucalyptus tree outside the window stirred in the night air. Somewhere above their heads, up in the branches where the moonlight sifted through, a squirrel gave a skittering cry. Maybe there was a nest up there somewhere. Maybe there were young ones.

"I think you're right" Reed finally said, staring back to the left, to the endless black of the unlit ocean. "I'll call her tomorrow." His face twisted into a grin. "If nothing else it will give her the chance to tell me to go fuck myself with a large piece of wood. Wouldn't want to deprive her of that."

Their hands accidentally bumped together, and when they did, Reed's fingers twined through Gideon's. Reed continued to stare out into the night as if they weren't touching at all. He also continued to smile. For that, Gideon was pleased.

"Thank you, Gideon," he said softly.

"You're welcome."

Seconds later, when Reed unwound his fingers from Gideon's, the heat of them lingered on Gideon's palm. Only when they had completely drawn away from each other did Reed turn to face him.

"Ready to eat?" he asked, his smile calmer now.

Gideon nodded. "Sure."

Snagging Gideon's hand again, Reed led him toward the kitchen.

REED PATTED his belly, groaned, and squeaked his chair away from the table. "I just gained six pounds."

"More like ten," Gideon said. "I've never seen a human eat like that before."

Reed burped. "Blow me."

Gideon opened his mouth to say... *what*? A split second later, Reed's ears turned a vibrant shade of red when he realized what he'd said, to Gideon's endless entertainment.

"I meant that in a metaphorical sense," Reed stammered.

Gideon finally closed his mouth. He snapped his fingers and offered an exaggerated pout. "Darn. I hate metaphorical blowjobs."

Reed laughed then. It was a good laugh. Honest and unfettered. Gideon thought he might still be a little embarrassed by what he'd said, and he knew he was right when Reed fiddled with a piece of pizza crust and muttered under his breath, "Gay people. You have to watch every little thing you say." But his eyes were crinkling at the edges when he said it. Reed had never been more handsome.

Tilting his chair onto its back legs, Gideon wiped at his grin with a napkin. "Speaking of gay people," he said, "how is your new gay life treating you? Did you get lucky the other night when you went out?"

Reed's ears got even redder. "No," he said, obviously reluctant to talk about it. "Wasn't in the mood, I guess."

"I didn't know gay guys had to be in the mood to be slutty. I thought they just had to be awake."

Reed lifted his eyes and studied Gideon's face. "I didn't know anybody. I'd probably have had a better time if you'd come with me. At least I'd have had someone to talk to."

At that, Gideon dropped all four chair legs to the floor and leaned forward over his dirty plate.

"Speaking of that," he said, "the only reason I said no to your invitation that night was because I didn't have any money. I was flat broke. It wasn't that I didn't want to go with you."

"Oh," Reed said. "You should have said something. I'd have spotted you."

Gideon shook his head. "Way too humiliating. I'm only telling you now because I didn't want you to think I simply didn't want to go with you. I did. Financially, I just... couldn't."

Averting his eyes, Reed fiddled with the pizza crust a little more. "I'm glad you told me. I did kind of wonder."

Gideon smiled inwardly at Reed's reaction, and then a furry feline body brushed up against his bare ankle under the table. Punkin saying hello. He bent down and scooped her into his lap, where she immediately curled into a ball and went to sleep.

"Have you heard from *your* lover?" Reed asked. Hesitant, as if he wasn't sure he should bring it up.

Gideon lifted his eyes to the ceiling. "No, but I received a friendly call from the Salvation Army telling me I can have my underwear back for a reasonable price."

"How did they know it was yours? What did they do? DNA test the hash marks?"

"Don't be crude."

"Did they really call you?"

"No, dumbass. I lied."

Reed grinned.

They stared at each other for the space of ten or twelve heartbeats while Punkin purred softly under the table. Finally, Gideon decided to be daring, and after Reed's hash marks comment, why the hell shouldn't he? He cast a casual glance at his fingernails as if pondering his next manicure. Any fool in the world could probably see he was up to something. "So, Reed. You've never been in love with a man, then? Only Carol?"

One of Reed's dimples popped into view. Then the other one. Strangely, not much of a smile accompanied them. "Is this going somewhere?"

"Nope. Just asking."

Reed tugged himself out of his chair and scooped the plates and silverware off the table. He carried it all to the sink and started running water to wash up. While waiting for the sink to fill, he said quietly, "I'm not really sure I know what being in love is."

Gideon eyed Reed's broad back, the uneven line of red hair hanging down the nape of his neck. He needed a trim. Gideon's gaze traveled down to the slim hips tucked inside the baggy lounging pants, then climbed upward again until it came to rest on Reed's ears. He expected to see a blush there, but he didn't. He knew immediately he might have gone too far.

"I'm sorry, Reed. I shouldn't have asked that."

When Reed spoke, his voice was low and calm. His words were scarcely loud enough for Gideon to hear above the rush of water filling the sink.

"No, it's okay. You can ask." He inhaled a deep breath as if stoking his courage. "My marriage to Carol was a mistake. Worse than that, it was a lie. It took me four years to realize that the love I thought I felt for Carol was a lie too. It had to be, coming from a relationship based on nothing more than blind untruths and wishful thinking. I thought I would come around, I guess. I thought once Carol and I were married, I would find that one little spark of heterosexuality inside myself that would keep me on the"—he spun and made sardonic finger quotes in the air for Gideon's benefit—"*straight* and narrow. That was probably the biggest lie of all."

As if suddenly heartsick, he stood with his back to the sink, staring down at his feet. "No, Gideon. I never loved Carol. If I had I wouldn't have put her through what I did. And no, I've never been in love with a man either. It's hard to fall in love at all, I guess, when you can't even love yourself. And when every breath you take is a lie."

Gideon eased Punkin from his lap and set her on the floor. He rose from his chair, crossed the room in three long strides, and pulled Reed into his arms. Reed hesitated only a moment before returning the embrace. They stood there like that, Reed's wet hands at Gideon's back, Reed's chin burrowed into Gideon's shoulder, while Gideon wrapped Reed tightly in his arms.

He tilted his head up and whispered words in Reed's ear, inhaling as he did the scent of the shampoo Reed had used to wash his hair. It smelled of strawberries.

"You're both still better off now that you've faced the truth, Reed. All the lying can stop. You can be who you were born to be. Carol can find the man who can love her the way she deserves to be loved. Like you told her. The only battle you have to fight now, I think, is this guilt that seems to be taking over your life."

Reed eased back just far enough to stare into Gideon's eyes. At the same moment, his wet hands clutched tighter at Gideon's back, dampening Gideon's skin through the fabric of his shirt.

"Guilt?" Reed asked.

Gideon didn't answer. He simply nodded. And then, slowly, he eased himself up on tiptoe far enough to lean in and softly lay his lips to Reed's mouth. He watched Reed's eyes open wide in surprise, then slowly close until his pale lashes rested atop his blushing cheeks. A gentle humming sound *burr*ed deep in Reed's throat. It sounded like Punkin's purr. Gideon's heartbeat quickened when he heard it.

Reed's tongue moved hesitantly against the kiss, gently prodding, and Gideon opened his lips to let it in. Reed's fingers dug more insistently into the flesh of his back, clutching harder, getting Gideon's shirt even wetter than it already was. Gideon sighed a contented sigh and let himself be pulled in, loving the sensation of Reed's strong arms wrapped around him, their torsos flush, the taste of Reed's mouth on his own. Reed's cock pressed against his. Not overtly, but just enough to stir Gideon into easing himself closer. Reed slid a hand down his back and nestled it, fingers splayed wide, atop the curve of his ass. From there he dug his index finger under the hem of Gideon's shirt and kneaded the spot at the base of Gideon's spine where a little patch of blond hair sprouted. Gideon shuddered at that single fingertip stroking him there.

Reed whispered, "You're so beautiful."

Gideon whispered back, nearly breathless, clearly lying through his teeth, "You don't like redheads. Neither do I." Reed smiled against Gideon's lips, and shifted his hips to press his hardness more firmly against Gideon's own. "I know. I'll keep the lights off when we make love."

"Are we going to make love?"

"Yes."

"Naked?"

"Yes."

"Then will you wear your tool belt?"

This time Reed snorted into the kiss.

Chapter 7

THE FIRST sensation of Gideon's warm cock pressed against his cheek caused a shudder of desire to stutter through Reed's body, almost flooring him with its intensity. He had never in his life felt anything like it. He knelt before Gideon now. Their kiss had survived the shedding of clothes, but the moment they were unclothed and the heat of their flesh lay one against the other, Reed could no longer hold back. He had dropped to his knees at Gideon's feet, laying kisses on Gideon's warm stomach, pressing his face into the heat of it, inhaling Gideon's scent while wrapping his arms around Gideon's hips, holding him close.

They were positioned now at the open living room window, where they had stood earlier. The evening breezes, cooler now that the night had deepened, blew across their naked bodies. The panoply of city lights leaked over the sill to paint soft streaks of color on their bare skin.

Surprised by his own daring, Reed kissed the base of Gideon's erect cock, then dipped his head lower to swipe his tongue across Gideon's balls where they lay tucked in tight, drawn inward with desire. He smiled when Gideon pressed closer to Reed's exploring lips, gripped Reed's hair, and steered Reed's mouth to where he wanted it to go.

Stroking the back of Gideon's legs, loving the way the hair there bristled against his palms, Reed abandoned Gideon's balls and slid his tongue upward along the pulsing shaft in front of his face. When his kisses touched the rubbery edge of the corona, he brought one hand around to the front and gently tipped the stiffness of Gideon's cock downward until the head of it lay against his lips. Feeling moisture there, Reed slipped his tongue out and rolled it across Gideon's slit, gathering up a smear of liquid, the musky taste of which caused another shudder of desire to ricochet through him.

Gideon's breath caught as his fingers tightened in Reed's hair. When Gideon spoke, his voice sounded shattered. Bruised and breathless. Still, the joy in his words was unmistakable. "That feels incredible."

In answer, Reed wrapped his fingers gently around Gideon's shaft and took the head of it into his mouth. Once again laying a hand to the back of Gideon's thigh, he pulled him closer, drawing Gideon's cock deep between his lips.

Gideon gave a hushed gasp, and Reed smiled hearing it.

Looking upward, Reed let Gideon's cock slip free. He stood it upright and smeared it across his face, loving the heat and firmness of it pressed against his skin, the trail of moisture it left behind. Against the lazy drag of arousal, he opened heavy eyelids to gaze upward across Gideon's stomach and chest to the eyes aimed down at him from above.

"You like that," Reed whispered, his voice husky. He was so turned on he was trembling.

"Yes."

"Will you come to bed with me?"

Gideon stroked Reed's lips, moistened now by his attentions to Gideon's cock. Gideon's fingers were so careful, his stroke so light on his tender mouth, Reed shivered even more.

"Please," Reed pleaded, pressing a kiss to Gideon's thumb.

Gideon gazed down, his eyes hazy with lust. He plucked gently at Reed's bottom lip—fingers probing, less gentle now. "God yes," Gideon murmured. "I want you next to me. I want to lie where I can get at you."

Reed slid the palm of his hand up Gideon's stomach, loving the heated softness of his skin, the way the spray of hair around his belly button rustled across his palm. The way Gideon's stomach jerked in and out as he inhaled tiny gasps of air, clearly trembling from the inside out as if hungry for more of what the night might offer.

"I hope—" Reed began, then stopped.

Gideon's fingers tightened in his hair. "What, Reed? You hope what?"

Reed pushed his face into Gideon's stomach again while Gideon's cock stood hot and stiff against his cheek. He spoke the words into the darkness behind his eyelids, afraid to say them to the living world, afraid to leave himself so open, so *needing*. "I hope you'll stay the night. I've slept alone so long."

Gideon pressed his palm to Reed's cheek as if gauging the heat. There was a tiny laugh in his voice. "That's assuming we sleep at all."

Reed relaxed then. He almost laughed too. He rose from the floor and gripped Gideon's hand, pulled him toward the bedroom.

"Come," he said.

Edging closer as Reed tugged him along, snaking an arm around Reed's trim waist, Gideon laid a kiss to his bare shoulder. "I intend to," he said.

By the time they stepped through the bedroom door, their mouths had found each other again. At the foot of the bed, Gideon hooked a leg around Reed's and tripped him lightly onto the quilted surface. They landed together in a tangle of arms and legs and hungry, seeking mouths.

"Oh man," Reed muttered into another kiss. "I think I'm going to like this."

THE BEDROOM drapes were closed against the night, and aside from their letting in a slip of light at the occasional stirring of a breeze, the room was left in total darkness.

Gideon, on hands and knees, straddled Reed's prone body and hovered over him. He found Reed's mouth with his own, easing himself down until their chests touched, their tongues collided, and Reed's hands came up to anchor him in place. Reed's long cock, laid flat against Reed's belly by Gideon's weight, pressed against Gideon's balls. His own cock stood upright between them, and when Reed wrapped gentle fingers around it, Gideon bucked at the touch.

"Taste me," Reed mumbled, never breaking the kiss. "Please."

"Now you're talking," Gideon muttered. Without waiting for further directions, Gideon slid his mouth away, breaking the kiss. Dragging his lips downward over Reed's chin and neck, he planted a new kiss in the spray of hair that covered Reed's lean chest. Pressing his lips there, Gideon sensed the power of the heartbeat hidden beneath. Reed's heart was hammering as hard as his own.

Gideon liked that.

His balls dragged across Reed's thigh as he squirmed farther down the bed. The stone hardness of Reed's knees jounced beneath his stomach like a speed bump as Gideon's kisses traveled ever southward. When he brushed Reed's belly button with his lips, he paused and stayed long enough to slip his tongue inside to explore for a moment. Gideon could tell Reed enjoyed the sensation of that unexpected invasion of Gideon's tongue, moist and tickling, digging into his belly. Reed's entire body shuddered with either sexual eagerness or repressed laughter, he couldn't tell which. When Reed muttered, "Tickles," Gideon knew.

With Reed's cock now pressed hard against his chin, begging for attention, Gideon burrowed deeper between Reed's long legs, scooching them wider apart to make room for himself. He slid his tongue down the shaft of Reed's heavy, long cock, tasting and savoring every inch of flesh from the corona to the base of Reed's balls.

A tremor juddered through Reed when Gideon dipped his hands under Reed's thighs and lifted his legs enough to let his tongue travel into even more dangerous terrain.

Reed gasped when Gideon laid kisses to his perineum, wading through a forest of hair to get there. And when he lifted Reed's legs even higher and brought his lips directly to Reed's opening, Reed took such a death grip on Gideon's hair that Gideon wondered if he would come out of it with any hair left at all. But that didn't stop him. He was just getting started.

He dragged his tongue across Reed's hole, and when Reed tensed beneath him, he wondered if Reed had ever had that done to him before. Thinking to err on the side of caution, he slowly let Reed's legs collapse to the bed again, and without pokeassing around about it, went right for the main prize.

He cradled Reed's erection in his hand, loving the weight and heft of it, standing it upright, admiring its length, its uncut perfection. Hunkered down on his knees between Reed's legs, he slipped the fat head of that beautiful cock into his mouth, savoring the taste of precome and knowing he must have done something right if Reed was leaking juices already.

Reed stroked Gideon's cheek as Gideon took him deeper. A moment later, as Gideon slipped his mouth down over Reed's cock to the very base, until Reed's pubic hair tickled his nose and Gideon's balls were snug against his chin, Reed suddenly tensed beneath him.

"Oh no," Reed gasped, his entire body suddenly as stiff as his dick.

Gideon suspected he knew what that meant, and he didn't mind at all.

"Let it go," he mumbled, his mouth still tasting, still adoring. "Let it go, Reed. Come for me. Let me taste you. We've got all night. We can take our time later. Right now do this one for the Gipper."

Reed bucked with laughter at the feeble joke, but the laughter didn't last long. He wrenched himself into a sitting position and hugged Gideon's head to his lap, his legs still quivering at Gideon's flanks on either side.

Gideon smiled and eased Reed back down into the tangled mess of covers, never once releasing Reed's cock from between his lips. It was hard to talk with his mouth full, so he didn't bother. He simply went back to pleasing the man beneath him. And the man beneath him, he couldn't help but notice, had finally stopped arguing about it.

"Oh God," Reed said a moment later. His grip tightened at the back of Gideon's neck, holding his head close, pulling Gideon's mouth even closer. "Oh Jesus!"

Reed's cries suddenly stopped as if his tongue had been ripped out of his throat and tossed through the bedroom window. Gideon held Reed's iron cock deep in his throat as Reed bucked and squirmed and gasped beneath him.

A moment later, the only sound to be heard in Reed's bedroom was the pounding of two hearts, hovering next to each other on the bed. Both men's breathing had stopped. It was the stillness before the call to battle. The last hush before the hand grenade explodes. The final torturous blast of silence before all hell breaks loose.

And all hell was about to do exactly that.

Gideon smiled around the bulbous head of Reed's throbbing cock and tried to keep it anchored in his mouth while Reed writhed and flopped around beneath him like a fish out of water. Suddenly, a horrific groan erupted from Reed's throat. He clutched Gideon's shoulders, clawing at him, dragging him ever closer as if afraid he would escape, afraid he would stop what he was doing. Reed's long hairy legs came up and clamped on to Gideon like a vise. Reed finally let go.

Gideon gripped Reed's waist in his hands and held on for dear life as Reed continued to twist and thrash beneath him. The cock in his mouth grew fatter and stiffer, and before Gideon could think of a way to tell Reed how much he dug the hell out of *that*, Reed cried out like a wounded animal and with a last shudder of unrelenting pleasure, strafed the roof of Gideon's mouth with hot jets of searing come.

Gideon rode the tide as best he could, getting bounced off once so that a goodly shot of delicious come went shooting across his face from chin to hairline instead of down his throat, but Gideon quickly corrected and managed to capture the remaining salvos.

"Good grief," he sputtered once, not believing how much come could explode from one man, but he wasn't complaining, He was enjoying the hell out of the ride.

Reed grunted, and to Gideon's unending delight, one more surge of milky come, as hot as lava, splattered across his tongue. The stream was a little weaker, but hell, who was Gideon to complain?

When Reed collapsed beneath him like he'd been shot, Gideon savored a few more moments by enjoying the feel of Reed's hard cock beginning to wilt between his lips. For some reason Gideon found that to be as erotic as everything else that had happened. Reed's softening erection finally slipped from between Gideon's lips and lay moist against his chin. Gideon whispered into the shadows, "I guess you needed that."

With trembling hands, Reed pawed at him, gripping him under the arms and finally dragging him up the bed to within cuddling distance.

Burying his mouth into the curve of Gideon's neck, Reed eased him over onto the bed beside him. When he apparently had him where he wanted him, with his heart still hammering like a tom-tom, Reed splayed his own long body, all six feet of it, over Gideon's. Only then did Reed's mouth slide upward to claim a kiss.

Gideon closed his eyes, stunned by how much he was enjoying all this, although he was pretty sure his own enjoyment had barely begun.

About two minutes later, he learned he was right.

REED SKIDDED downward, slathering damp kisses across Gideon's pale chest. A breeze had risen outside, and Gideon's skin glowed like alabaster when flashes of moonlight peeked through the shifting curtains. But the heat of that alabaster flesh was from living man, not stone. Reed inhaled the delicious scent and soft warmth and lost himself in the wonder of having Gideon so pliable and eager in his arms.

Never in his life had Reed experienced with such intensity what Gideon had just done to him. The way Gideon made love to him was the way it was done in books, not real life. Not in Reed's experience anyway.

He pushed his mouth into the nest of pubic hair at the base of Gideon's standing cock and breathed in the smells there. Sweet soap. The slightest hint of perspiration. The scent of his own kisses he had planted there before. It was the glorious aroma of an eager young man trembling in sexual anticipation.

Reed trailed lazy kisses up the shaft of Gideon's cock, slowly climbing to the summit. Adoring the way Gideon stroked his cheek as Reed pulled his dick into the heat of his mouth. Thrilled by Gideon's tremulous breath as Reed's tongue strove to savor that perfect muffin-shaped head. A drop of heated moisture touched Reed's tongue, and he knew it was Gideon's precome, leaking into his kiss. Reed squeezed his eyes shut to block out any distractions so he could savor the sweetness, so he could glory in the taste of what Gideon offered so freely and with such generous, gentle abandon.

"Sweet Jesus," Reed mumbled, more to himself than to anyone else, and as soon as the words were set free, he pulled Gideon's erect cock deeper into his mouth. Gideon arched his back, and his hips came up to meet his hunger as he pawed at Reed's shoulders, his fingers trembling now, his breath coming in ragged spurts.

Reed could only smile when he sensed the sexual craving he had brought to life in Gideon's beautiful body. He had never experienced a moment like this before, how powerful it made him feel. Reed's experiences with gay sex had been a series of hurried, sticky hookups, usually perpetrated in awkward, out of the way places with little or no conversation or emotional connection. He'd never had the desire to savor the moments, nor the time to make those moments *worth* savoring. The couplings were coldly desperate, loveless acts, tainted later by guilt and shame.

With Gideon, on this night, in this bed, it was different. There was no guilt or shame to be found. Their actions were not hurried. They knew each other now. They were no longer strangers. That meant the world to Reed. It changed everything. And now that their bodies had finally come together and they had committed themselves to each other for this one night of pleasure, they could unleash those desires slowly and without fear. As unbridled and unstoppable as the hungers were, they were still tempered by Reed's ability to hold back if he wanted, to take his time and enjoy the process.

Yet it was his other actions that surprised Reed the most. He had never before let himself go like this. He had never opened himself up as he had tonight, with this man. He felt daring and brave, and his desires were truly unreined for the first time in his life. He was totally shameless and thrilled to be so.

"Your mouth is heaven," Gideon whispered into the shadows, his fingers more relaxed now, laying gentle strokes along Reed's cheek. His legs trembled at Reed's sides while his cock pulsed eager and hard inside Reed's worshipping mouth. Gideon's precome leaked freely. The taste of it spreading over Reed's tongue made Reed's heart buck. He had never experienced anything so erotic.

Sliding his hands along Gideon's ribs, relishing the feel of the man beneath him, Reed counted off the wale of each living bone under his fingertips. He traced the sharp ridge of Gideon's hip, and with those same fingers, he gently cupped Gideon's balls, cradling them lovingly in his hand. His mouth slid ever downward over the unbending shaft of Gideon's blood-filled cock. When Gideon gave a tiny cry and then bit into his own arm to silence himself, Reed stretched a hand upward, and oh so gently, he tugged the arm away from Gideon's mouth.

"I want to hear you," he whispered, with Gideon's cock still lying deep in his mouth.

"Don't stop," Gideon pleaded. "Please, Reed. Don't stop what you're doing."

Reed smiled at the need in Gideon's voice. "Never," he muttered.

Returning his hand to cradle Gideon's balls, he gave all of his attention to the job at hand. He let his tongue do as it would, circling the head of Gideon's cock until the juices seeped again. Never before had he felt so capable in the art of making love. He relished it when Gideon bucked beneath him. His heart hammered harder, almost with glee, when Gideon stammered desperate words of pleasure, told him what to do, told him where to touch, what to taste.

Surprising even himself, Reed watched as if from a distance as he let Gideon slip from his mouth while his strong hands gripped Gideon's hips and flipped him gently over in the bed.

Lying now with Gideon on his stomach beneath him, Reed slathered kisses down Gideon's spine, moving relentlessly downward. Once his lips reached the base, and rested in that delicious sprouting of pale hair at the end of Gideon's backbone, Reed let the heated slope of Gideon's ass lure him farther. Dipping his tongue into the cleft there, he almost smiled when Gideon spread his legs wider, offering Reed full access.

Reed felt no shame when Gideon rose onto his elbows and knees and twisted his head around to watch as Reed cupped his hands over both mounds of gossamer flesh and spread them wide. When Reed's mouth spread kisses inward toward the small opening he discovered there, buried deep in that luscious trench of pale, firm flesh, Gideon dropped his head to the bed and waited, ass high. Reed smiled as a tremor of expectant desire stuttered through Gideon's body. Then, in the midst of that incredible rush of desire, Reed pressed his tongue to Gideon's hole.

"Oh God," Gideon muttered, reaching behind him and digging his fingers through Reed's hair, pulling his face tighter against him.

Just as Reed was beginning to fully enjoy this new experience—he had never done anything like this; *never*—and his tongue began to delve deeper, Gideon tensed beneath him and emitted a shuddering cry.

"I'm going to come!"

All but weeping with excitement himself, Reed roughly flipped Gideon onto his back and laid him flat to the bed, one broad hand pressed tightly against Gideon's chest to hold him down, trap him in place. Once again he slid his hungry mouth over Gideon's cock, claiming it for his own.

The explosion came a heartbeat later. Gideon's back arched off the bed, and he gripped Reed's ears like LeBron James clutching a basketball and going in for a layup. Reed laughed, then thought maybe that was counterproductive and stuffed Gideon's cock down his throat until it wouldn't go any farther.

That's all it took. Gideon yelped and, surprisingly, laughed as his cock erupted. Thick gouts of delicious cream spilled over Reed's tongue, splashing across the roof of his mouth. Gideon's hot juices dribbled down his chin. When Reed moved the wrong way only for only an instant, one glob of come shot straight up his nose, making him chuckle. He once again took control of the situation, and Gideon released jet upon jet of his steaming juices into Reed's greedy mouth. Reed never once wanted the stream to end.

But of course it did.

All too soon the detonation ended. Gideon melted into a muscleless mass of quivering sinew on the bed beneath him, his fingers still clutching Reed's ears as if he were anchoring himself to the planet.

Reed eased Gideon's softening cock from between his lips and buried his come-slathered face in Gideon's stomach. Both hearts pounded wildly in a syncopated duet, one just as loud as the other. Reed lay there, shivering, gasping, breathless, unwilling or incapable of movement or even thought.

When Gideon's fingers slid from Reed's cheek to caress his shoulder, Reed lifted his head and looked up to see Gideon staring down at him. His eyelids were lazy in the moonlight, his mouth slack. Reed thought he had never seen a more contented expression.

"Thank you," Reed muttered, his chin nestled in the groove of Gideon's belly button. Gideon's softening cock lay warm and moist against his Adam's apple.

In answer, Gideon slithered down in the bed until the two were face-to-face. He laid his lips over Reed's mouth, and Reed wondered if Gideon could taste his own juices in the kiss.

"Thank you back," Gideon whispered, easing a little farther down to snuggle his face into Reed's chest.

As their hearts quieted, they lay in each other's arms, motionless, drained. Reed reached over and yanked the curtains apart to let more light into the room and let the night breezes blow across their heated bodies. He eyed the moon outside the window over Gideon's shoulder, reliving every moment of what the two of them had just done. Gideon's breath, gentler now and less hurried, stirred the hair on his chest.

When Punkin crawled onto the bed and burrowed next to them, falling instantly asleep with a lazy, happy purr, Reed pulled Gideon tightly against him and finally let himself relax.

"Stay," he mumbled into the darkness. "Please don't go."

"Okay," Gideon mumbled back. He snuggled closer, causing Reed to smile. "But just till dawn. I have to work tomorrow."

"On Sunday?"

"Yeah."

Reed dropped a kiss on Gideon's nose. "Okay. Till dawn."

Still wrapped in each other's arms, they lay facing each other. Gideon fell asleep immediately. Reed watched him for so long he was able to follow the progression of a sliver of moonlight gliding across Gideon's shoulder before it disappeared over the side of the bed.

When Reed let his own eyes close, he did so with his mind at peace for the first time in months. As sleep finally glided in on silent wings to carry him off, his last thought was how safe and alive and *sensual* he felt in Gideon's arms.

And for the first time in his life, how honest he felt to be a gay man, content in his own skin.

Reed's sleep was dreamless. When he awoke hours later with the sun beaming across the windowsill, warming the foot of his bed, he was alone.

Gideon was gone, but Reed could still smell him on the pillow. He rolled into the scent, inhaling it deeply. The memories it evoked made Reed's cock stiffen beneath him. He imagined what he would do if Gideon were still in bed beside him. Naked. Receptive. Staring up at him with that mischievous, sexy grin he sometimes wore. The way his hands felt. The heat of his lips. The taste of his skin.

Reed shuddered, and tried to push those thoughts away. He had other matters to contemplate.

First of all, it was Sunday. Blessed Sunday. Thank God he wouldn't be dragging his welding equipment six decks down into the guts of a sweltering cast-iron boat and poking a few hundred seams of molten metal back and forth in front of his face, breathing in the fumes, dying of the heat, wishing he were anywhere else than where he was. Like in bed, for instance. Just as he was now. Only not alone.

Reed droned a contented growl, stretched, yawned, and rolled over onto his belly while digging his face into his pillow and squeezing his eyelids shut against the encroaching sun. He spared another moment to remember the night he'd spent with Gideon and how he could still taste Gideon's juices on his tongue this morning.

He luxuriously ground his hard-on into the mattress beneath him, then determinedly wrapped it in his fist and tried to concentrate on sleep instead.

Oddly enough, he succeeded. Ten seconds later, dick in hand, he was out like a light.

Chapter 8

It was a reluctant Gideon Chase who slipped out of Reed's arms, and out of Reed's bed, as dawn began to brighten the Sunday sky. He tiptoed around gathering his clothes and his cat and then eased the bedroom door closed behind him so he could dress in the living room without disturbing Reed's sleep.

He found a tiny pile of cat poop on Reed's living room floor. He hadn't brought Punkin's cat box along, so he couldn't really blame her. He gathered up a wad of paper towels, cleaned up the mess, and washed his hands in the kitchen sink after peeking around to see if Punkin had left any other surprises scattered about.

Suddenly starving, he poked his head in the fridge and hauled out a couple of slices of cold pizza, scarfing them down while he dressed.

He found a pen and a scrap of paper on the desk in the corner by the living room window and hastily jotted a note.

> *Thank you for dinner. And breakfast. The night was terrific, and so were you. I'm sorry we didn't get your computer hooked up. Maybe next time. Gideon*
>
> *P.S. I love the way you come. I'll be having flashbacks and beating off to the memory of it for the next ten years.*

Gideon stared down at the words he had just scribbled and giggled. Then he blushed. Too needy? Too desperately slutty? He thought of tearing the note up and starting over. He remembered

Reed's long lean body, his back arched upward like a drawn bow, tense and quivering at the moment of orgasm—holy cripes that was hot!—and he knew beyond the shadow of a doubt that the final words in his note were true—he *would* be fantasizing about last night for a good long while.

He grinned and left the note just the way it was, sticking it to the refrigerator door under a magnet depicting a gorilla from the San Diego Zoo making a kissy face for the camera. He tucked Punkin under his chin, quietly stealthed his way out the front door, and locked it silently behind him.

REED FOUND Gideon's note two hours later while stumbling around, bleary-eyed, making coffee. Needless to say, he didn't remain bleary-eyed long. He read the note over and over again. He smiled and blushed when Gideon told him how he loved the way Reed came. But it was a different line in the note that wouldn't leave his head. It kept rattling around inside his brain pan like a spent shotgun pellet long after the note had been set aside and Reed's day truly begun.

Maybe next time, Gideon had written. *Maybe next time.*

Would there be a next time? Reed hoped so. Judging by the note, Gideon hoped so too. Reed liked that. He liked it a lot.

Almost as much as he liked Gideon.

Before he could wear himself out parsing the hell out of that last thought and fretting over what it might mean, Reed set about prepping himself for the day, toting his coffee cup along with him as he tackled one chore after the other. Showering. Shaving. Dressing. Making the bed. Gathering up his dirty laundry and padding down six flights of stairs on bare feet to dump it in the basement laundry room, which was a shithole if he'd ever seen one. He stuck his quarters into the appropriate slots to get the rusty old washing machines running, then plopped himself down in one of the ancient plastic chairs lined up against the wall among the cobwebs and dust bunnies and settled in to wait.

While his dirty clothes sloshed around, hopefully removing the grunge and not being chewed to mush by machines that had clearly seen better days, he sipped at the mug of coffee he had lugged along with him, which was now cold, and gave himself up to mulling over everything he could remember about the night before. Everything.

His reminiscences were getting to the lascivious stage when his seclusion was interrupted by a short, pink-haired, Mexican-looking guy of maybe twenty-five summers who suddenly materialized in the chair beside him like a frigging ghost, causing Reed to jump like he'd been poked with a needle.

His visitor seemed to think Reed's reaction was pretty funny. "Hi," he said, all smiles, in a lilting Mexican accent. "My name is Ramon." He cast a snarky glance at Reed's coffee cup and smiled even wider. "Didn't mean to scare you. Maybe you should cut back on the caffeine. You're a little hyper."

Reed was gracious enough to laugh at himself for being startled. And while he was being gracious, he also clandestinely crossed one leg over the other to hide the hard-on that had popped up about two minutes earlier thanks to those lascivious Gideon-thoughts he had been entertaining before the pinko bandito came along to scare them out of his head.

Determined not to be a dick, even though his dick was front and center in his mind at that particular moment, he stuck out his hand in a friendly enough fashion. "I'm Reed," he said. "Nice to meet you."

He sat back and really studied his visitor for the first time. Ramon was a cute little guy. His blue-black Hispanic locks—Reed could tell that by the roots—had been bleached white, then coaxed into a vibrant shade of pink, a considerable feat of chemical engineering by anybody's standards. He wore tiny shorts that covered practically nothing, and across his chest he wore a T-shirt portraying a silkscreened Caesar Chavez waving a blow-dryer over his head and looking pissed. Some sort of militant, produce-picking wing of the California Board of Barbering and Cosmetology, Reed supposed with an inward chuckle. Ramon wore Birkenstocks on his feet, his legs were delectably brown and fuzzy, the toenails on his right foot were painted in a graduating range of pastels to denote the colors on a Gay Pride flag, and he had a tiny tattoo on the inside of his right wrist that read *te amo Barney* in gracefully flowing script.

This was clearly a man unashamed of his gayness.

"You were lost in thought," Ramon said, flashing snow-white teeth against gleaming copper skin. Leaning close again, like a buddy sharing secrets, Ramon coyly asked, "Have an especially good night last night, did you?"

"No, I—*what*?"

Ramon laughed. "You're saying no, but your eyes are saying yes. Was it your new neighbor? Gideon Chase? He's a hottie if there ever was one."

Reed couldn't think of a single reason to disagree. Sounding a wee bit shell-shocked even to his own ears, he stated wearily, as if he knew the truth would come out sooner or later so he might as well release it now, "Yes. He most certainly is. And yes, it was a terrific night. But how in the world did you know?"

Ramon *tsk*ed as if the answer was obvious. "You have a mellow, well-laid glow in your eyes. Sort of toe-curlingly smug, you know? There is also the fact that you and Gideon are the only two single men in the building. Everybody else is taken. Arthur must have seen a potential spark between you two or he never would have given you apartments next to each other." He tapped the side of his head and winked. "Always thinking, that one. Always playing matchmaker." Ramon rolled his eyes and patted his pastel hair. "No taste in clothes, of course. Take that wedding dress, for instance. There must be a million despondent silkworms slitting their throats in China to think they played a part in *that* fiasco." He suddenly looked pensive. "I mean if silkworms *have* throats. I'm not really sure."

"You can google it later and find out," Reed said, shooting for droll. "Say, um, how did you know Gideon and I had apartments next to each other?"

Ramon shrugged. "The grapevine, señor. Everybody knows." He leaned closer and went through the motions of brushing something from Reed's pant leg with dainty little flips of his fingertips. "You've got some pollen here. Let me just—"

Reed laughed. "Calm down, Nostradamus. Your predictions are getting away from you. It's not Belladonna Arms love pollen on my pant leg, if that's what you're thinking. More likely it's just a spot of bullshit that dribbled off of *you*. And just to be clear, what happened last night had nothing to do with love pollen or any *other* sort of metaphysical plant spore. It was just two friends hooking up for the first time and having an enjoyable experience together."

Ramon giggled. "The key word in that statement is 'enjoyable,' I think."

Reed had to smile at that. After all, truer words were never spoken. The evening had been *most* enjoyable. But then, Ramon seemed to know enough already. He certainly didn't need to know any more.

"So did you *want* something?" Reed asked, as if he had a board meeting in five minutes and couldn't be hanging around forever chatting with the help.

Ramon tittered and gave Reed's knee a friendly pat. "A lady always knows when it's time to leave. Besides, I've embarrassed you enough. Stop by 4C one of these days and meet my partner, Barney. You'll love him." He frowned and flapped an admonishing finger in Reed's face. "But not too much, I hope."

Reed grinned and crossed his heart. "I promise."

Ramon's frown sloughed away, and he blessed Reed with a sweet smile before reaching out to ruffle Reed's hair. "I like gingers," he said with a sigh. And with that, he bounced through the laundry room door and giggled his way out of sight.

Reed sat smiling, watching him go. When he was alone, Reed thought back yet again to the night before. A surprising thought pulled him up short.

Geez. I may be starting to like gingers myself. One particular *ginger anyway.*

The rattletrap washing machine with his clothes in it chose that moment to beep and clatter and give a horrendous *thud* before shimmying to a stop, crawling three inches across the floor before it died.

Reed heaved himself up and started dumping his clean clothes in the dryer. While he did that, he wondered what Gideon was doing. And more importantly, what Gideon was thinking. Say, about last night for instance.

Reed sighed and started remembering the night before all over again. Two minutes later he had another boner.

BY THE time Gideon finished with work, he had made up his mind about a few things. Most and foremost that continuing an affair with Reed Kelly would be a big mistake. Gideon had just been kicked out of one relationship. He hadn't even replaced everything he'd lost in *that* breakup. Clothes, dishes, dental floss, self-respect. The last thing he needed was to get involved with a man who up until a month before had managed to convince himself he was straight for twentysome years before deciding whumping the wienie was really the way he should be going after all.

Gideon would not have thought it possible, but he actually seemed to have found the one man in the world who was more fucked up than he was.

And who was to say Reed's ex—the illustrious Carol—wouldn't worm her way back into the picture at any moment. Reed obviously felt guilty about leaving her. He clearly still had issues about leading her astray for four years in a marriage that could best be described as dishonest and at worst as one big flapping fuckdoodle lie from the get-go, until he dumped her like a hot potato the minute he decided he wanted to sample a few peckers instead.

There was also the matter of fragility. Not Reed's fragility, but Gideon's. He freely admitted he was lonely and susceptible to a little kindness and attention such as Reed had shown him the night before. He was also still heartsore after being deceived by his ex and still furious about all those socks he had just bought and not even worn yet when the sly little prick tossed them into a donations bin, no doubt snickering maliciously like Muttley in a Dick Dastardly cartoon while he did it. And the cruelest of ironies was that the donations bin belonged to the Salvation Army! One of the most homophobic organizations on the planet. Couldn't Manny at least have given his new socks to an AIDS charity so Gideon would know they were being used by someone who needed them, someone down on his luck, someone deserving of a helping hand, someone *gay*.

As if all that wasn't enough to nip this new relationship in the bud, Reed was also a redhead! Gingers weren't Gideon's cup of tea. They never had been. Although he had to admit, Reed Kelly pretty much undid that particular aversion. Jeez, the guy was hot!

Gideon knew himself well enough to know that if he allowed himself to spend more time with Reed, even a few minutes, his slut gene would kick in and he'd find his head in the guy's pants again. He couldn't just refuse to see him, though. He still had to keep the promise of hooking up Reed's computer for him. That would probably afford them a good thirty minutes of alone time—less if Gideon hurried, or more if he purposely fiddled around, acting like he didn't know what he was doing.

Gideon considered all this while plodding up the six flights of stairs to his apartment. He let himself in, stooped to gather Punkin into his arms after she came running to greet him at the door, then stood stock-still for a minute listening to see if he could hear any sounds coming from next door.

Nope. Silence. Reed was probably out. Wonderful. That gave Gideon a little more time to worry about what he was going to do, and didn't he just *love* having time to worry about stuff.

He had barely made a mental spreadsheet of all his options—although there were actually only two, either dump the welder or *don't* dump the welder—when he was interrupted by a sound next door.

Apparently Reed was home after all.

Gideon set Punkin aside, and without thinking about it any more than was necessary to plant one foot in front of the other, he slipped through his front door and padded down the hall. Instead of knocking at Reed's door, he drummed his fingernails on the jamb, half of him hoping Reed wouldn't hear and the other half wishing he'd brushed his teeth before he came over.

Before Gideon could think about backtracking and sneaking off, Reed yanked the door open and stuck his grinning face out into the hall. "I was hoping it was you."

Gideon just stood there, his hand still raised at drumming level, his heart doing its own little drumming routine. "Were you?"

"Yeah."

"Uh, why? Did you think I wouldn't hook up your computer?"

Reed cocked his head to the side and looked surprised. "No. I just sort of wanted to see you."

"You did?"

"Yeah."

"I guess I wanted to see you too," Gideon said, wondering when his Mensa membership would come in the mail. "I guess that's why I knocked on your door."

"You guess? You don't know?"

"Yes. I mean, no. I mean, yes, that's why I knocked on your door. So I could see you."

Reed brushed his hair back off his forehead while a crazy sort of smile turned up the corners of his mouth. The smile was tinged with shyness, but not much, Gideon was happy to see.

"You want to step inside?" Reed asked, "Or would you rather I knocked you out with a wrench and dragged you in?"

"Butch," Gideon said with a smile of his own and immediately stepped across the threshold. The moment he was in, Reed reached around him and pushed the door closed, sealing them both inside.

Reed remained close, standing there, a quizzical smile on his face. Gideon felt the heat roll off Reed like he was next to a space heater. The warmth was scented with a particular man scent that he remembered all too well from the night before. It was Reed's smell, and Gideon felt his hormones begin to bubble as he breathed it in.

Without giving himself time to think twice, he strode forward and walked straight into Reed's arms for what he thought might be a quick hug.

It was a hug all right, but the last thing it was, was quick.

Gideon laid his head on Reed's chest while Reed's strong arms folded around him, pulling him close.

"Thanks for last night," Reed said.

Gideon lifted his head, and they shared a grin.

"Got your note," Reed added, his ears glowing red.

Gideon nodded. "It was quite a night. I thought a note was called for."

Reed gave his head a funny little shake while his eyebrows shot skyward. That tiny movement was all it took for Gideon to know Reed agreed wholeheartedly. It really had been quite a night.

"It's already all over the building," Gideon said.

Reed blinked. "I know. Ramon told me."

"Who's Ramon?"

"Little pink-haired guy on 4."

"Oh yeah. Well, apparently UPI has nothing on the Belladonna Arms rumor mill. I think we were even the lead story. Banner headlines, stop the presses, film at eleven."

Reed pulled Gideon deeper into his arms. "Well, it *was* a newsworthy night. I wouldn't mind seeing the film myself."

"Neither would I," Gideon said with a smile. He let himself melt into Reed's embrace while the gray matter inside his noggin tried to pretend he hadn't. His smile immediately faded away.

"You know, Reed, I just got out of one relationship. I probably shouldn't be rushing into another."

Reed buried his lips in Gideon's hair. "Me too. And me neither. I couldn't agree more."

"And I'm still not drawn to redheads."

Reed's lips moved over Gideon's scalp as if sorting through the hair follicles seeking the perfect one to nibble on. "Oh God," he muttered, giving a vaudevillian shudder. "Me neither. Redheads. *Blecch.*"

"So if you want to be friends, Reed, we can just be friends. How would that be?"

"Works for me."

"No stress. No angst. Just friends."

Reed's voice was little more than a susurration of sound that hummed through Gideon's skull like quietly beeping sonar, lighting up nerve endings from his nipples on down. "Friends it is, then."

"Last night was just a fluke. We don't have to do it again."

"Of course not." Reed dipped his head and slipped a tongue in Gideon's ear, all the while whispering, "Fluke, fluke, fluke. We don't have to do it again *at all*. I mean like *ever*."

Gideon's voice wasn't any steadier than Reed's. "Since you weren't holding a hammer, I can only assume that's your hard-on poking me in the belly." Reed's smile moved across his ear, down to his neck. "Must be," Reed breathed, his tongue sliding over Gideon's skin while his two index fingers slipped into Gideon's belt loops and pulled his hips closer. "And since you don't even *own* a hammer, that must be your hard-on I feel too."

Gideon's breath gave a hitch. "Anatomically speaking, yeah. Still, it doesn't have to mean anything. We can still just be friends."

Reed's mouth slipped across Gideon's cheek, headed for his mouth. "Of course we can. Buddies with boners. That's us."

"That's us," Gideon echoed.

A moment later they came together in a kiss. To Gideon, the kiss was warm and gentle and something about it made his knees weak. Kisses didn't usually do that to him. Especially ones from a redhead.

"Let's go to bed," Reed mumbled into the kiss.

"What about your computer?"

"Screw my computer. Let's go to bed."

Gideon slipped his tongue into Reed's mouth, and Reed slurped at it like a lollipop.

"It'th thtilll daylight," Gideon lisped. As long as Reed sucked on his tongue, Gideon's esses were out of order. Not that he cared. "And what happened to uth being juth buddieth with bonerth?"

"We may have hit a pothole in that line of thinking. Come to bed," Reed said again, releasing Gideon's tongue and laying kisses at the base of his throat instead. There was a pleading in Reed's voice this time that went straight to Gideon's heart. Or quite possibly his penis. He wasn't sure which. Well, yes, he was.

"Okay," he whispered back.

So much for dumping the welder.

THEIR PERSPIRING bodies lay in a swath of cool air blowing through Reed's bedroom window. Gideon rested with his cheek on Reed's shoulder, his finger drawing lazy circles in the damp scruff of golden-red hair that sprinkled Reed's stomach. Contented, he watched in the moonlight as that stomach rose and fell with Reed's easy breathing. Their passions were spent for the moment, their heartbeats no longer clamoring. The pool of mellow silence they lay in was like the first gentle sweep of sunlight following a storm, the slow rising of sensible morning after an endless night of wonder. The real world after a fairy tale ends.

Although it wasn't a fairy tale at all. And it wasn't morning either. It was simply a Sunday evening in the existence of two losers at love who unintentionally collided with each other and found the collision wasn't as troublesome as they thought it would be.

Flat on his back and holding Gideon close, Reed dipped his head to nestle a kiss into Gideon's tousled hair. "I didn't think this would happen," he whispered.

Gideon's lips brushed Reed's skin when he asked, "Think what would happen?" Not once did his finger stop drawing circles on Reed's skin.

"Us ending up in bed again so soon. I thought last night was just a drunken cock-up. I wasn't even sure you'd *want* to go to bed with me again."

"Why? Because we both hate redheads?" There was irony in Gideon's question, and he suspected Reed knew it.

Reed huffed in faux exasperation, confirming Gideon's theory. "I may want to rethink that whole 'hating redheads' mind-set. Somehow it doesn't appear to apply anymore."

Gideon trailed his finger a little lower and twiddled with a clump of pubic hair at the base of Reed's sleeping dick. The pubic hair was about six shades redder than the golden-red fluff on Reed's chest. And neither shade of red matched the hair on Reed's head or the blond hair on Reed's legs. The guy was a frigging color wheel. Gideon huffed back. "Yeah. I guess redheads are an acquired taste. Sort of like brussels sprouts. I didn't use to like them either."

"Fickle bitch," Reed teased, and they both grinned.

Gideon squirmed around until his leg lay over both of Reed's, trapping them underneath. In this position he could look up along the crisp ridgeline of Reed's jaw, which was cleanly shaven for a change. There was a tiny razor cut just below Reed's ear, and Gideon stretched his neck out far enough to reach it with a kiss. Nothing lingering. Just a peck really. A "here, this will make it better" kiss. That chore completed, he once again settled in alongside Reed, his mouth pressed tight to Reed's shoulder because he liked the way it was perfectly tilted to offer maximum support. And because it smelled nice and tasted even better. He closed his eyes for a moment of spoiled contentment when Reed's hand slid up and down his back. Reed's far hand was propped beneath his head, exposing that luscious armpit full of ginger hair for Gideon to contemplate while peering across the expanse of Reed's beautiful chest.

"I had this all worked out in my head," Gideon said.

Reed tilted his head down to study his face. "Had what worked out?"

"Us. Tonight. How I'd sweep in here, hook up your computer, and sweep the hell out before any entanglements ensued."

Reed tucked a finger under Gideon's chin and tilted his head up just a little more, as if securing for himself an unbroken line of vision straight into Gideon's azure eyes. "If I remember right, you walked into my arms. I didn't walk into yours. And you did it less than thirty seconds after I opened my door. This entanglement is all of your making."

"Yeah," Gideon sighed. He stretched his hand lazily downward and cupped Reed's balls, cradling them gently, loving their warm weight, the gossamer softness of the skin enclosing them. "I never was very good at working stuff out in my head."

Reed's eyes suddenly flared with a different light, a light that looked remarkably like freshly dawning passion. "You may not be a whiz at working stuff out, but you're terrific in bed. Did anyone ever tell you that?"

Gideon opened his mouth in the fakest yawn ever. "All the time. It gets tiresome actually."

Reed laughed. He choked on the laugh when Gideon dragged his thumb across the head of his dick, creating a tsunami of shudders that started at Reed's toes and worked their way up to the tip of his ears. All humor gone from his face, Reed swallowed hard. There was nothing left but a look of sheer anticipation. At least that's how Gideon construed it.

"There you go again," Reed said. "Being terrific in bed."

But Gideon was too contented to pursue another bout of sex. He released Reed's cock from his tender grasp and rested his face on Gideon's shoulder again. His hand came up to stroke Reed's cheek. He smiled when Reed turned his head and planted a kiss in the heat of his palm.

"Like I told you, I met Ramon today," Reed said, his voice sleepy, his heartbeat once again a series of gentle lethargic thuds, like careful footfalls inside his chest. Gideon could feel them against his ear. "He told me Arthur is setting us up."

Gideon nestled closer. "Does that bother you?"

"Why? Does it bother you?"

Gideon shrugged. "Not much."

"Yeah, me neither."

Gideon took a moment to relish the feel of Reed's long body splayed comfortably next to his, the way their leg hair bristled together, the way his breath on Reed's skin stirred the scent of the man beside him, lifting it to his nose, carrying it through his brain. Gideon had never inhaled such a delicious scent from the skin of a man before. Unperfumed. Unsoapy. Just pure man. Every inch of Reed's body reeked of it.

"You always smell so good," he whispered.

Reed planted another smile in Gideon's hair. "Thanks. So do you."

"Hey, wait a minute," Gideon said, lifting his head. "Setting us up for what?"

"Romance," Reed answered. "Ramon said Arthur's matchmaking the two of us into falling in love."

"Well, he certainly matchmaked our asses into bed with each other."

"He didn't have to try very hard."

"Nope."

"Want to spend the night again?"

"I don't want a relationship."

"I know. Neither do I. Want to spend the night again? This time it will be my turn to leave for work first. I have to be at the shipyard at seven."

"I'll make you breakfast before you go."

"You will?"

"Fuck no."

They laughed again. Quietly. This time their laughter carried them gradually into sleep. Not once during the long night did Gideon slip from Reed's embrace. Even in sleep, Reed kept him close. Gideon lay there, happily and contentedly trapped, Reed's delicious scent carrying him through to dawn.

Chapter 9

SHILOH SMART and Ben Moss, both dressed in kilts and looking scrumptious as hell, hovered over Reed and Gideon's table at the Twisted Kilt, delivering this, flourishing that, and cooing words of subservient encouragement with every course. The food might have been Martian cuisine as far as Reed was concerned. Cullen skink soup. Finnan and haddie. Black pudding, collops, and rumbledethumps, whatever *that* was. Ben and Shiloh served it up with flair and a coy wink now and then, clearly thrilled to be playing a part in what they perceived to be a pivotal moment in this romance Reed and Gideon had going on. Their enthusiasm could be best explained by the fact that the dinner date had been arranged and paid for by none other Arthur, the Belladonna Arms matchmaker supreme.

The last few weeks had been a period in Reed's life unlike any other he had ever known. His almost daily liaisons with Gideon gave him true happiness for the very first time. He no longer felt he was living a lie, simply going through the motions of being happy, being fulfilled. With Gideon playing a part in Reed's new single life, his happiness was a real and tangible thing. It touched everything he did. It was always there in the back of his mind. When Gideon was close, it was smack dab in front of his nose.

A smile from Gideon could light his day. Sex had never been as incredible as it was with Gideon in his arms. He felt stronger and lighter and more comfortable in his own skin than he had ever felt before. *This is me*, he said silently inside his head a dozen times a day. *This is who I really am, who I was really meant to be. Gideon showed me this. Gideon made it happen.*

And much to Reed's surprise, everybody in the Belladonna Arms seemed to know it, not least of all Arthur.

Another boost to Reed's happiness was the fact that his new computer had been hooked up for weeks now, thanks to Gideon, and Gideon had never learned Reed could have hooked the damn thing up himself. Sometimes being sneaky was the only way to go.

While no words of love or commitment had yet been spoken between Reed and Gideon, their friendship had become a true and honest thing. Reed thought he could see real happiness on Gideon's face when they were together, and for the moment that was enough to make Reed happy too.

His life settled into a pleasant rhythm. For one thing, he no longer slaved away down at the shipyards in the claustrophobic belly of the USS Dulmouth, sweating like a pig and wondering if he'd ever see the sun again. Now he spent his days working on the superstructure of the USS Thomas, a Navy destroyer, reconfiguring the pilothouse and masts down at the Thirty-second Street piers. After months below decks, it was a pleasure to be out in the open air, perched high above the water of the bay where he caught a breeze now and then and where the cries of sea gulls sometimes caused him to lift his face to the sky, flip up his welding mask, and contentedly behold the grand Pacific Ocean in the distance.

Not once in the months since filing for divorce had Reed tried to contact Carol. She still had his cell phone number. If she wished to get in touch, she could, and there were days when Reed wished she would. He truly missed her. But he also knew any contact would have to be instigated by her. In spite of what Gideon said about Carol possibly thinking Reed didn't care about her anymore if he failed to call, Reed thought the best action he could take to make her forget about him was to simply bow out and give her room to get on with her life without pushing himself back into it with unwanted calls.

He hoped—no, he prayed—he was doing the right thing. He had abandoned her once. The last thing he wanted to do was hurt her even more.

The occasion for Reed and Gideon's special dinner came on the second month anniversary of the day they first tumbled into bed together. Arthur all but ordered them to have dinner at the Scottish restaurant where Shiloh and Arthur's nephew, Ben, worked. The Twisted Kilt was a popular downtown dining spot, and Reed thought maybe some of that popularity might have something to do with the handsome waiters running back and forth, kilts twirling, knees flashing, an occasional luscious thigh making a brief appearance. And without a doubt, two of the sexiest waiters on the premises were Shiloh and Ben, Reed's fellow tenants at the Belladonna Arms.

After Gideon and Reed strolled into the restaurant precisely on time for their reservation, and after a glance flitted from Shiloh to Ben, as if to say, "Oh look how cute they are together," the two waiters did everything in their power to make the anniversary dinner an occasion to remember.

Shiloh, another ginger, was small and elflike, with a handsome, sincere face that seemed to always be sporting a smile. Ben was a mountain of a man with pale skin and blond hair and an endless array of muscles that never stopped flexing or bulging in one part of his body or another. Regardless of bloodlines, Ben carried none of Arthur's fat on his towering frame, although he certainly retained Arthur's stature. And Arthur's sweetness too, if first impressions counted. Reed thought he had never met two nicer guys, or two guys so much in love, as Shiloh and Ben. The way Ben smiled knowingly down on them from on high every time he fussed around at their table, carrying off this and serving up that, Reed thought maybe Ben might have received a little of Arthur's penchant for matchmaking in his DNA too.

While they washed down dinner with round after round of Innis & Gunn ale, another new treat for Reed, Gideon looked on with an air of superiority since he had eaten at the Twisted Kilt often while he was still in a relationship with fuckface Manny and consequently knew the menu up one side and down the other. Even neeps and tatties were no mystery to him.

Somewhere between the collops and the black pudding, Gideon leaned across the table and said loud enough for several heads to turn in their direction, "Sorry, dearest, but you have some sort of sheep's offal dribbling off your chin."

Reed thanked him with a snarl and wiped his mouth with a napkin. Then, blushing, he kicked Gideon in the shin under the table, making Gideon laugh like a hyena.

When dinner was almost over and they were properly stuffed, they hung around the restaurant downing a few more Scottish ales—still compliments of Arthur—and getting a wee bonnie bit inebriated while waiting for Ben and Shiloh to get off work so they could all walk back to the Belladonna Arms together. Gideon was leaning across the table again, this time while telling Reed a truly filthy joke about a nelly little hairdresser with a tube of K-Y and a sailor with an umbrella. Gideon had just snagged Reed's hand to deliver the punchline—which was "Open it! Open it!"—when a shadow fell over the table.

CAUGHT IN midhowl, Reed almost swallowed his tongue when he gazed up to see Carol standing over him, clutching her purse to her chest.

"Hello, Reed," she said. Her familiar voice was so unexpected his heart clenched in either shock or guilt, he wasn't sure which.

"C-Carol...." he stammered, absurdly aware that he and Gideon were still holding hands across the table. He pulled his hand away the same moment Gideon did. Their eyes met, the laughter gone from Gideon's face now too, and then they both turned to stare up at the woman standing in front of them.

Carol's eyes flitted from one to the other, although Reed thought they lingered longest on Gideon before resignedly turning back to him.

"I didn't mean to interrupt," she said, her words cool and clipped. There was a coldness in her eyes Reed had never seen before, a stern tilt of the chin that caught him off guard.

In spite of that, Reed salvaged his manners and screeched his chair back, dragging himself to his feet. Following his cue, Gideon stood as well.

"You're not interrupting," Reed said, forcing a smile to his face, trying to hide his own surprise, which he knew was sort of pointless because Gideon was looking surprised enough for both of them. He was also looking guilty, Reed noticed. Reed's own guilt was understandable, he thought, but Gideon's guilt was not to his liking at all. Gideon had nothing in the world to feel guilty about.

"Excuse me," he said, reaching out to trail his fingers down Gideon's arm. "Gideon, this is Carol. Carol, Gideon Chase."

Carol tore her eyes from Reed and trained them again on Gideon's face. As if taken by surprise, she lifted her hand, but just as quickly dropped it when Gideon began to lift his own. Her eyes hooded, she turned back to Reed, abandoning Gideon in midgreeting.

Reed's cheeks began to burn, but it wasn't from embarrassment. "Would you care to join us?" he asked with teeth-grinding politeness, forcing the words out as if prying them off his tongue with a crowbar.

Carol narrowed her eyes and once again her gaze flitted to Gideon, who still stood there looking uneasy. "I think not," she said. She glanced toward the opposite end of the restaurant to an older couple seated in a booth by the back wall. "I'm here with my parents."

Carol's mother and father were watching the reunion with stern faces. When Reed lifted his hand to wave a greeting, after all he had known those people for years, he was met with stony glares.

Carol offered an unkind little tinkle of laughter, as once again her gaze fell on Gideon. "As you can see, Reed, I'm pretty sure they'd rather set themselves on fire than spend an evening with you and your… friend."

From the corner of his eye, he saw the hurt on Gideon's face as he cast his gaze downward at the floor, at the dishes on the table, anywhere but in Carol's direction. Gideon's ears were red now too, and not once in the two months he had known Gideon had he seen a more tortured expression rise up to mar that perfect face.

A surge of anger rushed through Reed. He clenched his hands, and his throat tightened. He returned his eyes to Carol's face, and when he saw the smirk of triumph there, knowing she had wounded Gideon as she had clearly set out to do, Reed still fought to remain civil. It was an uphill grind. And just as quickly, he knew a civil attitude was the last thing he should be shooting for anyway. Because frankly, he simply didn't give a shit about anything but that wounded expression on Gideon's face. Fuck Carol. Fuck her parents. Fuck being civil.

"So how is the catering business treating you?" Reed asked, his voice as level and slick as a slab of ice.

Carol didn't respond, but by the two splashes of color that rose to her cheeks, Reed gathered his ex-wife's catering business wasn't treating her well at all. He was instantly sorry for goading her about it. But a second later, when she muttered the word, "Asshole," he got mad all over again.

Twisting his mouth into a nasty smile, he reached out yet again, this time taking Gideon's hand over the table. It felt cold and small in his hand, but the appreciation he saw in Gideon's eyes when he clasped it, made up for everything. Gideon's cool fingers slipped through his, and he straightened his back, no longer looking embarrassed or ashamed.

Reed had never felt closer to Gideon than at that moment. Seeing how Gideon drew strength from the simple act of Reed reaching out to claim his hand, to make a point of including him in his life and making sure his ex-wife knew it, made Reed's heart again clench. But not in pain this time. In pride. He felt the anger spill out of him so quickly it almost took his breath away. His mouth turned up in a smile, a real one this time.

"I'm sorry, Carol," Reed heard himself say, again tightening his grip on Gideon's hand. "About what you said earlier. You must have misunderstood. Gideon isn't just my friend. He's more than that. We've been dating for a while now. Are you sure you wouldn't care to join us?"

Reed was torn somewhere between elation and pity when he saw the change his last invitation brought to Carol. Clearly she could dish it out but wasn't too keen on taking it in return. Hurt flashed in her eyes, but the hurt was just as quickly replaced by cool fury. Her gaze slid to Gideon, and when her eyes met his, Reed saw the dawning of truth register on her face. Gideon's face had morphed as well. He no longer looked ashamed. He looked proud and strong standing there with his hand encased in Reed's. When Gideon smiled now, it too was an honest one, and this time the victory that had flashed in Carol's eyes earlier when she thought she'd wounded him flared in Gideon's eyes instead.

"Y-yes," Carol stuttered, looking quickly away. "I'm sure." The last word was snipped from her lips as if with a pair of icy scissors. She turned back to Reed, but her eyes never quite reached his. "I'm sorry I bothered you," she said. And with that, she turned away, heading not for the table where her parents waited, but toward the restaurant entrance where she slipped through the door without once glancing back. A moment later, her parents gathered their belongings and followed her out. They hadn't even ordered yet.

Suddenly weary, and still clutching Gideon's hand, Reed dropped back into his chair. Gideon followed suit, leaning forward to brush a fingertip over Reed's chin, as if trying to coax a smile.

"Are you all right?" Gideon asked.

Reed lifted his eyes and slowly nodded. After a heartbeat or two, he found a sympathetic smile and shot it across the table. "Are you?"

"Uh-huh." Gideon still had his fingers entwined in Reed's; neither man had yet tried to pull away. "Thank you, Reed." Gideon said, his voice gentle. "You stood up for me."

Reed frowned. "She had no right to act like that. Not to you. I'm the one who hurt her. Not you."

Gideon shrugged. "I understand her, though. She was jealous. If I saw you with someone else, I'd be jealous too."

Reed lifted his eyes to stare across the table. His face softened. "Would you?"

Gideon's warm gaze floated back to him with just a hint of astonishment, as if Reed had asked the dumbest question in the world. The clatter and bustle of the restaurant around them faded into the background as Reed let that incredulous gaze melt into his own. Gideon lazily stroked the back of Reed's hand with his thumb. His fingers were no longer cool in Reed's grasp, but warm. Reed wasn't the only one hanging on now. Gideon was holding on too, clutching Reed's hand like a guy about to slip beneath the waves, but knowing, just *knowing*, his safety was assured as long as he kept a connection with the man in front of him. In Reed's mind, in Reed's imagination, he wondered at the way Gideon seemed to need his support, yet at the same time offer his own support tenfold with nothing more than a touch and a kind, open glance. Reed marveled at the perfect way their two hands fit together. How the simple heat of Gideon's palm against his own could make him feel so contented. So complete.

Their beers sat warming on the table as they continued to stare into each other's eyes.

"You're perfect," Reed said in a whisper barely loud enough for the words to reach Gideon's ears.

"So are you," Gideon answered. His delivery was straightforward and direct, like a schoolteacher explaining something obvious that the student should have already known.

Again, Reed was left momentarily speechless by Gideon's attitude, the way he made everything seem so obvious, so clear. "I think...," he began, but then his words trailed away.

Gideon tilted his head, gazing at him, his eyes delving deep. Eager but kind. Patient but knowing. "You what, Reed? What were you going to say?"

The words were still on the tip of his tongue, but suddenly Reed couldn't speak them. Not yet. Not now. He simply shook his head and brought Gideon's hand to his lips.

"Maybe later," he said. "When we're home."

Gideon's face was somber but not unhappy. Reed thought he saw understanding there. At least he hoped he did. "All right," Gideon said. "If that's what you want."

Reed continued to press his lips to Gideon's hand, marveling to himself that he could do such a thing in the middle of a crowded restaurant. He used to be so inhibited in public. Even with Carol. He used to glower at people who made a pretense of showing their affection for each other when strangers were around. But now here he sat kissing Gideon's hand, not the least bit embarrassed. If anything, he was proud to show his connection to Gideon, proud to know he was part of Gideon's life and that Gideon was part of his. He required neither acceptance nor tolerance from the people who might be looking on. He was suddenly awash with feelings for the man sitting across from him. Somehow those feelings had flooded in when he wasn't watching, catching him by surprise.

And for Reed Kelly, that was a pretty amazing turn of events.

Gideon softly cleared his throat. "Thank you again, Reed. For doing what you did. I mean, with Carol."

This time it was Reed's turn to frown. "I'll never let anyone slight you," he said.

When Gideon's chin puckered and his eyes misted up, Reed looked on in wonder, amazed that his simple statement had caused such a reaction.

Slowly, oh so slowly, Gideon's smile returned. When it did, it burrowed straight into Reed's heart.

"Take me home," Gideon softly said.

"But Ben and Shiloh…," Reed began.

Gideon tightened his grip on Reed's hand. "They'll understand."

And Reed nodded. They would indeed.

GIDEON LAY breathless, reaching up to caress Reed's face as their lips pressed together in one long unbroken kiss. Gideon's legs were bent upward, clamped around Reed's hips in a scissor hold, his heels at Reed's ass. They lazily rocked together as Reed's long cock slid gently deep inside him before as gently sliding out, then beginning the long slide in again. Unhurried, the rhythm unchanging, Gideon stroked Reed's jawline, his entire body throbbing with desire, expectant, waiting for the next piercing. And the next. And the next.

With each penetration, the bulbous head of Reed's engorged cock scraped across Gideon's prostate, and he shuddered as the ecstasy of that gentle nudge stuttered through him. Reed's face hovered over his as he pulled back from the kiss to study Gideon's face, but not once did he change the rhythm of his piercing. Gideon stared up at him, mouth slack and moist from their long kiss, his hands still at Reed's face, caressing, his body unerringly offering itself to the gentle stabbing of Reed's hungry cock.

"Don't stop," Gideon gasped, eyes pleading, his voice a fractured whisper. But at that moment, Reed did exactly that. He stopped. He froze with his cock buried deep inside Gideon. He balanced himself over Gideon, a gleam of sheer devilment in his eyes as he watched Gideon writhe beneath him, impaled.

When Gideon couldn't stand the stillness a moment longer, he stammered, "Oh please," and Reed resumed the gentle rocking, his iron cock retreating before slowly delving deep again.

Reed rose onto his knees, lifting Gideon's hips along with him. His back arched as he drove himself into Gideon's core. His warm fingers slid around Gideon's cock standing upright between them. Reed stroked it gently, his thumb sliding across the oozing slit, and Gideon's entire body convulsed at the dual sensations.

"Oh God," Gideon stammered, and a second later, with a whimpering cry, he spilled his seed in Reed's hand. Reed captured it all in his palm, and when Gideon's thrashing had ceased, Reed carried the precious juices to his mouth and lapped them from his own hand.

At that moment, Reed lost his rhythm. As Gideon clung tightly, once again gasping for breath as that heavy, fat cock dragged its way through him, Reed's face twisted into a wanton rictus of delight. Reed's cock bulged inside him as Reed cried out some nonsensical words that Gideon couldn't understand. Enthralled, Gideon fixed his gaze on Reed, who stared down at him in turn, his mouth wide, the sinews in his neck standing out like guywires.

When Reed came, Gideon reveled in that final rush of passion deep inside where Reed's cock now trembled, as stiff as iron. As he spilled his juices inside his condom, Reed dropped over Gideon like a shadow and gathered him tightly in his arms. His mouth found Gideon's, and in the heat of that kiss, Reed carried himself to the end of his climax. Spent, they collapsed in each other's arms. Gideon laid his mouth to Reed's throat as Reed lay over him, and on the tender skin of his face, he could feel Reed's surging pulse hammering. He stroked Reed's broad, heaving back and held him as close as he could, never wanting him to move, never wanting him to pull away. Never wanting Reed's softening cock to slip free from his grasp.

But of course it did. And at that unwanted moment of parting, both men shuddered, then relaxed even more.

They lay for the longest time in each other's arms. Soon reality slipped in, and Reed eased himself from the bed, padding into the bathroom to clean himself up. Gideon waited, and as he knew he would, Reed quickly returned with a damp washcloth and a towel to clean Gideon up as well. Gideon lay supine under his ministrations, his legs bent upward, watching Reed's gentle movements with as much amazement as he had the first time Reed did such a thing for him. Reed's patience and gently caring ablutions never ceased to surprise Gideon.

This time, when Reed finished, Gideon took his arm and lazily pulled Reed back over him so that he lay there on top of him as he had at the moment of orgasm.

"Thank you," he whispered into the shadows, burrowing happily into Reed's heat, squeezing his eyes shut at the sensation of Reed's strong arms gathering him into a new embrace.

"Thank you too," Reed whispered back, his soft lips at Gideon's neck, the probing nubs of his fingertips gently massaging Gideon's hips.

Their cocks lay warm and unthreatening, nestled side by side. Gideon pressed his face into Reed's chest, loving the way the ginger hair there scraped across his tender skin. And as always, the way Reed's singular smell burrowed through him like perfume.

He wrapped his arms tightly around Reed's waist, holding on for dear life. Through the bedroom window came the sound of raindrops plopping softly on the glass.

"It's starting to rain," Reed muttered, his lips in Gideon's hair. It was a place Reed always seemed to gravitate to in quieter moments.

Gideon merely nodded, too content to speak. Too content to care about the world outside their room. Outside their bed.

Silence lay between them for a flurry of heartbeats. In that silence the rain continued to patter across the glass. Somewhere in the shadows, Punkin purred in her sleep.

Minutes later, Reed spoke again, his voice as soft as smoke, barely wafting through the darkness. His caressing hand slid up Gideon's ribs to rest at the side of his neck, his fingers warm, his palm broad but gently weightless on his skin. "I've never told you, but the night you moved in next door, I heard you crying in your sleep."

Gideon tensed in Reed's arms. "I did?"

"Yes. It was the saddest sound I've ever heard."

Gideon lay quiet, considering what Reed had said. Finally he spoke. "It was a rough time for me. I-I had never been hurt like that before."

Reed eased himself closer, seeking Gideon's mouth in the shadows. When he found it, their lips came together as if it was the most natural thing in the world. In the midst of the kiss, Reed muttered words that touched Gideon's heart. Gentle words. Words that fluttered through him like startled sparrows.

"You'll never be hurt like that again," Reed whispered. "Not by me. I promise."

Gideon opened his eyes to study Reed's face in the shadows. He lifted his hands and stroked Reed's cheeks, his thumb lying soft at the edge of their kiss. "I know I won't," he said, their warm breaths blending, their heartbeats pumping out a common rhythm as their gentle kiss went on and on.

"I just wanted you to know…," Reed said as his eyes slowly closed and his pale lashes brushed across Gideon's skin.

Wide-awake now, and suddenly as far away from sleep as he had ever been in his life, Gideon heard his own words flow breathlessly through the darkness, as if uttered by someone else. "I do know, Reed. I've known it all along."

His pulse accelerated when Reed nuzzled closer, his kiss becoming a smile that Gideon could feel against his skin. And just as quickly, Reed's voice trailed away as sleep overcame him. But not before he muttered a single lazy string of words into the shadows—and directly into Gideon's soul.

"I'm glad, Gideon. I'm glad you know."

Chapter 10

SIMILE-WISE, THE flaming red sunset looked like a smear of cherry marmalade spread across the horizon outside Reed's living room window. Closer in, slathered across the bottom of the window itself with nothing simile-wise about it, lay a glutinous smudge of grape jelly, delivered there by Artie's miniature paw. Said paw was moist and sticky, and every time Artie touched a solid surface—such as a previously spotless window pane—his little jelly-covered hand stuck to it until he yanked it away with a grunt. The resultant sucking sound was remarkably similar to that of a cow pulling its foot out of the mud. In turns either stunned or appalled, and sometimes both at once, Reed sat on the sofa beside an equally appalled Gideon, judging by the tension in his body, while the kid destroyed Reed's apartment with the single-minded dedication of a team of teeny tiny terrorists.

Punkin had the good sense to hide under the bed. Reed thought he might join her there momentarily.

He tore his eyes from the destruction and centered his shell-shocked gaze on Gideon, mostly for the purpose of lowering his blood pressure. "Tell me again how we got roped into babysitting this little fucker. I mean, tyke."

Gideon gave a wry snort. "Pete begged. And you folded."

"Why would I do such a thing?"

"Because Pete wanted to take his wife out for a quiet dinner. And because you're a wienie."

Reed did his best to look offended. "Am not."

Gideon snickered while his eyeballs jittered left, then right, following Artie, who was unstuck at the moment from all nonporous surfaces. The kid was thumping back and forth across the room on his stubby little legs, arms flailing, a bungee cord of snot dribbling out of his nose, and another one, this one Welch's purple with specks of english muffin stuck to it, swinging back and forth off his chin. He was emitting a merry wail that sounded vaguely like the scream of a tsunami siren warning the populace to head for higher ground.

"Death wish, then?" Gideon ventured, still trying to answer Reed's question. "Insanity? Morbid self-hatred? Although I think my first answer was the right one. You said yes to Pete's request because you're a wienie."

The tsunami siren was interrupted by what sounded like the basso profundo blast of a discordant tuba. The noise was so surprising, it stopped little Artie in his tracks. He twisted his head around to look down at his own butt, which was where the noise originated. He stood in the middle of the room, swaying on his feet since his balance was none too good anyway. His tiny eyebrows were furrowed in concentration as if he had suddenly been struck by the exact unraveling of the Fibonacci sequence.

Reed and Gideon stiffened and clawed their way to the edge of the couch, perching there on pins and needles, all internal antennae quivering in dread. "Tell me he's not gonna do what I think he's gonna do," Reed muttered, true horror clenching his heart.

Gideon's fingernails dug into Reed's arm. His breath came in wheezy little gasps. "Quick! Rip off his diaper and set him in the cat box before he lets go!" (Reed and Gideon were spending so much time together, Punkin now had a cat box in each apartment.)

Reed blinked, actually considering it.

Before Gideon could yell at him again, Reed's nose puckered up, his lungs locked up for the purpose of self-preservation, and he crammed two fingers up his nose to keep the horrendous odor that suddenly rolled through the apartment from eating its way into his brain and rendering him more useless than he already was.

"Good lord, what a stench!" Gideon gasped. "I can hear cockroaches falling dead in the kitchen."

"I don't have cockroaches."

"Not now you don't."

Reed's vision blurred. The reek was unbearable. "What in God's name do they feed that kid?"

Gideon pulled his T-shirt collar up over his nose and left it there. With his voice muffled, he sounded like he was cowering in a sewer. The stink in the air heightened that impression.

He tried to form words without the benefit of oxygen, or even opening his mouth. "It smells like the Chernobyl blue plate special. Radioactive weasel guts poured over a cow pattie pooped out of a cow with three heads." He extended a trembling hand, pointing to a mound of baby miscellanea Pete and Sylvia had dumped off with the kid. "Go fetch that little plastic pottie Pete left with us and plunk the little bastard down on it while I call a cab. I'm getting the hell out of here before the EPA arrives."

Reed squinted his face up into a pretty good impression of a serial killer about to off his next victim. "If you try to leave me alone with that kid, I'll break your legs."

"Fine!" Gideon snapped.

They at long last sprang into action, although it was obviously too late. Artie's diaper already looked like someone had stuffed a shovelful of mud down the back of it. The weight dragged the diaper down around his knobby knees and with his center of gravity altered, it all but pulled him backward across the room. Reed noticed the kid was looking mightily relieved, however. But that was temporary. A moment later even Artie screwed his face up in horror when he got a whiff of himself.

"Poo-poo!" he screamed and, pinching his face into a perfect impersonation of Walter Brennan having his fingernails pulled out with a pair of pliers, let out a horrific wail.

Reed, on his feet now, bent over and glared at the kid, their noses inches apart. "Poo-poo? You think?" he asked, convivially enough, since even he knew committing infanticide might be a little over the top. Plus he would have to explain to Pete and Sylvia why he'd strangled their only child. That might get awkward, even if it did seem like a community service.

Standing this close to Artie, the tears positively streamed from Reed's eyes. Quickly scooping the toddler off the floor, while holding him out as far from his nose as his arms would allow, he hustled into the bathroom, where he hastily but cautiously deposited Artie in the bathtub, rather like a bomb disposal expert removing a mujahideen IED from an

Afghani highway and cautiously scooting it into a ditch where it could
do the least amount of damage if it blew the fuck up.

Twenty minutes later, after much gagging and retching, Reed
and Gideon got little Artie cleaned up. Reed carried the soiled diaper,
which now weighed two pounds if it weighed an ounce, to the bathroom
window with a pair of ice tongs and flung it down the hillside into a
patch of brambles, where it would probably lie until the end of time,
periodically killing off any and all wildlife that came within twenty feet
of it. Gideon came along right behind him and flung three stained and
reeking wash cloths, a bath towel, and a brand-new bathroom rug, now
stained beyond redemption, through the window too. After that, the ice
tongs went flying.

"Next time the kid goes out the window first," Reed said, eyeing
his suddenly denuded bathroom.

"Good idea," Gideon agreed. "Save us a lot of work."

Artie was naked now from the waist down because no matter
what they did they couldn't get his clean diaper to stay in place. He kept
wiggling and flinging his legs all over while they tried to pin it on, so
they finally gave up and set the tyke on the floor wearing nothing but a
baby-sized pullover sporting a picture of SpongeBob SquarePants on the
front. With his tiny unfettered penis bouncing merrily in front of him, he
took off giggling, eager to complete the devastation he had only begun
to wreak on Reed's apartment. He seemed to be lighter on his feet now,
which was no surprise to anyone.

Reed and Gideon collapsed wearily onto the couch after scrubbing
their hands in the bathroom sink for ten minutes.

"Did I tell you I never want kids?" Reed asked.

Gideon grunted. "Well, there's a surprise."

Punkin made the tactical error of crawling out from under the bed
and poking her head through the door. Artie spotted her and the chase was
on. All Reed said was "Poor cat," and nonchalantly turned to Gideon.
"So how you been?"

Reed was pleased to see Gideon's expression mellow. He edged
closer on the couch and rested his hand on Reed's knee, suddenly all
snuggly. "After last night, you shouldn't have to ask."

It was Reed's turn to edge closer. "That *was* fun."

"We have good sex."

"We do indeed. I never knew it could be like this."

Gideon gazed up into Reed's eyes. "Didn't you?" he asked softly.

Reed started to blush, so he turned to watch Artie, who seemed to have forgotten about the cat completely. He was currently plucking the leaves off a rhododendron, which Reed had pretty well killed anyway. Reed didn't intervene until Artie started stuffing the dead leaves in his mouth. Then he sprang into action.

He swept across the room, lifted little Artie up by his ankles, dangled him upside down, and gave him a good shake so he would drop the leaves. He carried the kid, still head down and balls up, into the kitchen and with one hand, peeled him a banana. Artie sputtered something resembling a thank-you and stuffed most of it into his mouth. Since he was still upside down, his aim was off. What didn't go into his mouth, went into his ear. Upended, little Artie's motor skills sucked even worse than they did when he was upright.

Reed set him gently on the floor and returned to the couch where Gideon waited with that same sweet smile on his face. "Worst babysitter ever," Gideon said.

Reed grinned. "Like you're any better."

They settled in once again side by side. This time they were so close that only by climbing into each other's laps, ripping off their clothes, and applying lubricant to a few strategically located body parts could they have gotten any closer.

"You were perfect last night," Reed cooed, his lips on Gideon's ear.

Gideon dropped his head back so Reed could kiss his throat. He really liked it when Reed kissed his throat.

"So were you," Gideon whispered, his voice already husky and pitched with need. There was a hunger in his words that Reed found sexy as hell. In fact, he found *everything* about Gideon sexy as hell. Not that they could do anything about it *now*, what with the blasted kid being there and all.

Reed burrowed backward into the lumpy cushions of the couch, dragging Gideon down with him. He pried his mouth off Gideon's Adam's apple and flailed around for a topic of conversation that wouldn't leave him hornier than he already was. "I haven't seen Arthur around much. Busy with the wedding, I suppose."

Gideon who was at the moment stroking Reed's furry belly under his shirt and purring in contentment, suddenly slapped himself in the forehead with a smack. "Oh God! That damn wedding. He's driving everybody crazy."

"Well, that's our Arthur."

"At least the earthquakes have stopped. Arthur is feeling pretty good about that."

"Good thing," Reed said. "Roger and Stanley on 5 told me Arthur has had two heart attacks already. Years ago, apparently, but still some damage was done. If he keeps going nuclear every time the earth gives another jolt, he's liable to set himself up for a third. Apparently, Tom is pretty worried."

Gideon frowned. "I'm sorry to hear that. I love Arthur. I'd hate to see anything happen to him."

"We all would," Reed sighed. "But do you think he'll listen to anybody? He's too worried about the color of his wedding bouquet and which shoes to pack for the honeymoon to try to calm himself down over a few minor earthquakes."

"They're going on a honeymoon? He and Tom have been together for years."

"Arthur wants to take a train to San Francisco. He has it in his head to get a compartment and fuck Tom all the way from the San Diego city limits to the Golden Gate Bridge, then after they arrive, eat his way across Fisherman's Wharf, get shitfaced in every slutty bar in the Castro, and tour Alcatraz in his wedding gown. I understand Tom is thinking of buying a gun and shooting himself in the head."

"Really?"

"No. I made that last part up."

Little Artie was sitting in the doorway leading into the kitchen with his head down around his crotch, studying his ding dong with all the concentration of a man trying to remove his own appendix. Taking the little pink head between thumb and forefinger, Artie pulled it out as far as it would go, then let it spring back like a rubber band. Over and over again. He was so fascinated by what he was doing, his tongue was poking out the side of his mouth, and the snot was dribbling from his nose again.

Reed and Gideon both stared at him. Finally Reed said, "That can't be good. He'll have the thing worn out before he hits puberty. Pete and Sylvia will never forgive us."

"We have to get a diaper on him," Gideon said.

"We do indeed," Reed agreed.

"Got a staple gun?"

"Don't be silly," Reed said. "Whoever heard of putting a diaper on with a staple gun? Fetch the Gorilla tape instead. It's in my tool box."

Five minutes later, after much wrestling and pleading and coercing with two cookies and another banana, they finally managed to attach Artie's Pamper by wrapping a long sticky swath of Gorilla tape completely around the kid *twice*, binding the diaper in place and thus preserving the lad's penis for future exploration, say, thirteen or fourteen years from now when he'd need it most.

Stepping back to look at their handiwork, they watched little Artie tug at the diaper with all his considerable strength and not budge it an inch. He finally forgot about it and went back to destroying the apartment. A mixed blessing at best.

Less than fifteen seconds later, the earth gave its biggest jolt yet. The building rocked, and Artie toppled over backward, bonking his head on the floor. Looking befuddled but not entirely unamused, he said, "Boom!" with an astounded smirk on his face.

While the Arms continued to quake and groan around them, the cookie jar tumbled off the kitchen counter with a crash. It exploded on contact with the ratty linoleum and sent a spray of Sylvia's chocolate chip cookies—a bribe for babysitting—flying across the room. The cookies, reduced now to crumbs and mixed with flecks of crockery, resembled the remnants of Princess Leia's home planet of Alderaan after being blown into pixie dust by Peter Cushing, who at the time looked so emaciated as to be in dire need of a bacon cheeseburger.

The earth gave another lunge, and Reed's beer bottle danced its way across the coffee table. When it toppled off the edge, Reed snatched it out of midair at the same instant that Gideon flew across the room to scoop Artie up into his arms and out of harm's way from the jagged edges of the broken cookie jar.

Voices were raised all over the building. Screams, yells, curses. Far, far below, somewhere down around ground level, they heard a high-pitched yodel of terror that could only have come from Arthur. It lasted forever, growing gradually more desperate as the tremor continued to shake the Belladonna Arms.

The building shimmied and swayed for another minute or so, but it seemed like hours. The old cast-iron neon sign, which must have weighed several tons, squeaked and rattled above their heads while Reed prayed desperately it would not come crashing through the ceiling and kill them all. The window panes rattled in their frames, and another piece of crockery crashed to the floor in the kitchen.

Then, just as suddenly as it began, the earth stilled and the swaying stopped. It left a silence behind that was almost as frightening as the earthquake itself. Arthur stopped bawling down in the bowels of the building. The curtains stopped swaying. The dishes in the pantry stopped clattering. Even little Artie was struck dumb for what was probably the first time in his life. He lay scrunched into a protective ball in Gideon's arms with his eyes as big as meatballs and his tiny fingers clamped on to Gideon's shirt either in terror or because he was having the time of his life, Reed wasn't sure which.

Reed and Gideon stared at each other. Slowly, grins crawled across their faces.

"Wow," Gideon whispered, his eyes not much smaller than Artie's.

Reed trailed leery eyes across the ceiling as if waiting for the building to collapse around his ears. When it didn't, his tremulous grin grew a little braver. Still breathless with wonder, his voice wasn't much more than a feathery gasp. "That must have been a six on the Richter scale. I've never felt one so strong."

Gideon nodded, obviously as stunned as Reed. "Arthur must be thrilled. Did you hear him howl?"

Reed snorted. "*Everybody* heard him howl."

In the distance, they heard another scream. This one belonged to a siren attached to a fire truck. Then the distant bleating of an ambulance joined in. It seemed everyone had not escaped the earthquake uninjured.

Reed was about to mutter something sympathetic for whoever the EMT's were hustling to fetch when a furious pounding on Reed's front door made all three of them freeze. This time even the baby looked worried.

The doorknob jiggled, and since the door was locked, the pounding began again, even more furiously than before. Whoever wanted in, wanted in badly, and they weren't afraid to slam a few fists against the door to make it happen.

"Now what the fu—" Reed sputtered. Clearly there was too much excitement going on for one night. He was starting to OD on adrenaline. Much more bedlam and he'd be filling his shorts like Artie.

For lack of a better plan, he rushed across the room and yanked open the door.

Charlie and Bruce, the resident kleptos, stood peering in, their faces tight with anguish. Charlie stood there shirtless. His fiery hair stood on end, and his pants were unzipped. Bruce had his shirt on but it was backward and inside out. Both men looked greasy and reeked of cinnamon-flavored lube. Clearly they had been fooling around when the earthquake interrupted them, which was far more information than Reed wanted to know. Behind them, along the shabby halls and stairwells of the Belladonna Arms, Reed heard clattering footsteps and slamming doors. The building was like an anthill after someone pokes a stick in it, tenants scattering every which way. What the hell was happening? Bruce looked shell-shocked underneath the brim of his ten-gallon hat.

Did he even fuck with that thing on? Reed wondered. Bruce also had a red pubic hair stuck to his cheek, plain as day. Reed tried not to stare at it or let himself compare it to the flaming red hair sticking off the top of Charlie's pencil-shaped head to see if he came up with a genetic match, which under the circumstances, would seem to be a given.

A moment later, the earth gave a small final jolt. Like an afterthought. All five humans waited, stiff as statues, ears cocked, wondering what would happen next. All ten eyeballs were white and round and rolling this way and that like a pool table full of cue balls. The sirens wailed louder, clearly drawing near. Suddenly they heard the squeal of tires as the emergency vehicles came tearing up the hill and screeched to a halt outside the Belladonna Arms!

Gideon hugged Artie close, his lips in the baby's hair, while Reed slipped an arm around Gideon's waist and pulled them both against him as if shielding them from danger.

Was the building about to collapse? What the hell was going on?

Bruce leaned in and plucked at Artie's diaper, which didn't give an inch. "Is that Gorilla tape?" he asked, his eyebrows furrowed in concentration. Clearly he was missing the big picture.

"Yeah. Why? You got a problem with Gorilla tape?" Reed asked, his words clipped, his left eye twitching, a little speck of spittle wetting the corner of his mouth.

Bruce shuffled his feet while his gaze flitted upward to the stratosphere, then down at his feet, clearly trying to stare anywhere but at Reed's glowering countenance. "Just asking, bwana. Just asking."

"It's Arthur," Charlie screamed, as if he suddenly remembered the reason for their visit. "He's had a heart attack! Come on!" Then he took a fistful of Bruce's shirt and dragged him toward the stairs.

"Where are you going?" Reed called out.

But they were already gone.

Gideon and Reed raced to the edge of the stairwell and stared down. Charlie and Bruce were already three flights below, but even farther away than that, down all the way on the ground floor, they saw a cluster of firemen at Arthur's apartment door, which abutted the first flight of steps off the lobby. Behind the firemen came two paramedics with a gurney piled high with medical equipment. To the side, Tom, looking harassed and terrified, ushered them into their apartment.

"Oh no," Gideon whispered. "Oh dear God no."

THE EMERGENCY room at Mercy Hospital resembled a Belladonna Arms tenants' meeting. Almost everybody was there. Roger and Stanley. Charlie and Bruce. Barney and Ramon. Milan and Harlie. Shiloh and Ben. Lester and Dan. A dozen other residents were in attendance as well, all of them couples, all of them male, all of them gay. There were a passel of sick strangers scattered around the emergency room too, but since they didn't live at the Arms and had no connection to poor Arthur, nobody gave a shit what happened to them.

Reed and Gideon—with little Artie, his diaper still bound in place with Gorilla tape and still cradled in Gideon's arms—were the last to arrive.

"How is he?" Reed cried out to the group in general, rather like a soldier tossing a hand grenade blindly across enemy lines, figuring he'd take out *somebody*.

The question stuck to Lester, who was standing in the arms of Dan, both men in bow ties and pleated pants and perfectly polished wingtips. *Jesus*, Reed thought, *don't they ever relax?*

The only flaw in Lester's or Dan's facades was the fact that Lester was wringing the tail of his dress shirt, clearly distraught by all that was happening.

"We don't know yet," Lester answered, his voice not much more than a nervous little squeak. "Nobody has come out to tell us anything. Tom is in there with Arthur and the doctors, but he hasn't had time to give us an update. Oh lord, I hope Arthur's all right. He brought me and Dan together. If it wasn't for Arthur, we wouldn't even *love* each other!"

Lester and Dan swallowed in unison, twin gulps, a bizarre thing to witness.

It was almost as bizarre as the sea of heads bobbing in agreement around them. A soft muttering of sympathy swelled up from the crowd, rather like the barely discernable roar of machinery kicking to life deep in the guts of Hoover Dam. A score of voices chimed in with "Oh God, we all owe Arthur!" and "Amen to that!" and "Poor Arthur!" and "Poor Tom!" Off in the distance by the vending machines, someone with a skewed sense of priorities, cried out, "This thing took my quarters!"

On closer inspection, Reed noticed that last complaint was made by one of the faceless sufferers who didn't know Arthur from a bag of lug nuts. So screw him and his quarters. Reed pulled Gideon and Artie closer and cast his worried eyes back to his equally worried neighbors. As a group cemented by common purpose, their eyes slid from one another's faces and wandered with trepidation to the door that led to the treatment area instead. Poor Arthur was in there somewhere. Suffering. Maybe dying. Reed could barely stand to think of it.

"Let me see if I can find out anything," Roger said, rather like Noah announcing, "Let's get this fucking ark underway." Roger was a nurse at this very hospital, although tonight he was off duty. Still, he might have an inside track on learning Arthur's condition. He slid his hand along Stanley's arms in a comforting gesture and took off for the door everybody was staring at, where he ducked out of sight with no one challenging his right to do so.

The other tenants in the waiting room stared hopefully at the still-swinging door like a herd of cattle waiting for someone to chuck them a bale of hay.

A moment later, the treatment door swung open again and out walked Tom.

Compared to Arthur's rotundity, Tom Berger was a towering six five and as lean as a pretzel. For a man in his fifties, he was also quite handsome. Dark-haired and bright-eyed, he gave the impression of being someone who is perfectly contented with his place in the world. The most amazing (and admirable) thing about Tom Berger was his unwavering devotion to Arthur. He had even been known to don a dress now and then when Arthur insisted. How much more proof of devotion could anyone possibly ask for?

At the moment, he was looking fairly exhausted. His hair was messed up, his clothes rumpled, and there was still a hint of shock shimmering dully in his eyes. He had obviously just had the scare of his life.

He cast his gaze around the emergency room before homing in on the contingent of Belladonna Arms residents standing against the far wall. Pulling himself up straight, shoulders wide, he got his long legs moving and took off in their direction. His hatchet nose sliced through the air like the proud, pointed bow of a ship cleaving its way through the waves.

Watching him, it dawned on Reed that Tom Berger would be the perfect man to have at your side when things started going south.

Milan, Tom's son, with his arm still around his lover, Harlie, stepped out from the crowd to greet him. The three came together in a mutual hug before Tom finally turned once again to the crowd.

"Arthur's fine," he said, lifting his voice to carry across the room. "It was a heart attack, but the doctors tell me it was a mild one. They want to keep him for a few days, which Arthur isn't too thrilled about, but I told him I'd bring his favorite snood and a satin housecoat, so that perked him up a little." Tom let his mouth twist into an amused little moue. Several watching faces did the same, as if to say, "That Arthur sure is a card."

"Is he awake?" Harlie asked.

"Yes. He's asking for cheesecake. The doctor's not pleased, and his nurse is having a cow."

Tom's lips twisted into another fond smile while most of the Arms's tenants, familiar with Arthur's peculiarities, not to mention his dietary habits, chuckled knowingly.

Tom's eyes drifted through the crowd and finally came to rest on little Artie, now sound asleep in Gideon's arms, snoring softly with his thumb in his mouth. Tom stretched his long neck out and gaped.

"Good grief," he said, eying Artie's diaper. "Is that Gorilla tape?"

At that moment, Pete and Sylvia came bustling into the emergency room. Sylvia wore a pretty little cocktail dress in purple satin, and Pete had on his usual work suit. Being an accountant, and since it was a special occasion, Pete had forgone the pocket protector and requisite lineup of favorite ink pens, settling for a purple tie and breast-pocket hanky that matched Sylvia's dress. The only thing surprising in Pete's attire was the massive wine stain that covered his chest and flat belly all the way from the knot of his tie to the bottom button on his white dress shirt. Clearly, the earthquake had caught him in mid sip with a full glass of red.

Pete and Sylvia rushed to Tom's side and, Pete taking one arm and Sylvia the other, wrapped themselves around him like eels and cooed words of comfort in his ear. When Tom told them Arthur would be all right, Sylvia dabbed at a sudden rush of tears with the purple handkerchief she companionably plucked from Pete's breast pocket without asking.

Blowing her nose, she gazed around with a worried expression. When her eyes fell on Gideon, with Artie asleep in his arms, she slapped a hand to her breast in relief.

"*There* you are!" she cried.

Then she blinked, sniffed, and handed the now damp handkerchief absentmindedly back to Pete, who retrieved it without question to blow his *own* nose. Sylvia took a hesitant step forward, then leaned in the rest of the way to study her sleeping son sprawled out in Gideon's arms.

"Golly," she said. "Gorilla tape. I'm surprised Pete hasn't thought of that."

Chapter 11

ARTHUR CAME home from the hospital on Sunday, almost a week later. Gideon was one of a dozen tenants waiting for him in the lobby of the Belladonna Arms to give him a rousing welcome. Their off-key version of "For He's a Jolly Good Fellow" hit a snag or two when everyone saw how wan Arthur appeared, but they covered it well and were pleased with the results when Arthur paid them back for their kindness by weeping like a baby. Great fat tears rolled down his pale cheeks (Tom had refused to supply him with makeup at the hospital, saying Arthur needed to rest rather than sitting in his hospital bed in his satin bed jacket slathering makeup on his face twenty-three hours a day). Gideon learned later it was the closest Arthur and Tom ever came to an argument. In a gesture of goodwill, Tom had given in and presented Arthur with a pair of false eyelashes, and that seemed to do the trick. Arthur was wearing them now, along with his snood and housecoat, not to mention a pair of marabou-feathered house slippers, as Tom clutched his hand, leading him up the front steps into the lobby where his welcoming party was congregated.

Arthur kissed everyone in attendance, raining slobbers and tears onto each and every shirtfront. His near-death experience seemed to have humbled him. Or maybe it had simply left him weak. Gideon couldn't be sure. But his voice no longer boomed. The sparkle in Arthur's eyes had somehow diminished. He looked tired, and he was clearly an emotional wreck.

Gideon also spotted a worried light in Tom's eyes, although Tom tried to hide it while cajoling Arthur through his apartment door after waiting patiently for Arthur to flap his hanky while waving one last thank-you to the welcoming crowd. Only when Arthur had flung a flurry of kisses through the air and sucked in the final glob of emotional snot, did Tom, with an appreciative glance at everyone present, follow Arthur inside and gently close the door in their faces.

Quietly, whispering among themselves, the crowd dispersed.

Gideon headed up the stairs wishing Reed was at his side, but Reed was working overtime at the shipyard and wouldn't be home for hours. Gideon felt an ache inside his chest knowing he and Reed wouldn't be together throughout the rest of the day. He knew what that ache meant, of course, but he had been fighting it for a couple of weeks now. That odd little twinge could twist itself into full-blown heartache on the turn of a dime when he considered the dangers inherent in sharing his feelings with Reed. The last thing Gideon wanted to do was scare Reed off by getting too grabby and clingy. Reed still had his own feelings to work out, and he was clearly doing the best he could. He didn't need Gideon pressuring him for things he wasn't ready to give.

Six flights later, Gideon walked past his own apartment door and stood in the seedy old hallway long enough to rest the palm of his hand on Reed's front door. Somehow even that small connection to Reed made him feel better. Closing his eyes, Gideon moved closer to the door and rested his forehead against the wood.

What should I do? he asked himself, aiming the words not at the world or any particular set of ears, but into the mindless darkness behind his eyelids. *Wait*, the answer came back. *Just wait.*

Gideon sighed and opened his eyes. Hearing a faint mewing coming from behind his own door a few steps away, he gave a final stroke to the door in front of him and turned away to retrace his steps back to his own apartment.

And to the loving kitten, now almost fully grown, waiting for him inside.

THE DAY was sunny, as most days in San Diego are. But it was coming on to fall and the temperature had dropped, which was a pleasant relief. Decked out in his welding gear, which included mask, fireproof jacket, and heavy blue jeans, not to mention work boots, leather gloves, and twenty pounds of tools strapped around his waist,

Reed switched off the acetylene torch for a moment. Being sixty feet up, strapped on to the destroyer's radar antenna, he was in a perfect position to flip his plastic face mask up and enjoy the breeze wafting in off the bay.

He stared off into the distance where the crystal air showed a crisp, clean line of horizon miles out past the San Diego Bay and Coronado Island, off to the where the farthest edge of the Pacific Ocean dipped behind the rim of the earth. Out past where other worlds began and other horizons rose up, one after the other, until the earth was as alien to Reed as his feelings were.

He knew beyond a shadow of a doubt that never before in his life had he ever been in love. He knew it because of the way he felt now about Gideon. Carol had never conquered his heart as Gideon had. Carol had never rendered him speechless with need like the mere presence of Gideon could. Carol had never made Reed blush with longing from little more than the memory of an intimate moment or the recollection of a gentle word. Carol had never rendered Reed stunted with doubt by a questionable reaction to something he'd said that was meant to be funny but was maybe taken the wrong way. Even the remotest possibility that Reed had done something to displease Gideon, or make Gideon feel bad about himself, dug at Reed's heart like an ice pick.

Reed repostioned his numb ass on the crossbeam where he perched, strapped in with a safety harness, and stared down at the ship's deck thirty feet below. Other workers were scurrying around or huddled in groups, arguing about this or that. And not for the first time in Reed's life was Reed grateful to be a welder, where nine days out of ten he worked alone, without some annoying supervisor hanging over him barking orders and making a general nuisance of himself.

Being alone was also the downside of being a welder. It gave Reed far too much time to think.

When his cell phone chirped from his back pocket, Reed's heart gave a tiny optimistic lurch. Maybe it was Gideon. Maybe he wanted Reed to pick up dinner on the way home, or maybe he just wanted to wangle an invitation for himself to spend time with Reed tonight. Or maybe he just wanted to hear Reed's voice. Wouldn't that be something?

But Reed's hopes were shattered when he gazed at the readout on the face of the phone. It wasn't Gideon calling at all.

It was Carol's mother. *What the hell does she want?*

With a sinking heart, Reed punched a connection. Ten seconds later, his world, his new life, *all of it*, fell apart.

And he had only himself to blame.

CAROL'S HAND lay moist and still in his, like a small, dead bird, its lifeless body cooling on dewy grass. Since the moment Reed stepped into the hospital room and parked himself in the chair beside her bed, Carol's emotionless eyes stared blankly at the ceiling, never once skittering toward his face. It was as if she didn't know or care that he was there at all.

Other eyes in the room—eyes belonging to Carol's mother and father, who stood in the corner looking on with furious disdain—never skittered away from him once. Those eyes weren't empty at all. They were filled with anger and yes, maybe even hatred. But Reed couldn't worry about that now. He was too busy coping with the hate he felt for himself to take note of anyone else's.

After the phone call, it had taken Reed a long time to gain admittance to Carol's room. She was resting comfortably after they pumped the pills from her stomach hours before, the hospital staff told him, but only her parents were allowed at her side. Reed loitered in the waiting room until late into the night before he was finally allowed entry.

Even then, Reed wasn't sure if it was Carol's parents, Carol herself, or one of the nurses who finally took pity on him and allowed him in. He made the requisite promises as the staff admonished him not to get the patient upset and not to stay too long, and now here he was, cradling Carol's hand while she continued to turn away, his body wracked with such shame he could barely breathe.

"Carol?" he said softly, leaning toward her over the bed. He stroked the back of her hand with his thumb and felt her fingers move on his palm. A moment later she turned her head and let her eyes fall on him for the first time. Still, her gaze was vacant. Emotionless. He thought he had never seen such sad and empty eyes in his life.

"Reed," she said, her voice gravelly, probably from the tube they had used to drain the pills from her stomach. While her eyes remained lifeless, he thought he detected a faint, appreciative smile at the corners of her pale lips. "You came."

Reed fought back tears. "Of course I came."

They returned to silence for perhaps a minute while Reed continued to cradle her hand. During that minute he studied Carol's bloodless face and limp hair. He allowed his vision to travel over her as she lay so still beneath the gray hospital blanket. He eyed the plastic wristband she wore, proclaiming her a patient of Mercy Hospital. She looked so small, like maybe she had lost weight. With a resurgence of guilt, Reed realized he had only seen her once since he left her, and that had been the uncomfortable little scene in the Scottish restaurant when he was having dinner with Gideon.

Gideon.

Gideon had called a dozen times, but Reed had not answered his cell phone because he couldn't bear to say what he knew he had to say. He would think about that later. For now he had to concentrate on Carol. And try to right some of the wrongs he had inflicted upon her.

"I'm sorry," Carol said, her raspy voice sounding like that of a stranger. Even her eyes were strangerlike in the way she stared at him. Cool. Disconnected.

Reed again had to blink back tears. He could barely get the words out. "You have nothing to be sorry for."

Carol gave her head a tiny shake. A fire came to her eyes for the first time, but the fire wasn't directed outward. It was directed in. At herself. "No," she said. "You don't understand. I'm not sorry I did it. I'm sorry I didn't *succeed*. Hell, I can't seem to succeed at *anything*. Marriage. Business. Even suicide is beyond me."

Across the room, Carol's mother gasped and dropped her head to her husband's chest, quietly sobbing. Carol's father glared over his wife's head, his murderous eyes shooting hatred at the man across the room who still sat at his daughter's side. In his eyes, the very man who had caused all of this to happen.

Reed's throat was tight with anguish, his mouth dry, his eyes burning. "You don't mean that, Carol. We'll get you through this. I promise."

For the first time, Carol's face twisted up in pain. Her cool fingers clutched at Reed's hand as she pulled him closer. Her eyes filled with tears. Her breath was sour, her teeth dull. "I've missed you so much!" she hissed, clawing now at his hand, half rising from the bed. Begging.

Reed eased her head back down to the pillow with shushing noises while the mother continued to sob across the room. A nurse peeked in the doorway to see if everything was all right and quickly slipped away again.

"You won't need to be ashamed of me anymore," Carol pleaded. "I'll make myself prettier. I promise. Just come home."

This broke Reed's heart. He couldn't believe what he was hearing. He swallowed hard, trying desperately to gain control of his voice. "Carol, you've always been beautiful."

Burrowing back into the pillow, she relaxed, but her eyes never left his face. There was fire in them now. Anger suddenly swelled in her like lava rising to the lip of a volcano, seething, bubbling, spilling over. She had slipped from pleading to fury in the space of a heartbeat. "Yet I wasn't enough. You needed something more."

"No," he said, lifting her hand to his lips. "I needed something… *other*."

"And did you find it?" she asked. "Did you find it with that boy I saw you with?"

"Gideon isn't a boy. He's a man. And to answer your question, I don't know. I think maybe I have. I guess maybe it depends more on his feelings than it does on my own. Carol, our marriage left us both a little damaged, I think. I'm not sure I know anymore what love really is."

With that, Reed's last ounce of self-respect shattered. He dropped his head to the bed. With Carol's hand still pressed to his lips, he let the guilt thunder through him. "I'm sorry," he said, his gasping breath slicing his words to shreds. "I'm sorry I hurt you. I never meant for you to do this to yourself. I never meant it to end like this." He lifted his head, and with the heel of his free hand, wiped tears from his cheeks. "What do you want, Carol? What can I do to make this right?"

"Come home," she immediately whispered. "Today. Come home *today*!"

"I'll not have it!" Carol's father boomed from across the room.

"Roy," his wife sobbed, aghast. "Let them settle it on their own."

"No! I won't have this queer shredding my daughter's heart again! Nurse," he cried, "Get this fucker out of here. Nurse!"

"Daddy…," Carol tried to plead, but her father continued to yell for the nurse. His face was bright red. He looked like he was on the verge of a stroke. The fear in the mother's eyes was for her husband now, not for the suffering of her daughter.

With his heart thudding in shame, Reed knew her father was right. He'd done enough damage to the woman lying on this bed. He'd done enough damage to all of them. No matter what he did, it wouldn't be enough to set things right. And if he went back to her, they would all be back to square one. No one would find happiness. Least of all Carol.

Through streaming eyes, he stared at Carol's pale face. Her tears were falling now too. He struggled to find the right words, but it seemed to him all the words had already been spoken. There was nothing left to say. Still he had to try.

But it was Carol who said them first. The emptiness returned to her eyes as if she had finally accepted the truth. "Just go," she said. "Go now. Get out of here."

"No," Reed pleaded. "I can try to change. I owe you that much."

A sorrowful smile finally softened Carols' face. "None of us can change, Reed. It's suicide to try. No one knows that better than I do."

Reed sobbed the words he'd been longing to say since he stepped inside the room. "Don't hurt yourself again. Please, Carol. Not for me. Not for anybody."

"I won't," she said, and just as quickly, she slipped her hand from his and turned toward the window, staring out onto the darkness.

Under her breath, almost soundless this time, Carol said again, "Go now, Reed. Please."

And so he did. Just as the nurse came bustling in, probably to throw him out anyway, Carol's father made a furious move toward him, fists clenched, eyes insane, but his wife pawed at him, pulled him back.

As Reed finally left the room, he saw Carol's mother and father swoop toward the bed, once again trying to undo the damage Reed had caused.

Sadder and filled with more hurt than he had ever been in his life, afraid for Carol's safety all over again, Reed slumped down the hallway, dragging himself toward the elevator.

He needed to go home. He needed to be... alone. At least for a while. After that, he had to make some changes, and he knew beyond a shadow of a doubt those changes would tear him apart.

He thought back to Carol's promise. The promise she made not to hurt herself again. He had lived with the woman for four years. He knew when she was lying.

With that horrifying truth tucked immovably inside his head, he shed tears all the way across the underground lot where he had parked.

There was another truth tucked inside Reed as well. The truth in knowing the hardest part of what he had to do would be the act of saying goodbye.

To Gideon.

Chapter 12

GIDEON WAS too mad to cry. "And what did you tell her?" The words might have formed a question, but there was nothing questioning in Gideon's heart. It was an accusation, pure and simple.

Reed shrank away as if stunned by Gideon's reaction.

But Gideon wasn't done with him yet. "Are you going to start living a lie again? Is that what you're planning on doing? And if it is, then might I ask *why*? It certainly didn't make you happy the *last* twenty-five years you tried it!"

Reed sucked in a deep breath, his eyes burrowing into Gideon's. Looking unsure. But looking determined too. That determination was the part that scared Gideon the most.

Reed took a step forward. He took Gideon's arm and tried to lead him to the couch. Gideon pulled away, refusing to be led. He recognized the irony in that even as he did it. Five minutes ago, before he opened the door to Reed's knock, he would have allowed Reed to lead him anywhere. He would have followed Reed happily to whatever destination he chose. They could have traveled to the worst shithole on the planet, and as long as they traveled there together, Gideon would have been happy.

But apparently that journey, wherever it might have conceivably ended, would now never be made at all.

It was late. Reed had just come home from the hospital. He hadn't even set foot in his own apartment yet, he said. There was a light under Gideon's door, so he had knocked to explain about Carol, and now he was trying to explain the rest of it, but Gideon refused to make it easy for him.

"So what's your plan, then?" Gideon seethed, because he already knew where this was headed, and he wasn't about to accept it gracefully, even if he *could* have. "Let me hear it, Reed. Lay it on me."

"Gideon," Reed pleaded, reaching up from the couch to where Gideon stood directly in front of him. When his fingertips brushed Gideon's hand, Gideon yanked away and took a step back. Gideon still hadn't shed a tear, but they were close. He could feel them burning, threatening, molten embers about to burst into flames behind his eyes.

"You're going back to her, aren't you, Reed. That's what you came here to tell me."

Reed closed his eyes as if the mere speaking of those words had shredded his heart. But he didn't deny them. How could he?

"Yes," he said. "Eventually, I guess, if that's what she wants. I have to make sure she won't hurt herself again. Surely you understand that. But I won't go right away. I have to figure out what to do with the lease I have here. I have to try to make it right with Carol's parents. Right now her old man just wants me dead."

"I'm beginning to see his point," Gideon hissed, his words slipping out in a vicious whisper.

"And I have to figure out what to do about you."

Gideon smirked. "Oh, I think you've figured *that* out already."

Reed cringed as if he'd been slapped. He had such a pained expression on his face Gideon almost apologized, then thought better of it. What the hell did *he* have to apologize for?

Gideon tried to get a grip on his anger, tried to force himself to calm down. He dropped to the edge of the coffee table in front of Reed. Reaching out, he laid his trembling hands on Reed's knees. The look of gratitude that blossomed on Reed's face at Gideon's touch was heartrending to see, but Gideon didn't let it sway him from saying what he was determined to say.

He made a conscious effort to remain calm, or at least try to *appear* that way. Maybe if he could reason with Reed, remind him of what they were building together. At least what Gideon *thought* they were building together.

He reined in his voice, keeping it as emotionless as he could. "You made a promise to me once. Do you remember, Reed?"

Reed blinked, his eyes glistening. "A-a promise?"

"Yes. You promised you'd never hurt me."

"Yes, but—"

"No. No buts. A promise is a promise!" Again Gideon forced himself to calm down. "You told me something else once too. You told me after all the years of living a lie with Carol, you thought maybe you didn't understand love at all. Do you remember saying that?"

Reed's expression could best be described as fragile. He was wringing his hands between his legs, sitting there in front of Gideon, looking guilty, looking ashamed and scared now too, as if wondering how his life had suddenly gone so far off the tracks. Wondering, maybe, how it had suddenly become such a fucking train wreck. Or maybe he was just afraid to hear what else Gideon might say to tear the heart right out of his chest.

And that Reed had reason to fear.

"I think you were right," Gideon continued on, unflinching, his gaze piercing, the muscles in his jaw clenched. A thin film of perspiration dampened his brow. His stare was relentless, unwavering. He was still furious, and he was hurt too. Hell, he was dying inside. And why the hell should Reed be sitting there in front of him looking so confused about the whole thing? Why should he be the one looking so hurt? Didn't he know what was happening here?

Reed gazed down at his hands, then back into Gideon's eyes. Pleading yet again. "I don't understand what you—"

Gideon's hand streaked through the air, cutting him off. There was no gentleness in the way he did it. His hand was a guillotine blade, snipping the life from Reed's words before he ever uttered them. "No, I guess you don't understand," he said, his voice cold. "Did you think I hadn't fallen in love with you, Reed? Is that what you thought? We've been seeing each other for almost three months. Sleeping together practically every night. Making love. Learning to trust each other. Getting over our miserable pasts and maybe even cautiously peeking at what might become a future for the two of us. Did you think it wouldn't leave a mark, the way I feel about you? The way I thought you felt about me? Did you think you could just walk away from it all and never look back and I wouldn't care? Did you think it wouldn't hurt me?"

"The way you feel about me?" A single tear slid over the brim of Reed's lower lashes and slipped down his cheek to come to rest at the corner of his mouth. As Gideon watched, the tip of Reed's tongue came out and licked it away. "I-I don't understand."

Gideon leaned forward, clutching Reed's knees in a tighter grip, listening to his own pulse pound like a blacksmith's hammer inside his head.

"Don't keep telling me you don't understand, Reed. I love you, and you know it. Did you think I didn't because I hadn't said the words yet? I even...." But at this, Gideon's voice faltered. His words faded into an anguished silence.

Reed leaned forward, trapping Gideon's hands in his. "You even what?"

Gideon pulled away yet again, not angrily this time, just... wearily. Straightening his back, he scooted the coffee table far enough away from the couch that his knees no longer touched Reed's.

"I even thought you loved me back," Gideon whispered, and it was that admission that made his tears begin to fall at last. He brushed them angrily away, suddenly mad all over again for letting Reed do this to him. Giving the coffee table another scoot backward, he stood and stepped away, putting some real distance between Reed and himself.

But Reed unfurled his long body from the sofa, and before Gideon could do anything to fend him off, he crossed the room and wrapped his strong, gentle arms around Gideon and pulled him close. When Gideon breathed in Reed's familiar heat and scent, when he felt Reed's heartbeat pounding inches from his own, he buried his face in Reed's chest and let the tears go.

"I do love you too," Reed whispered, making gentle shushing noises to stem Gideon's tears. His lips were in Gideon's hair as Gideon quietly sobbed in his arms. He stroked Gideon's trembling back with his broad hands. "Hush now. Hush," he breathed the words in Gideon's ear.

It was a moment before Gideon could speak. When he did, he could only utter five words. It was all he had the breath for. He uttered them into the softness of Reed's shirt. He imagined them burrowing through the fabric and piercing Reed's heart. If only Reed would let them in.

"Then why are you leaving?"

"Gideon...."

Anger swelled in Gideon yet again. It suddenly raged through him like a wild animal crashing through the underbrush. He tore himself from Reed's arms and stumbled back. His face was flushed and wet with tears. When Reed made another move toward him, Gideon pushed him roughly away, although the hurt look on Reed's face when he did it made Gideon want to start crying all over again. The anger drained out of him as quickly as it had come, leaving Gideon tired and hurt—tired and hurt for both of them.

"You can't make yourself live a lie, Reed. If you do, you'll never be happy again."

Gideon could see Reed wanting to reach out for him yet again. He also saw the moment when Reed realized he couldn't. Reed stuffed his hands in his trouser pockets as if that was the only way to insure they wouldn't betray him. His body curled in upon itself as he stood there gazing down at his feet. He looked smaller. Worn out. When he raised his head to look at Gideon again, his eyes were filled with tears.

"I'm sorry if I'm hurting you," he said, "but I don't know what else to do. Carol needs me."

Gideon blinked, astounded by the words Reed had said. "I need you too, Reed. Don't you know that?"

A tear swelled on the cusp of Reed's eyelashes, shimmered there for a second, then slid down his cheek. Without another word, Reed turned and slowly walked toward the door. He pulled it open with a trembling hand and stood in the doorway for a moment as if trying to think of something else to say. Finally his back slumped, and with a weary sigh, he stepped out into the hallway and closed the door quietly behind him.

Leaving Gideon alone.

GIDEON CALLED in sick to work, holing up in his apartment for a week, claiming he had the flu. During that time, he didn't answer his phone, and he only shopped at night so he wouldn't run into any of the other tenants. He had to think things through, and to do that, he had to be alone. The only company he abided was Punkin's. As if knowing her master was unhappy, although she couldn't possibly have understood why, she never left his side. When Gideon lay on his lumpy couch and felt sorry for himself, she snuggled into his arms with her head tucked under his chin and purred like a Volkswagen. Many a time he had to wipe his tears from her coat, but not once did she seem to mind.

During the days since Reed's announcement, Gideon had not seen Reed once. There had been intermittent knocks on his door he suspected were Reed checking to see if he was all right, but he refused to answer them, and gradually the knocking ceased. The phone calls too, which he *knew* were Reed's, he simply refused to answer, finally switching his ringer off altogether.

On Sunday morning, Gideon heard another knock on his door. Once again, he ignored it, and a minute later he heard a key rattling around in the keyhole. Before he could move, the door burst open, and Arthur stood there, dressed in a leopard print sarong with a matching Afrikaans style head-wrap intricately knotted around his head. Bigass earrings in the shape of elephants, carved from slabs of baobab wood or something equally exotic, dangled from his earlobes. They looked like they weighed a pound apiece.

Arthur appeared none too happy.

"Uh, hi," Gideon said, at rather a loss for words. After all, it wasn't every day someone swathed in leopard spots barged into your apartment without asking. "How are you feeling, Arthur? How's the old ticker?" As an afterthought, he added, "I love your sarong."

Arthur straightened his head-wrap, gave a snooty huff, and planted his fists on his hips like he was down to his last ounce of patience, which he clearly was.

"If you must know, it's called a kanga. And the old ticker would be a darn sight better," he exclaimed, "if the people close to me would not lock themselves away and refuse to answer their doors and phones! What the hell are you up to in here, and what the hell is going on with Reed? He won't answer his blasted phone either! Don't you realize we are less than a week away from my wedding, and you two are part of my contingency of best men, twelve in all? Your white tuxes, as you darn well know, are sized and ordered, the boutonnieres are paid for, the preacher is on call, and Tom has finally agreed to wear the baby-blue tuxedo that matches the bride's bouquet I'll be carrying down the aisle. It's going to be a hell of a wedding, and I want all my boys there to give me away. It's no time for one-sixth of my wedding party to go AWOL. We have a wedding rehearsal coming up in a few days too! I hope you haven't forgotten about that."

"N-no. I remember."

"Well, that's a relief!" Arthur snapped. He arched his eyebrows high and tapped his foot, still waiting. When Gideon refused to say anything further because he didn't exactly know what Arthur wanted him to say, Arthur lost all patience and demanded, "Well, what happened, blast it? Did you boys have a fight?"

At that, Gideon wilted on the spot. His shoulders slumped, his eyes filled with tears, and he stood shivering as if he'd just been doused with a bucket of ice water. He tried to speak, but the words couldn't get past the lump in his throat.

Arthur's mouth formed a perfect O and he slapped his hands to his cheeks, sending the elephants spinning. "Oh, honey!" he cried. Rushing across the room with his leopard print kanga billowing out behind him, Arthur scooped Gideon into his massive embrace and stuffed Gideon's head between his equally massive tits, cooing, "Let it out, honey. Let it out."

Buried in Arthur's cleavage, Gideon sounded like he was speaking from the bottom of a well. Still sobbing, he wailed, "I've lost him, Arthur. He's going back to his wife!"

Arthur gave him a consoling pat even while stiffening like a tree. "Don't be silly. That's the dumbest thing I've ever heard. The man's as queer as I am. Well, almost. Why in the world would he do a thing like that?"

Gideon gave his head a furious shake, which set Arthur's tits to wobbling. "Because she tried to kill herself."

Arthur offered up an exasperated grunt. "A ploy for attention, nothing more. I've been known to do it myself a time or two. Not that I'm particularly proud of—"

"But she almost *died*!*"

"Oh pishposh. I'm sure she's just an excellent actress. Who is this woman anyway? Where does she live? Where can I find her? She sounds like fun."

"She's a needy bitch."

Arthur *tsk*ed. "Oh, child. She's just being melodramatic. Asserting her authority. Probably misses his big schlong."

"But they hadn't made love for over a year before he left."

"Well of course not. Why would he? Reed Kelly might be as butch as a bulldozer, but he's also gay as a maypole." Arthur patted the back of Gideon's head like he would a Dalmatian. "He also has excellent taste in men. That's a compliment, sweetie. Now let's see. How can we rectify this situation? How can we make this right? Hmm. I wonder...."

Gideon plucked his face from between Arthur's tits with an almost audible *pop*. He stared up into Arthur's pondering face, his own countenance growing more suspicious by the second. "Arthur? What are you going to do? Why are you looking so sneaky?"

Arthur gave him a wink. The false eyelashes on the winking eye were so long they created a tiny breeze that Gideon could feel blowing across his nose.

"I brought you two together," Arthur said. "Surely I can *keep* you together if I set my mind to it. They don't call me the matchmaker from hell for nothing, you know." He offered Gideon a bracing smile and another wink, this time with the other eye. The elephants bobbed at either side of his head, as if nodding their agreement. "Now then. Let your Auntie Arthur take care of this. Okay? She knows exactly what to do to get your man back."

An expression of hope lit Gideon's face for the first time in a week. "Do you really think you can? He doesn't want to leave me, you know. He said he loved me."

Arthur's eyes misted up. "Did he now?"

Gideon nodded sadly. "Uh-huh."

Arthur pouted, dimpling his chin. "And you love him back, don't you, cuddleumpkins?"

Gideon nodded again, his eyes swimming in tears. "I love him more than anything."

Arthur smiled a bracing smile, winked, and heaved a deep romantic sigh. "Well then, we can't let all that love go to waste, now can we?"

With a magician's flourish, Arthur plucked a handkerchief the size of a tablecloth from his cleavage and went about swabbing the tears off Gideon's face. As he swabbed, he grilled.

"What does this woman do, besides try to break up my gay boys' love affair?"

"She's a wannabe caterer. Reed said her business isn't doing too hot."

"Oh, really? Is she any good?"

Gideon's eyes flashed in a teeny explosion of fury. "No, she's a twat!"

"Now, now, dear. Let's not muddle your hatred with her conceivably discriminating culinary skills. If she has any. Sometimes all a woman needs is a project on which to focus her attentions. To give her life meaning. To keep her mind off the big P."

"The big P?"

"Penis, darling. Try to keep up. Where was I? Oh, yes. Women need to feel successful. If they can't be successful in business, they can at least reap a feeling of success by latching on to a man and keeping him in her clutches whether he wants to be there or not. Women are strong, you know. Men are emotional babies. She's clearly worked out how to wrap Reed around her little finger. And what we need to do is give her something else to sink her claws into."

Gideon stammered. "You mean... like a *career*?"

"Exactly!"

"B-but she's already won! Reed's going back to her as soon as he figures out what to do with the lease he has here."

Arthur barked out a laugh. "He'll have no luck getting out of *my* lease. I wrote it myself. There is a clause that says I can sue him to within an inch of his life if he tries to duck out early. I also know people who break knees for a living."

"You're scaring me, Arthur."

Arthur spouted an uneasy laugh, as if suddenly realizing he might have said too much. "Oh, I was joking, honey. Well, sort of. Anyway, Auntie Arthur wouldn't be so mean as all that. Auntie Arthur's a *sweetheart*."

Gideon was still eying him sideways. Somehow he had the impression he had just seen a clip from *Animal Planet* where a great white shark sweetly nestles its young pup just prior to gaily chomping its head off. "Well... if you say so, Arthur."

Gideon's face was dry now, but he didn't think it would stay that way long. Already, he sensed tears rising up again. Arthur, on the other hand, was smiling benignly, idly petting Punkin, who had strolled over to say hello, and gradually stuffing the humongous hanky back down his cleavage from where it had mysteriously appeared not two minutes earlier.

Arthur reached out and laid his meaty paw on the top of Gideon's head like he was leaning on a newel post while taking a break between landings.

"Don't worry about a thing," he said, a glimmer of inspiration suddenly shining in his eyes. "I'll have your man back before the week is out."

"But *how*?"

"I have a plan, darling. That's all you need to know."

"This is one of those Lucy and Ethel moments, isn't it? And I'm Ethel." Gideon wasn't amused. In fact, he went so far as to stomp his foot, demanding answers. "Tell me what the plan is, dammit. I have a right to know!"

Arthur gave him a wicked little leer, then reached out and pinched his cheek. "You're cute when you're feisty. But never you mind your pretty little ginger head about it. My plan is for me to know and you to find out," he quipped. "Or not." Then he straightened his sarong—sorry, kanga—and adjusted each elephant earring to make sure they were both still there. He spun in a big, billowing leopard-print cloud and headed for the door. "Now if you'll excuse me, love, I have to go call a few friends and fire my caterer."

"Huh?"

But Arthur was already gone, leaving Gideon standing in the middle of his living room in a cloud of Opium cologne as thick as a fog bank, scratching his head.

Chapter 13

REED FIDGETED, staring through the dining room window of the house he had worked so hard to make a home. He had only been absent from the house four months, and already he felt out of place visiting it again.

Standing there in the old familiar surroundings made him feel even more out of place inside his own skin. It was the way he used to feel before he left Carol. This reprise of his old discomfort saddened him. He had hated feeling this way then, and he hated it even more now. At the Belladonna Arms, in the new life he had been building with Gideon at his side, he had started to become a different person. A freer, truer person. He had found joy for maybe the first time in his life. And that joy came from simply being able to exist as himself, to be who he was born to be. It was no great mystery why he felt that way then, and certainly no mystery why he felt this way today. Reed had turned his back on the truth, and now everything was becoming a lie again, exactly as Gideon said it would.

At the thought of Gideon, Reed's heart stuttered with a throb of anguish so real, so *physical*, it caught him off guard. His breath hitched. The muscles clenched in his jaw. For a second, he even thought he might be having a heart attack, that's how real the pain felt. He knew exactly where the pain came from too. It came from the misery he knew he had caused Gideon—and the misery he had caused himself by doing what he thought was the right thing to do.

But was it? Was it really?

He gripped the curtains at the dining room window. When he realized he was leaving sweaty wrinkles in the fabric, he forced his fingers to relax, then dropped his hand to his side, defeated. He considered ripping the curtains off the wall and flinging them across the room in a fit of petulance. Like that would help.

Unbidden, words came into his head. Words that made his heart ache again.

You've left him. Gideon is no longer a part of your life. It's over. There's nothing else you could have done.

Reed was so miserable, standing there in his old dining room, he had an almost overwhelming urge to drop to the floor and weep.

Oh God, what am I going to do? And just as quickly as the question popped into his head, the answer came back in a silent scream. *There's nothing you can do. You made your decision, now live with it.*

He could hear Carol in the kitchen, either piddling with the dishwasher or simply trying to avoid his presence, although she was the one who had pleaded for him to come. There were things they had to discuss, she'd said. Things they had to get settled.

He turned at the sound of her footsteps entering the room. She looked pretty today, he had to admit. She had regained her strength after her stay in the hospital. Her color was back. It was a warm autumn day, and she wore a pair of khaki shorts and a simple blouse that showed off her curves. She gave the impression of having thought out what she would wear beforehand. If that were true, for all the reaction it got from Reed, she might have saved herself the trouble. But maybe she didn't know that. At least he hoped she didn't.

She stood in the doorway drying her hands on a dish towel. "Daddy's still furious," she said, as if she thought he was dying to know that little factoid.

"I'm sorry to hear it," Reed said, his voice empty. He managed to put a little life into it when he asked, "Tell me the truth, Carol. Why did you do it?"

She tried to look innocent, but failed pretty spectacularly. The only thing she truly looked was ashamed, and for that Reed was grateful. Maybe it meant she wouldn't try to kill herself again.

"You mean take the pills?" she asked.

"You know that's what I mean."

She stared down at the dish towel in her hands, folding it, refolding it. "I felt lost," she finally said. "You were gone. The catering business was breathing its last gasp. I felt so useless. So unwanted. I just couldn't face it anymore."

"I'm sorry," he said. And he was, although he'd said the words so many times they were now tasteless on his tongue. Still, Reed knew he could never express the remorse he felt for what he had done to Carol. He could see in her eyes that she knew he was sorry, but still it didn't make it any easier to forgive himself for what he'd put her through. Her reaction to his words of contrition were a mystery, though. He honestly couldn't tell if she forgave him, or if deep down she still hated him for what he'd done. He wondered if he would ever know.

She had been out of the hospital for a week. The first few days, she had stayed with her folks. As soon as she returned to the house, she had asked Reed to join her. He supposed he knew what she wanted, but he wasn't happy about it. He was perfectly willing to put his life on hold to see her over the hump of recovering from her suicide attempt, but no amount of sympathy would ever make him think he was doing the right thing by leaving the life he had been building with Gideon.

Still, he couldn't let Carol hurt herself again. Some things were more important than love. Loyalty for one. Empathy for another.

"Have you stopped seeing that boy I saw you with?" Carol asked.

The question took Reed by surprise. His heart gave a familiar lurch inside his chest. "His name is Gideon. And yes, I've stopped seeing him."

"Daddy knows, of course."

"I don't care if he knows or not, Carol. I'm not living my life to please your father."

"What about me?" she asked. "Will you live it to please me?"

Reed gazed down at his hands. They were trembling. "I'll live it to keep you safe," he said. "I don't think we can ever resurrect the pleasure part of what we had. You might as well know that going in. I'm not the man you married, Carol. I haven't been that man for a long time."

"But you won't see this Gideon anymore?"

A surge of anger swelled inside him, but he forced it back down. Getting into a fight wouldn't help Carol get back on her feet. It wouldn't do anything for his own predicament either. That part of his life was already drywalled and plastered over, sealed away forever. He sighed, as if gathering together all the patience he could muster with as little drama as possible. "I already told you I won't see him anymore. Please don't ask that question again."

Carol crossed the room and shyly took Reed's hand. She reached up to straighten his collar, then just as quickly turned to the window to stare outside. Reed turned with her and followed her gaze. The weeds had taken over the lawn. It didn't look as if it had been mowed in a month. Reed wondered if she had even *attempted* to keep the property up while he was gone.

"I can make you want me again," she said softly, still staring through the glass, averting her eyes, afraid perhaps of seeing what she might see if she looked. "I know I can, Reed. We can make love any way you like. I'll do whatever… you want me to do. It will be like it was at the beginning."

"No," Reed said, his voice empty again.

When he said nothing more, she turned to study his face. She lifted her hand and stroked his cheek. "Won't you even give me a chance to make it up to you? To make you want me again?"

He faced her then, a deep sorrow digging at his heart. "You have nothing to make up. I just don't want you to hurt yourself again. If it takes my presence to keep you safe, that's what I'll do. But please, don't ever think it will be the way it was, because it won't. I'm not strong enough to make that happen. No gay man is."

"Don't call yourself that," she said, swiftly gazing back through the window as if she didn't even want to *see* him utter such words.

Reed gave up. He let his gaze follow hers, away from the two of them, out past the window where the world was plodding along as it always had, without heartache or angst or guilt. Just doing what it did. Naturally. Without emotions muddying it all up. God knows the planet's residents could muddy it up enough on their own.

"I should go mow the yard," Reed said, a weariness settling into his bones that was almost crippling.

"While you do that, I'll fix dinner."

"No, Carol. I can't stay. I have things to do. The apartment. The wedding."

She whirled to stare at him, her eyes cool again. Or was it budding anger? "You're not still going to that fat man's joke of a wedding, are you?"

"I promised. He's one of the best people I've ever met. I won't let him down. And it's not a joke of a wedding. It's two people who love each other making a commitment for life. Why would you call that a joke?"

"But... but you told me he was so *outrageous*."

"He is who he is, and Tom loves him for being that way. Sometimes we have to accept the people in our lives for who and what they are. Sometimes it's the only way you can make them happy. Hell," he added, "sometimes it's the only way we can make *ourselves* happy."

He glanced at Carol to see what she thought about what he'd just said, wondering if she might glean a seed of understanding for their own situation. But she wasn't even listening. She was staring through the dining room window again, and this time she was doing it with a horrified expression on her face that was almost comical.

A movement outside caught Reed's eye, and he pushed the curtain farther aside to see what had grabbed her attention. His heart skidded to a stop inside his chest. He stepped forward and all but stuck his nose to the pane like a kid staring through a candy store window.

"It can't be," he mumbled, fogging the glass.

"That's him, isn't it?" Carol's voice was muted, or quite possibly stunned would describe it best. She sounded like she had taken a few too many tranquilizers again. God forbid.

Still gawping through the window like a goldfish peering amazed through his aquarium wall at the wonders to be seen outside his watery little world, Reed had to chuckle. It was all just so bizarre.

"It's him all right!" he laughed. "It's Arthur in the flesh. And you have to admit I was right. *Outrageous* describes him perfectly."

OF COURSE, Arthur wasn't exactly *in the flesh*. Actually, he was dressed as if he had just returned from a fox hunt. Running of the hounds and all that, hey what? He wore jodhpurs, tight at the knees and poufy around his massive ass, which in a normal world would have been a fashion faux pas of astronomical dimensions. He had on knee-high black boots with spurs tinkling on the heels, a fluffy blouse of khaki-colored silk barely holding in his colossal boobs, be they flesh or bags of produce, one could never be sure. A nifty little riding cap was perched squarely on his head. Beneath the cap, a long golden wig flowed down his back and dipped alluringly over one eye, recalling that hottie of '50s cinema, Veronica Lake. Arthur was whistling a merry tune as he strolled blithely up the sidewalk toward the front door. In his hand he held a riding crop, which he whapped sharply against his leg as he stomped along, making him sound rather like a maniac with an UZI, forging a path through a spray of gunfire.

"What's he doing *here*?" Carol hissed. She looked as if a skunk had just crawled across her dining room table and plopped himself down in her mashed potatoes.

Reed was still laughing. He looked up and down the street for Arthur's horse, quite possibly sporting a side saddle, but all he saw was a black Cadillac Seville parked at the curb. There was a feather boa tied to the antenna.

"Well there, now you have me," he said. "Let's go find out, shall we?" And before a knock even came to the door, he rushed across the room and swung it open.

"Darling!" Arthur cried, lashing his riding crop dangerously through the air, almost smacking himself in the head. He smiled broadly and flipped his wig back off his cheek, ala every movie queen who ever lived. Carol stood at Reed's back, peering over his shoulder. He twisted around to see her reaction to this surprising development, and had to bite back a snort of merriment at the astonished look on her face. The last time he had seen her this flabbergasted was two years back when they took a train ride to Sacramento to attend the California State Fair, and while they were there, forked over six bucks apiece to see a three-headed chicken. It seemed to Reed that Carol's reaction to the three-headed chicken was pretty much the same as her reaction to Arthur. Mindless stupefaction.

Ignoring Reed, Arthur stared at Carol, all atwitter with excitement.

"And this must be the little woman!" he wailed. "And a pretty one too!" He barreled past Reed as if he weren't there and scooped a horrified Carol into his arms like they hadn't seen each other in years.

Actually, of course, they had never seen each other *at all. Ever.*

Reed was amused to see Carol so taken aback she didn't even try to wiggle out of the embrace. She merely hung there limp, trapped in Arthur's great arms, his long wig tickling her nose, his phony boobs pressed into her real ones, which were nowhere near as voluptuous. Of course, Reed had to admit, Carol's were *real*, so that accounted for something.

Arthur finally released Carol, leaving her disheveled and breathless, then turned his attention to Reed.

"Gideon sends his love," he said, patting Reed on the cheek and positively beaming with goodwill.

Reed gasped. "D-does he?" he asked before his eyes skidded to Carol. The look on her face proclaimed her less than ecstatic to have Gideon's name brought up at all. Her demeanor cooled before his very eyes. When she spoke, her words were snipped to within an inch of their lives.

"Was there something you needed?" she asked, eying her guest with a good deal less amusement than she had before.

Arthur flapped his false eyelashes, which caused a downdraft that almost fluttered the curtains. He reached out and surprised the hell out of Carol by pinching her cheek. "Aren't you the sweet one?" he gushed. "I love your hair!" He cast his eyes around the room, taking in the furnishings. "What a lovely little house too. So airy and clean." He turned back to Carol one last time. "I have business to discuss with you, dear. I wonder if you could spare a moment?"

Carol couldn't have been more surprised if he had hauled out a copy of the Constitution from between his tits and asked her to sign it. "B-business? With me?"

"Yes, dear. But it's rather personal, so I'd prefer we discuss it over the kitchen table while you're serving up a pot of tea. Would that be acceptable to you?" He patted his more than ample stomach. "A cookie or two would be nice as well. I'm *famished*, darling. Famished!"

"Uh, sure. Tea. Cookies. Of course. Just, umm, give me a minute."

Arthur flapped his hand through the air like the Queen of England flipping hellos to the peons. "Certainly, dear. Take as long as you like."

Looking shell-shocked, Carol headed off into the kitchen. Reed couldn't tell if she was mad or simply dumbfounded down to her socks.

The moment they were alone, Reed gently touched Arthur's arm. "Did Gideon really send his love?"

Arthur rounded on him, scrunching up his face in a pout, blasting Reed with a glare of stern disappointment. "What the hell are you doing?" he fussed. "Why are you here with that woman when you should be back at the Belladonna Arms with the man who loves you?"

Reed tore his eyes from the accusation on Arthur's face. He simply couldn't bear to look at it. "You don't understand."

With that, Arthur harrumphed. "That's what you think. And since you are clearly not up to the task, I'm here to remedy the situation."

Reed leaned in to whisper so Carol wouldn't overhear, "There's nothing to remedy, Arthur. I'm doing what has to be done. It's a good thing to do, even if you don't think it is. I'm sorry if I've hurt Gideon, but—"

Arthur gave an impatient cluck, his face ferocious and unforgiving. "For all your butchness, you are one silly-minded little twit. You've hurt more than Gideon. You've hurt yourself. And if you try to take this woman back, you'll be hurting her all over again as well. And quite possible, more than you did the first time. This time she might not recover at all."

Before Reed could question what he'd said, Arthur waved his hand dismissively through the air. "Oh yes. I know all about what happened. You broke her heart once, and now that she's recovering from trying to kill herself the first time, you're setting her up to do it again. Some friend you are. A real prize. Yes indeedy."

Again, Reed shook his head, avoiding Arthur's furious gaze. "You don't understand," he muttered again, more confused now than he was before.

"Stop saying that!" Arthur snapped.

At that moment, Carol reappeared in the kitchen doorway. She still looked addled.

"Um. The tea is brewing."

"Lovely," Arthur chirped, clapping his hands. To Reed he hissed ferociously, "Go make yourself scarce. You might want to mow the lawn. I swear I saw a herd of mooses lurking in the weeds when I was coming up the walk. Or is it meese?"

"I w-was about to do that," Reed stammered, more hurt than before to think that Arthur might think he was too lazy to even mow his own yard.

"Good, then," Arthur said, relaxing his fury enough to give Reed a pat on the cheek. "Your wife and I have business to discuss that has nothing to do with you. Now toddle off." Reed stared at Carol, every bit as confused as she looked. Carol opened her eyes as wide as they would go, as if to say, "Help me out here!"

Reed took the hint. "I think I'd rather stay," he said to Arthur.

Arthur adjusted an earring. "And I'd rather you go. Carol and I don't need you. Like I said, we have business to discuss. *Private* business. *Important* business. You'll just hinder the negotiations."

Reed sniffed, his ears burning. "What the hell are you talking about?"

Arthur patted his wig, looking bored and more than a little impatient. "I'll not say another word until you've vacated the premises."

Reed cast a helpless glance in Carol's direction. He finally shrugged, and said, "Fine. I guess I'll leave, then."

"Good boy," Arthur said magnanimously, dismissing him on the spot. Smiling sweetly, Arthur turned all his attention to Carol. Taking her arm, he led her toward the kitchen. He leaned in, bumping heads with her like they were two girlfriends out on the town. "I love tea and biscuits, don't you, dear? It's so bloody British." As if to accent the statement, he whapped himself in the thigh with his riding crop.

"Ouch," he muttered under his breath. "That stings!"

Carol cast one last beseeching glance at Reed, but then quickly returned her attention to the six-foot drag queen at her side. "So," she muttered, her expression a toss-up between befuddlement and intrigue. "What's this all about, then?"

Feeling like a side order of brussels sprouts nobody had requested, Reed gave a helpless shrug, which was directed at no one but himself since everyone else had clearly forgotten he existed.

Turning on his heel, he headed for the front door. Growling to himself like a snoozing cat abruptly tipped out of a cozy lap, he cast one last disbelieving glance backward and stormed from the house. High-stepping through the knee-high weeds toward his truck, he thought, *Fuck the lawn. I'm going home.*

And on the tail end of *that* momentous decision, he thought, *Negotiations? What negotiations?*

REED SPENT the afternoon at the Arms, listening to soft sounds coming through his bedroom wall from Gideon's apartment and wishing he had the nerve to go knock on his door. Feeling lonely and unwanted by everyone in his life—even Arthur, apparently—he finally in desperation fished his cell phone out of his pocket and punched in Carol's number.

She answered immediately, but didn't give him a chance to say a single word. Not one.

"Sorry, Reed. Can't talk. Arthur just left, and I've got a million things to do! Toodles."

When he realized he was the only one on the line, he flung the phone aside and wondered why Carol had sounded so chipper. What the hell had Arthur *said* to her?

As the sun began to sink, he leaned out his living room window and watched the tenants gather on the broad lawn that abutted the canyon at the side of the Belladonna Arms. Mindlessly wondering what was going on, it dawned on him suddenly that he should be down there too. This was the day everyone was supposed to meet for the wedding rehearsal.

And holy shit, Gideon would be there!

Reed quickly threw on a clean shirt, ran his fingers through his hair, and brushed his teeth. That was all he had time for. He flung himself through the front door and took off bounding down six flights of stairs to the ground floor. Other tenants were popping up here and there, all of them obviously heading to the same place. Greetings were tossed back and forth, everyone clearly excited about the wedding rehearsal.

Reed wondered if it meant he was a selfish prick that the only thing he was excited about was seeing Gideon again.

Out on the lawn, which was two acres if it was an inch, the poles and canvases of a massive white tent were laid out on the verge of the canyon. Not yet erected, the tent would clearly be a whopper and was intended to house the wedding banquet after the ceremony was held some three days hence. Fifteen or twenty fellow tenants were milling about, waiting for Arthur and Tom to arrive. The preacher was there, looking uneasy about all the male couples holding hands and smooching each other on the cheeks in greeting. He had obviously never seen so many gay people in his life.

At long last, Arthur and Tom arrived, Tom in normal street clothes looking happy and relaxed, and Arthur in a crepe cocktail dress with what must have been six petticoats underneath it to lift the skirts up around his ears every time he bent over to smooth his stockings or tug at his five-inch heels. How he walked on grass in those shoes Reed didn't have a clue. The look on the preacher's face at seeing who was headed in his direction was priceless. Reed might even have given a chuckle or two if he hadn't been focused entirely on Gideon, who was standing off at the edge of the crowd with Ben and Shiloh flanking him as if offering their moral support to one who has been grievously wronged, which Reed didn't doubt for a minute Gideon had. Hell, he *should* know, since he was the one who wronged him.

At that thought every ounce of eagerness Reed felt seeing Gideon again leached out of his system on the spot. A whole new round of guilt rushed through him.

Reed also caught cool glances shot his way in the disapproving gazes of one or two other tenants. The purveyors of the Belladonna Arms grapevine must have drawn their own conclusions about what had really transpired between Gideon and himself, and in the process most of the sympathy had fallen on Gideon.

Which, Reed had to admit with a sinking heart, was only fair.

As nervous as Reed felt about confronting Gideon again, and as determined as he was not to hurt Gideon any more than he already had by pushing himself on him, it was Reed's feet that finally took the bull by the horns and set about to betray him. He hadn't even realized his feet were acting on their own until he blinked away the glare of the setting sun pouring over the lawn to find himself face-to-face with Gideon.

"Hi," Reed said shyly. "How have you been?"

Gideon edged closer to Shiloh, while Ben moved his towering hunk of muscled manhood protectively inward on Gideon's other side.

Burying his hands in his pockets and barely lifting his eyes, Gideon said, "Hi, Reed."

The look of embarrassment and hurt on Gideon's face tore at Reed like a knife. It seemed not so long ago that Gideon would light up when Reed entered a room, and Gideon would gravitate toward him as if pulled by invisible wires. Apparently those days were over.

Reed shot guilty glances at Ben and Shiloh, and he thought he saw pity in their eyes, not for him, of course, but for Gideon. He supposed he couldn't blame them for that.

Suddenly losing his momentum, Reed glanced down at his feet, mumbled a confused apology about bothering them all, and headed off to the opposite side of the lawn, wishing now he hadn't come.

He stared out across the canyon. The bushes were turning pink in the setting sun, and shadows glided across the grounds, going so far as to climb the walls of the Belladonna Arms behind him.

While Reed was trying to decide whether to leave or not, a hand landed on his back. He whirled, hoping beyond hope to find Gideon there, but it wasn't Gideon at all. It was Tom, Arthur's soon-to-be groom.

Reed was no munchkin, measuring in at six feet, but Tom still hovered over him. He wore a caring, gentle expression on his handsome older face, and now that they were so close, Reed could see the resemblance between him and his son Milan. The resemblance was especially keen around the eyes, which were kind and dark and even at softer times, such as now, brooding. Reed thought Tom's eyes explained a lot about why Arthur loved him so. Even Reed would not be averse to staring across the breakfast table every morning at those gentle, honest eyes.

"Walk with me," Tom said, and without waiting for an answer, he slipped a fatherly arm across Reed's shoulders and steered him along the edge of the lawn, farther from the crowd. Glancing back once, Reed saw Arthur watching them from a distance.

Tom's voice was deeply baritone and sounded intimate, like a lover's voice as it drifted around Reed on the evening breeze. Tom's long arm lay warm at Reed's back, and something about the thirty years difference in their ages made Reed feel safe and cared for, as if a great truth were about to be bestowed upon him.

Reed bit back an inward chuckle, laughing at himself for letting his imagination run away with him. Only days later would he realize perhaps his imagination was smarter than he was, because it had certainly seen the truth of what was about to happen far better than he had.

"You're making a terrible mistake," Tom said softly. "Everybody here can see it but you."

Any humor Reed might have been harboring about the situation sailed off into the ether. His answer to Tom's statement came so quickly and was so desperately expressed, even he didn't see the words coming. "I know, Tom. But I'm only doing what's right."

Tom merely nodded, as if he'd expected as much. He continued to steer Reed along the edge of the lawn. In the glare of the setting sun, Reed could hear the starlings playing in the bushes down the hillside. The air was growing cooler by the minute as darkness slowly settled in. In the distance, the city lights began blinking on inside the skyscrapers piercing the San Diego skyline. A string of blue lights illuminated the Coronado Bridge spanning the bay. It was the same bridge Reed saw every day when he drove to the shipyards. It never looked as beautiful then as it did now, seen from a distance with the cherry-red sunset shimmering at its back.

Closer at hand, floodlights sprang to life at the side of the Belladonna Arms, illuminating the lawn where they were walking. Reed could see Arthur shuttling people here and there, pointing, gesticulating, blocking out their positions, setting them up for the big rehearsal.

"I should go back," Reed muttered.

Tom's arm tightened across the shoulders. "In a moment, son. Please." He continued leading Reed along the verge of the canyon. He pointed up ahead at a rabbit peeking around the edge of one of the game trails leading down toward the freeway in the distance, sitting as still as a statue, watching their approach with a gimlet eye.

Where the lawn stopped and the earth tumbled down the hillside to a tangle of bushes and weeds, Tom stopped, and by default, Reed stopped alongside him.

"I want you to do me a favor," Tom quietly said.

Reed edged just far enough away to gaze up at Tom's silhouette in the glimmering sunset.

"All right," he said. "If I can."

Tom looked down at him, a lazy smile softening his mouth. "Stay away from your wife for a while. She has things to do."

"What?"

"I think you heard me, son." His voice was kind.

Reed blinked in confusion. "What if she calls?"

Tom gave a teeny shrug. "I really don't think she will. She's got a lot on her plate right now. She'll be too busy to argue with you."

"Busy doing what?"

"Busy finding herself," Tom said. "And busy fulfilling obligations. She doesn't need you for that. I'm pretty sure she's strong enough to handle it on her own."

Reed frowned. "Obligations? I'm sorry, Tom, but I don't know what you're talking about."

"You will," Tom said with a conspiratorial wink. "Now come on, son. Let's go back before Arthur kills us both." Without saying another word, he steered Reed back across the grass.

GIDEON STOOD quietly obedient as Arthur blathered on and on and on, explaining crisply and concisely exactly what he wanted everyone to do during the upcoming wedding ceremony. Gideon wasn't really listening, of course. He was mostly just stricken dumb by having Reed standing next to him, where Arthur had directed Reed to go after his little talk with Tom, which Gideon had witnessed but had no idea what it was all about. As if standing next to Reed wasn't making Gideon uncomfortable enough, he was also trying to survive everyone being yelled at by Arthur, who was acting like a general with leadership issues trying to organize a group of brain-damaged recruits.

Gideon and Reed stood side by side, shoulder to shoulder, in a long line of wedding attendants, twelve in all. They would all be wearing crisp white tuxedos when the wedding day came, but for now they were all just looking scraggly and cowed and not a little pissed off, because Arthur was really starting to get on everybody's nerves.

Arthur had chosen to direct his wedding with all the fervor of a televangelist dragging a shitload of heathens, kicking and screaming, into the arms of unwanted redemption. His voice boomed out across the grounds, brooking no opposition, directing this person here and that person there while his skirts whirled around his fat knees and the unfortunate preacher stood off to the side looking lost and vaguely appalled and undoubtedly wondering what the hell he had gotten himself into.

If the troops didn't revolt before the wedding day came, the ceremony would be a blockbuster. That much was clear. After all, even in the mundane actions of everyday life, Arthur wasn't exactly known for his subtlety. Given the added incentive of this wedding being the most important event of his life, Arthur had become positively dictatorial.

Reed and Gideon's role in Arthur and Tom's wedding was fairly simple. Along with the other ten attendants, like bridesmaids in a heterosexual wedding, they were to follow the bride across the lawn to the rented arbor covered in rented plastic morning glories that would serve as the altar. And like any other wedding on the planet, they were supposed to do it without stepping on the bride's train or getting their foot stuck in a gopher hole or doing anything equally stupid along the way. After that they would stand in line with the other ten attendants while the vows were exchanged, and this they were instructed to do at parade rest, without talking or passing out.

Later the guests would drink and schmooze and wait for the banquet to commence beneath the unerected poles and piles of white canvas stacked on the lawn. After the banquet Arthur would fling his bride's bouquet into the crowd, and immediately afterward he and Tom would depart for their honeymoon, leaving everybody else to clean up the mess—Gideon extrapolated that last part on his own.

When Gideon thought he had the gist of what Arthur was trying to say—after all it wasn't rocket science—his mind wandered back to the presence of Reed at his side. He closed his eyes against the glare of the setting sun, and in the orange darkness behind his eyelids, he caught a whiff of Reed's familiar scent. It was a scent he had loved since the moment he first smelled it.

When Reed leaned toward him, causing their shoulders to touch, Gideon's breath caught. While Arthur continued to orate endlessly off in the distance (God, that man could talk!), Reed leaned even closer and whispered in his ear.

"You stopped answering your phone."

Gideon was comforted by Ben and Shiloh standing a few feet away, so he managed to remain calm. "So did you," he whispered back.

He glanced at Reed in time to see Reed's gentle blue eyes light up. "Why? Did you try to call me?" he asked.

Gideon looked away. "No. Arthur told me."

There was no mistaking the disappointment in Reed's answer. "Oh."

An uncomfortable silence settled between them. Arthur's droning instructions were loud enough to hear a mile away, but to Gideon it was little more than a mindless roar of white noise in the background. He was too busy concentrating on Reed to listen to Arthur prattle on.

Gideon scavenged through his mind for a tidbit of conversation. "H-how have you been?" finally came out, and he winced at the mundanity of it but just as quickly realized Reed didn't seem to mind.

"I've been okay," Reed said, clearly eager to respond, happy to be carrying on any sort of conversation at all. "And you?"

It was the mundanity of *that* question that finally sparked Gideon's anger. Turning to Reed, he said less timidly this time, and with a pretty good dose of sarcasm, "Happy as a clam. Why do you ask?"

Gideon had the pleasure of seeing Reed's eyes open wide as if he'd been slapped. Then just as quickly, Gideon felt guilty for making him feel that way. Jesus, his emotions were so screwed up. He couldn't even hold on to his own sense of outrage without weaseling out of it like a twerp.

Too tired to argue, even with himself, he asked wearily, "Why are you here, Reed? What do you want?"

Reed blinked. "I'm here for Arthur."

This time it was Gideon's turn to look disappointed. "Oh."

Reed shifted on his feet. When he did, his fingertips accidentally brushed the back of Gideon's hand. Gideon closed his eyes as a surge of memories shot through him, each and every one of them brought about by the fleeting warmth of Reed's skin against his own.

"I never meant to hurt you," Reed whispered. "I'm sorry."

Gideon shook his head to erase the words from his memory banks before they could take root. "It's all right. I'm getting over it."

Reed turned to him then, not even trying to stay under the radar of all the other tenants standing around, not a few of them leaning at ninety-degree angles trying to eavesdrop on their conversation. "You are?" he asked.

It didn't sound like a hopeful remark; it sounded disappointed. Gideon, feeling the urge to strike back once again, took Reed's moment of weakness and ran with it. "Did you think I'd be brokenhearted forever, Reed? Did you think I'd never get over you?"

"No, I—"

Gideon closed his eyes, shutting out the rehearsal, the sunset. Reed.

When he opened his eyes a minute later, Reed was gone. Only then did a single hot tear course down Gideon's cheek.

Ben and Shiloh edged closer to him, once again taking up their protective positions.

"Don't cry," Shiloh muttered.

"I'm not," Gideon lied. "I'm not."

REED LAY sprawled on his bed, confused and wondering at the happy lilt in Carol's voice when, an hour earlier, she had finally deigned to answer her phone. When he asked her where she had been, she simply laughed. When he asked her what she was so happy about, she refused to say. In fact, during the whole conversation, if you wanted to call it that, she hardly said more than hello and goodbye. It didn't take a psychic to realize she wanted to get off the phone so she could go back to doing whatever it was she was doing.

As Reed lay in the dark trying to figure out what that might have been, he heard a whimper coming through the window above his head.

It was Gideon in his bedroom next door, a mere six inches of plaster and lath away. He was crying in his sleep, just as he had done on that long-ago night after first moving in.

This time, Reed knew beyond a shadow of a doubt that the tears were because of him. He didn't move for the longest time, his fist clenching a wad of bedclothes, his other arm slung over his eyes, trying to block out the swell of his own guilt.

Even after Gideon's weeping subsided and a far-off clock chimed twelve times, piercing the night with its stentorian bongs to mark the turn of a new day, Reed lay awake in his lonely bed, longing for the familiar warmth of Gideon's body next to his. He had never felt so alone and abandoned. By Carol, by his friends at the Arms, by Gideon. Yet even he wasn't dumb enough to think it was anyone's fault but his own.

When a furry forehead nuzzled his chin, he slid his hands into Hitler's soft pelt and let the cat's gentle purring finally urge him close to sleep. But only close. Sleep's full and boundless release never quite reached him. Nor did the memory of Gideon's receptive heat, or the way his hands used to happily travel Reed's body, or how once upon a time he had whispered hungry words when their desires coaxed them into each other's arms. Those memories brought an ache to Reed that was almost crippling.

What have I done? What have I done?

Sleepless hours later, as the shadows in his bedroom began to dissolve beneath the creeping light of dawn, he groaned his way out of bed and sat at the edge of it gazing dejectedly at his feet.

"Gideon," he whispered softly into the empty room. But no gentle words responded. Even Hitler's purring stopped, as if he too were waiting to hear Gideon's voice.

With a heartsick sigh, Reed dragged himself off the bed and padded naked to the kitchen to make coffee. He wasn't looking forward to the day at all. Being close to Gideon during the wedding rehearsal had been torture enough. Being with him again today during the long hours ahead while Arthur married his lover Tom was more than Reed thought he could bear.

Despondent, he watched the coffee drip, no longer even wanting it. *What in God's name have I done?*

Chapter 14

SHORTLY AFTER dawn, as Gideon stared bleary-eyed through his living room window at the city stirring itself awake in the distance, a group of burly laborers from Party Rentals came swooping onto the west lawn. Within two hours, amid a chaotic scene of yelling (mostly in Spanish) and hammering and the whine of two cherry pickers accordioning noisily upward toward the heavens—which made the crows in the eucalyptus trees squawk in protest, adding to the din—a grand white pavilion rose high on the west lawn of the Belladonna Arms. Inside the tent, long rows of tables and chairs were lined up for the banquet to come. The massive tent flaps snapped like gunfire in the morning wind sweeping up the canyon walls.

Moments later, trucks backed onto the property, and the same laborers began unloading further stacks of white folding chairs and a grand round gazebo, which they snapped together like Legos and placed at the brink of the canyon alongside the tent. A tall arching arbor, equipped with creeping plastic morning glories, rose at the spot where the bride and groom would exchange their vows.

Gideon watched it all unfold beneath him, dreading the day ahead but still chuckling to himself when he remembered Arthur mentioning it would always be his greatest disappointment that he hadn't booked Westminster Abbey and flown the whole wedding party to England. It was even funnier that Arthur didn't sound like he was kidding when he said it.

Soon, an army of white folding chairs were neatly lined up with military precision across the grass to augment the three hundred chairs arranged at the tables inside the massive tent. After that, a ten-foot-wide red carpet was unrolled from the Arms's front porch all the way to the altar, two hundred yards away. A fleet of florists' vans arrived next, each one packed to the gills with snow-white floral arrangements. Carnations, roses, peonies, calla lilies, draping bowers of snowy wisteria, jasmine, and a dozen other varieties that Gideon couldn't have identified if his life depended on it. Arthur must have spent thousands on the flowers alone.

He grinned. Florists citywide must be booking cruises and buying new cars, made delirious by their good fortune.

Gideon stood leaning out his window, his coffee cooling and forgotten in his hand, thunderstruck by the immensity of what was happening down below, a wondrous smile bloomed on his face. It was all so exciting. But the smile didn't survive the sudden realization that he would be seeing Reed again in a couple of hours.

He thought back to the night he'd just spent alone in his bed, longing for Reed to be there with him. Aching to be wrapped in Reed's arms, to feel Reed's heartbeat against his cheek, to feel Reed's beautiful cock nestling sleepily in his hand.

A shuddering sigh escaped his lips. He looked down when Punkin brushed her flank against his ankle to say good morning. He bent, scooped her into his arms, and stood at the window, snuggling her beneath his chin.

"We don't need him," he said softly, but he knew the words were a lie the moment they crossed his lips. He did need Reed. He needed him a lot.

Christ, why does love always have to be such a pain in the ass?

He heard a door opening nearby. Gideon tensed. It was Reed's door. A murmur of voices drifted through the wall. A moment later, Reed's door closed with a click and heavy footsteps approached along the hall.

A sudden pounding on his own door made Gideon jump.

He set the cat aside and tightened the belt of his robe before unbolting the door and pulling it open. It was Arthur.

Gideon stared, then he stared some more. Arthur was wearing some sort of facial mask made out of either axle grease, as black as mud, or maybe tar he had pilfered from a road crew somewhere. Gideon couldn't be sure, but whatever it was, it was pretty disgusting. Not being satisfied with treating his face alone, Arthur had covered his entire head with the gooey stuff. Ears, dome, the back of his neck, the lot.

As if his head wasn't disconcerting enough, Arthur was wearing a satin dressing gown in deep indigo with pale blue feathers sewn onto the hem and sleeves. The gown's yards and yards of indigo fabric shimmered like moonbeams rippling across the surface of a crystal blue lake at midnight, the beauty of which was pretty much a waste of satin, since Arthur's head looked like it had been dipped in cow shit.

"Change of plans!" Arthur chirped, his mouth a big pink hole in a sea of mud. "When I kiss the groom after the vows have been exchanged, I want all my attendants to kiss their partners as well. It'll be *so* romantic!"

Gideon stared. "But my partner is Reed."

"I know. I just told him."

"But we're not seeing each other now. We're not dating anymore. We're not boyfriends!"

Arthur flapped a dismissive hand. "Oh pishposh. What does that have to do with anything? You've kissed him before, haven't you? He doesn't have hoof-and-mouth disease. What's the big deal? Do it for me. Afterward you can gargle and spit and run your mouth through a carwash if you're so inclined."

"But, but...."

Arthur wasn't listening. "Did you see the tent? Isn't it to die for?" He squealed like a teenage girl who has just been asked out by the captain of the football team. Before Gideon could say another word, Arthur went swishing off down the corridor humming the "Wedding March." An occasional feather dislodged in his wake, wafting through the air behind him as he headed toward the stairs.

"Wash that shit off your head!" Gideon screamed down the hall, but his only answer was a tinkle of laughter three flights below. Arthur was as slow as molasses coming up the stairs, but hell on wheels going down.

Furious at the predicament Arthur had put him in, Gideon slammed the door, scaring the cat. He turned and stared at the white tuxedo hanging on his closet door, still wrapped in plastic.

"Dammit," he mumbled to the world at large. Setting his coffee cup aside, he headed for the fridge. He didn't care if it *was* eight o'clock in the morning. He needed a beer.

He snagged a bottle off the bottom shelf, then lifted the small florist's box containing his boutonniere, which had been resting beside the beer. The box contained a dainty white orchid. Beautiful.

Gideon lifted the lid and sniffed the orchid.

As sad as he had ever been in his life, he set the box aside, took a long pull from the beer, and threw himself back on the bed.

ON THE morning of Arthur's wedding, Reed called Carol at eight fifteen. No answer. He called her again at nine. She didn't answer then either. At ten o'clock she finally picked up the phone.

"Where have you been?" Reed demanded. "I haven't seen you in days! Why don't you answer your phone anymore?"

Carol couldn't have been less friendly if she had been shooting six guns and lobbing hand grenades. "I thought you were the butcher. What do you want, Reed? I'm busy!"

"What do you need a butcher for?"

"None of your business."

"That's all you have to say?"

"Yes."

"Busy doing what?"

"That's none of your business either. Let's just say I'm busy working."

"Since when do you work?"

"Fuck you, Reed."

Reed couldn't believe it. Carol never cursed. Ever. "What? *What?*"

"Don't worry about it," she said, still snippy as hell and clearly impatient to get off the phone. "I'll see you later and explain everything then."

"What do you mean you'll see me later? You'll see me later *where*? And explain *what?*"

But she'd already disconnected.

"Bitch," Reed spat at the rhododendron in the corner, which was still barely clinging to life after little Artie had tried to eat it, the poor thing.

Reed stood holding his cell phone in his hand, suddenly lost in thought. What the hell was he doing? Why was he chasing after Carol? This wasn't how his new life was supposed to go. This wasn't where his big epiphany was supposed to have led him. He was supposed to be happy now. He was supposed to have turned his life around. He was supposed to be a new man, a *gay* man, not the same old miserable married twit he'd always been.

He shot a morose glance at the clock on the wall. It was almost time to get ready.

Dragging himself into the bathroom, he stared at the rented white tuxedo hanging on the curtain rod, still wrapped in plastic after the tailor altered it.

He could feel sweat forming in his palms just thinking about what Arthur had told him at the door, the change in the wedding ceremony down on the lawn. How he'd have to kiss Gideon as soon as the "I dos" were said.

There were other things Reed remembered too. He remembered how his fingers had brushed the back of Gideon's hand at the wedding rehearsal. And how Gideon had pulled away when they did.

He remembered one night long ago when Gideon's pale, beautiful body lay beneath him on the bed, shuddering, and Gideon's back arched high as his hot seed spilled over Reed's tongue.

That last memory was a killer. Torn between wishing the memory would go away and pleading with it to stay forever, Reed yanked his T-shirt over his head and flung it to the floor. He kicked off his jeans and stripped the tux from the hanger. Standing in front of the bathroom mirror, clutching the tux to his naked chest, he watched his reflection blur as tears rose in his eyes.

With a sigh, he began to dress.

GIDEON STOOD in front of his bathroom mirror adjusting his pale blue tie, which Arthur had said would match not only the groom's tuxedo, but also the bride's bouquet he would be carrying down the aisle. He brushed his ginger hair back off his forehead, checked himself out one last time, then clipped the boutonniere to his lapel like Arthur had shown him.

He froze when he heard Reed's door open and close. He must be heading down to the grounds, where people had been congregating for the last hour. Gideon wondered if Reed would stop at his door and see if Gideon wanted to accompany him down to the shindig. Either to Gideon's relief or to his sorrow, he couldn't decide which, Reed's footsteps moved on past without pausing.

By the roar of laughter climbing up the side of the Belladonna Arms and leaking across his windowsills, Gideon suspected the complimentary bar was open and Arthur's arriving guests were taking full advantage of it. Gideon had had three beers himself already, and he hadn't even left his apartment yet. Since he drank them out of his own fridge, he figured he had saved Arthur a couple of bucks, which was a good thing. This wedding had to be costing Arthur and Tom a fortune.

He stared back at the mirror. Gideon had never worn a tuxedo in his life. Especially one as white as the one he had on. He had to admit it looked pretty good with the pretty little orchid sleeping at his chest and the splash of blue neatly knotted at his throat. When all twelve attendants (or were they boysmaids?) got together, it would look great. Arthur might be a mess at dressing himself, but when it came to sprucing up a wedding party, he seemed to know all the tricks.

Gideon's heart suddenly swelled with happiness for Arthur and Tom. It was wonderful, Gideon thought, that two people could declare their love for each other in this brave new world and it no longer mattered who was doing the loving. Or who was doing the committing. Two men, two women, a man and a woman, three sheep and an aardvark. Anything was possible now. Love, it seemed, had finally come into its own. For everyone but him.

Gideon was in the process of shaking that thought away when a knock came at his door. His heart skidded upward into his throat, and he whirled to face his front door like a terrorist was about to barge into the room with a bomb strapped to his chest.

The knock came again, and trying not to think about who it might be—Reed? Could it really be him?—Gideon stepped to the door and pulled it open. A moment later he was dredging up a show of enthusiasm and in the process forcing a smile to his lips he didn't really feel.

"Ben. Shiloh. You both look great!"

And they did. They stood at Gideon's door side by side in identical white tuxedos with the identical blue neckties and identical white orchids shimmering on their lapels. And there wasn't a kilt in sight.

"You look great too!" they cried back.

All three took a moment to barge back into Gideon's apartment and primp and preen in front of the bathroom mirror, squeezed together like sardines, especially with the cat joining in. As soon as every tie was perfectly knotted and every boutonniere perfectly boutonniered and readjusted by a flurry of helping hands, they headed out through the apartment door arm in arm. Best buddies ever.

In the hallway, Gideon watched Shiloh slip a glance at Reed's door.

"He's already gone down," Gideon said quietly.

Both Ben and Shiloh gave him a tender pat, which Gideon shrugged off, swearing he was all right, and then they headed down the stairs.

Far below they heard the band tuning up, playing something classy and matrimonial. Damn near a hymn.

"Jesus, I hope *that* doesn't last long," Ben groaned. "I need something with a better beat. I feel like dancing."

"After the ceremony," Shiloh said, reaching over Gideon to kiss his lover's cheek. "Arthur promised."

Heartsore, and wishing he had another beer, or maybe someone like Ben to plant a kiss on, Gideon slipped out from between the two and took a position at the end so they could be together.

He couldn't help wondering if he would be doing that the rest of his life.

What was the old saying? Oh yes. Always the bridesmaid, never the bride.

Fuck.

STROLLING ALONG the red carpet toward the cacophony of voices out on the lawn, Gideon thought he had never seen a grander layout for a wedding in his life.

Ben squinted into the glare of white tent, white chairs, white flowers, white tuxes, white altar, white gazebo. "All this white is blinding me! Uncle Arthur and Tom have been living together for years. Why get all virginal now?"

"I think it's great," Shiloh sighed, weaving his arm through Ben's and resting his head on Ben's broad shoulder.

"So do I," Gideon agreed, eying the two, as always amazed and touched—and probably a little envious—by how loving they were together.

Three abreast again, they proceeded down the red carpet and headed straight for the bar, where they found four handsome bartenders in white top hats and tails who were more than willing to serve them anything their little hearts desired, up to and including a roll in the bushes, or so their attitude implied. Two minutes later, Gideon and his two buddies were nursing cocktails and mingling with the crowd.

There were a lot of tenants in attendance, all of them, in fact, but there were a lot of strangers milling around too. Most of the people there Gideon had never seen before. Arthur must have put invitations out on the internet. There was a rather large contingent of drag queens in attendance as well, but apparently Arthur had warned them beforehand, for not one of them was wearing white. Gideon suspected stealing the thunder from *this* bride might be the last thing an unsuspecting drag queen would ever do.

He spotted Roger and Stanley, gloriously attired in white like himself, kissing so deeply they appeared to be tonguing each other's uvulas under the arch of morning glories at the altar. Wrapped in each other's arms, their tongues clearly down each other's throats, they were beautiful to behold. Gideon stood sighing, jealous as hell. A moment later he was giggling after the preacher came along and shooed Roger and Stanley away from the rented plastic altar like they were committing a sacrilege or something. Roger and Stanley didn't seem to mind. Still smooching, they ambled off into the crowd arm in arm, where they were absorbed by the mob, leaving the preacher shaking his head.

Sylvia and Pete, with little Artie strapped to Pete's chest as usual, and as usual still kicking poor daddy in the nuts every five seconds, were strolling about the grounds greeting everyone they passed.

Sylvia spotted Gideon and raced toward him, her beautiful ankle-length gown, ashimmer with silver sequins, blazing around her.

"Wow! You're gorgeous!" Gideon cried, making Sylvia blush before she swept him into her arms.

He saw Pete giving him a shy wave and looking a little sick to his stomach, as men who have just been kicked in the balls usually do. Both Gideon and Sylvia stared at poor Pete with sympathy as he approached. Artie was flinging his arms around and reaching up to tug at Pete's hair like he was trying to rip it out of his head, occasionally varying the torture by poking a finger up Pete's nose. Not being satisfied with all the other damage he was inflicting, he gave his old dad another perfectly placed kick in the nuts.

Pete turned green, and Gideon and Sylvia winced.

"Why doesn't he strap Artie to his back?" Gideon asked.

Sylvia sighed. "He did it once, and Artie puked on his neck."

"Oh."

Sylvia turned her attention to Gideon. She patted his cheek and brushed his red hair out of his eyes. "You look handsome."

Gideon blushed. "Thank you."

She leaned close and whispered in his ear. "Hang in there. Arthur has everything under control."

Gideon blinked in confusion. "Huh?"

Sylvia tinkled out a little laugh. "Never mind. You'll find out soon enough." Spotting someone in the distance, she cried, "Oh look! There's Barney and Ramon, I have to go say hello."

With that, she was gone in a glitter of silver sequins and a teeny cloud of perfume. Gideon watched with empathy as Pete and little Artie hustled past trying to catch up to her. Poor Pete wasn't walking too well.

The band suddenly blasted their way into an energetic medley of Elvis Presley hits. Gideon wasn't surprised at the musical selections when he looked their way and saw that every one of the eight or nine band members was hovering around seventy years of age. Still, they played pretty well. Gideon was impressed. He was also impressed by the beautiful white gazebo that had been erected at the edge of the canyon to house the band.

Harley and Milan, Milan being the bridegroom's son and Arthur's soon-to-be son-in-law, swooped in to throw their arms around Ben, Shiloh, and Gideon, catching them off guard. Heads bonked together and drinks sloshed everywhere. A roar of giggles erupted. They hailed each other in exuberant greeting and told each other how fabulous they all looked. Before Gideon could return the compliment, they were gone, either heading for the bar for another round of drinks, which they certainly didn't need, or homing in on another group of friends to pounce on and shower with compliments.

Gideon laughed. Surprisingly, he was starting to cheer up.

His eyes wandered past the gazebo, where the band was now tooting and sawing away at "Heartbreak Hotel," which was a poor selection for a wedding, Gideon thought. He spotted several long lines of tables, with flapping white tablecloths and beautiful sprays of white daisies every ten feet or so, all of it strategically arranged along the northern edge of the lawn in the cool shade of the massive pavilion erected earlier. An army of servers in red vests were setting the tables, preparing for the dinner that would follow the wedding ceremony.

Gideon smiled at how grand and beautiful it all was, astounded again by how Arthur had spared no expense, when suddenly, across the heads of the crowd, a pretty female face caught his eye. He did a double take. Then another.

His heart sank, and all the sadness he thought had dissipated a little bit came suddenly flooding back. Carol, he remembered her name was. Carol. *What the hell is she doing here?* Then another thought struck him. *Oh God. Is she Reed's date?*

A moment later, his smile no more than a memory now, his happy mood shattered, he slipped away unnoticed from Ben and Shiloh. All alone, avoiding every eye he passed, he headed for the bar.

Drink at last in hand, and a double this time, which was probably the last thing he needed, Gideon edged his way through the boisterous crowd, feeling like an outcast. He moved toward the southern edge of the lawn where the grounds ended. The day was getting hot. Staring out over the canyon below, he let the sun burn the back of his neck while his mind traveled paths he didn't want to take.

Desperately, he tried to shake the thoughts away.

Turning back toward the mob behind him, he cast his gaze here and there. He didn't see Reed anywhere. But having seen the woman he'd spotted earlier, he knew Reed must be near.

He turned his back on all the celebrating faces and once again let his eyes travel the empty canyon below.

He sipped at his drink and through sheer will power managed to twist his face into a smile. Even if it wasn't real, and even if nobody could see it, he felt better knowing the smile was there.

The ache in his heart was another matter altogether.

REED STOOD alone in the shade of the tall eucalyptus tree. It was the same tree Hitler climbed to occasionally gain access to Reed's apartment window. Reed had been downstairs for thirty minutes, and he was already on his third gin and tonic. Each and every one a double.

He felt out of place. No one treated him any differently than they ever had. Many of the tenants still came up and passed the time, chatting about this and that, blathering endlessly on, mostly about the wedding and how excited they were that Arthur and Tom were finally getting married. They told Reed how handsome he looked, and he returned the favor to them. But somehow he knew they were judging him for what had happened between him and Gideon. And for that, Reed couldn't blame them at all. If he hadn't been part of the upcoming ceremony, he would slip away. And he was pretty sure no one would care if he did.

By sheer accident, he turned back toward the front porch at the exact moment when Gideon, alongside Shiloh and Ben, arms linked and laughing, stepped out into the morning glare and headed down the long red carpet toward the festivities on the lawn. He ducked behind the bole of the tree as they passed, but even so he never once took his eyes from Gideon's face.

Gideon truly did look handsome in his white tuxedo, with his freckles and his red hair flaming in the sun. Reed felt such an overwhelming desire to rush up to Gideon and drag him into his arms, he had to polish off his drink in one throat-searing gulp to chase the urge away.

As the three melded into the crowd, Reed slipped off to the bar to refill his drink, stopping here and there when fellow tenants greeted him, trying not to appear shamefaced under their scrutiny. Maybe he was being paranoid. He didn't know. But he did know one thing. Even if it was all in his imagination, even if everybody else *wasn't* appalled by the way he had treated Gideon, *he* certainly was.

He also knew that deep down inside, down where his feelings couldn't be hidden even from himself, he was at the brink of a momentous decision. He just couldn't decide what that momentous decision should be. Well, maybe he could. But that didn't mean he had the guts to act on it.

Drink replenished, he suffered through two minutes of stilted chitchat with the two librarians, Lester and Dan. They too were part of the wedding party and decked out in white tuxes. Somehow they wore theirs better than Reed did, probably because they were used to wearing ties and sport coats every day while Reed was more accustomed to having a string of clanking tools strapped to his ass. Actually, Reed doubted if Lester or Dan had ever sweated a day in their lives. Somehow their pores looked unused. Still they were cute and clearly in love, and by the time they wandered away, Reed was smiling. Funny how love could have that effect on you even when it wasn't your own.

Reed chuckled at that, although he wasn't sure why. God knows the realization was sad enough.

A second later the chuckle died in his throat. He stood frozen, drink forgotten in his hand while he did a double take. All of a sudden he didn't feel the sweat sliding down the back of his neck or the tightness of the necktie knotted at his throat, or the way his new dress shoes pinched his feet.

Stunned down to his toes, Reed stared over the heads of the milling throng of wedding guests and all but gaped at his ex-wife Carol, barking orders at a regiment of waiters, none of whom were looking too thrilled about being barked at. Oddly, Reed thought, even while barking orders she had never looked happier.

But the main question was *What the hell is she doing here*?

The waiters were setting up a buffet line. He could figure that much out. A long row of stainless steel steam tables and serving wells stretched along the inside wall of the great tent. Gleaming service islands, their colorful cargos tucked under sneeze guards sheltering scrumptious mounds of salads and fruits and deserts, all shimmering beneath films of plastic. At the foot of the buffet line stood a tiered wedding cake. Reed cast a practiced eye on the dimensions and concluded it was a good six feet tall. As tall as he was.

And there alongside the cake, among the sneeze guards and the steaming serving wells and enticing mounds of food, stood Carol, fussing over everything, pointing to this, gesturing at that. At one point she teasingly dragged a waiter forward by his necktie and giggled with him as she explained something about the serving utensils.

Still dumbfounded by Carol being there at all, Reed stared as she stepped up to inspect great piles of shining china and bins of glittering silverware, bending down, peering closely at a fork, a knife, making sure all was neatly arranged, all was spotless.

She wore a pretty floral dress and sensible flats since she was working on grass. Her hair was drawn up in a simple bun at the back of her head, and she had donned the silver earrings Reed bought her on their honeymoon in a little shop on Catalina Island. She looked happier than Reed had seen her look in a very long time.

A sudden understanding clawed its way into Reed's addled brain. So this was what Arthur had come to the house about that day. He had hired Carol to cater the wedding. Reed didn't quite understand what that had to do with *him*, as Arthur had implied it did, but he was glad to see Carol so happy. She loved working with food. It had always saddened them both that her catering business had never taken off like they hoped. Maybe with this huge wedding on her resumé, that would all turn around.

Reed was still gawking at her when he saw her lift her head and turn directly toward him.

Without a backward glance, she abandoned the fleet of waiters and chefs and 500 pounds of food and weaved her way purposively through the crowd toward him.

To Reed's astonishment, she had a mischievous smirk on her face.

Without saying so much as hello or how nice he looked in his tux, she slipped her arm through his and said, "Walk with me."

Speechless, Reed let her pull him along, her fingers cool on the back of his hand, her fragile, familiar scent billowing around his head.

Chapter 15

CAROL LED Reed through the crowd, out past the gazebo and the band, which had now ramped up the tempo a bit to include a little Billy Joel in their repertoire. It was still the wrong generation of music, but none of the drunken wedding guests seemed to mind. A young Mexican man sporting a poufy shirt unbuttoned down to his navel and a pair of white pants stretched so tight around his slender hips that you could see every wrinkle in his dick, which had certainly snagged the attention of the crowd, was singing along with the band. Judging by the knowing and appreciative leers coming from a few of the musicians—the randy old coots—Reed suspected the young singer had been hired not just for his ability to sing on key, but for other talents as well. Spit-shining the old guys' skin flutes, maybe.

If Reed hadn't been so surprised by Carol dragging him through the crowd like a tow truck, he would have snickered at that thought.

At the edge of the lawn, far enough away from the band and the raucous crowd for them to hear themselves speak, Carol turned and offered Reed a smile. It was the first honest smile he'd received from her in months.

"You look handsome," she said as her fingers came up to straighten his tie, then pat it in place.

"You look handsome too," Reed answered. It was an old joke between the two, and they both dutifully laughed. Reed's laughter didn't last very long. "What are you doing here, Carol?"

While Reed's smile faded away, Carol's didn't budge an inch. "It's obvious, isn't it? Arthur hired me to cater his wedding. He also told me if the marriage didn't work out, he would hire me to cater his divorce. I assumed he was joking. But with Arthur you can never be sure."

"He was joking," Reed said. "He and Tom love each other very much."

Carol nodded fondly. "I know."

"So you've seen them together?"

"Yes."

Reed swung his arms wide to encompass the whole wedding party stretching from the edge of the canyon to the walls of the Belladonna Arms higher up the hill, where the battered old structure stood gleaming in the sunlight, warts and all. "So all this doesn't shock you anymore?"

The guests were getting more boisterous now. The bartenders had done their job well. In fact, Reed thought, if they didn't start watering down the drinks, the crowd would soon be stripping off their clothes and screwing in the salmon bisque.

Carol stared out over the crowd. "You mean the gayness of it all? No, it doesn't bother me, Reed. And as for Arthur. He's the sweetest man I've ever met." She allowed herself a wider smile. "You just have to get past the glitter and feathers and rhinestones to see it."

Reed matched her grin. "So you don't hate him anymore."

Carol blushed. "No. I don't hate him anymore. Although his sense of style leaves me a bit squeamish. I also have to admit your gayness appears fairly bland compared to his. Are you really sure you belong with this crowd?"

Reed blushed. She was joking, and he knew it. He also knew it was the first time she had even *remotely* joked about him being gay, and that surprised him. "Thanks. And yeah. I'm pretty sure. Do you really love Arthur as much as you sound like you do?"

"I really do. His kindness is as big as he is."

She smiled sweetly, and Reed matched her smile with one of his own. "I doubt you'll find anybody here to disagree with you on that." He reached over and flicked a piece of lint from the front of Carol's dress. His face grew instantly somber. "How are you feeling? It's good to see you happy again."

Carol let her gaze skip away for a second. She gave an embarrassed shrug but quickly pulled herself together again. Squaring her shoulders, she announced, "Now that I'm working, I feel great. Arthur has promised to spread my name around for other catering jobs. Thanks to him I've already booked another wedding and an anniversary fete for a wealthy family in La Jolla. Very swank. Arthur has a lot of friends, you know."

"He does indeed."

"He also taught me a lot about catering big affairs. Turning me on to the best rental deals for equipment, the best places to hire staff, the simplest way to bake perfect Toll House cookies."

Reed laughed. "I'm sure Arthur learned the cookie thing from Sylvia. She's the cookie queen of the Belladonna Arms."

Carol giggled. "I know. He told me. She's also very pretty. I met her earlier. Hard to believe she was once a man. The kid is a terror, though."

Reed groaned. "I babysat him one night. I still haven't recovered. Neither has my rhododendron."

They shared a laugh, and as quickly as the laughter came, their conversation quieted. They stared out over the crowd. There seemed to be very few sober faces now. Reed glanced at his watch. It wouldn't be long before the wedding began. He wondered if Arthur was a nervous wreck and hoped he'd managed to get all the road tar off his head before he had to don that bigass white wedding gown of his. He also wondered how awkward it would be standing with Gideon through the ceremony and then kissing him at the end. The very thought of it brought color to his cheeks.

Reed gazed off toward the south end of the lawn and spotted Gideon standing there all alone, staring out at the city skyline in the distance. Reed only tore his eyes away when Carol began to speak.

She laid gentle fingers to the fire on his cheeks. She spoke softly, as if to a child. "Arthur taught me other things too. So did Sylvia."

"Sylvia?"

"Yes. Did you know she tried to kill herself once?"

"Sylvia? But she's always so happy."

Carol's cheeks colored. "That's one of the things she taught me. That the happiness always returns. She also told me we're sisters now, her and I." She blushed brighter. "I've always wanted a sister."

Reed smiled at the tender look on her face. "And what did Arthur teach you?"

"To stand up for myself."

"Oh."

Reed gazed down when her fingers slipped from his face and gently circled his wrist. He lifted his head and his eyes skidded over her shoulder to Gideon once again, standing so forlornly at the edge of the lawn, his white tuxedo gleaming in the morning sun, his hair as red as flames atop his head.

Reed knew at that very moment what the momentous decision he had been worrying about earlier really was. It came to him all of a sudden, without warning. Without doubt.

He turned his eyes back to Carol. The words came without an ounce of forethought. And the moment he uttered them, he knew they were exactly right.

"I can't do it," he said. "I can't let you take me back."

They stared at each other. To Reed's amazement, Carol smiled. "I know."

Reed blinked in surprise. "You do?"

"Yes, Reed. I do. I've… I've been lonely without you, but even so, I know I made a mistake when I pleaded with you to come back. You finally found the courage to admit a great truth in your life. I can't let myself stand in the way of you exploring who you were meant to be. I didn't understand it at first, but after spending time with Arthur, I think I'm beginning to."

To his surprise, she turned to gaze out in the same direction Reed had been staring. He watched as her eyes fell on Gideon, standing at the edge of the canyon, his shoulders slumped, one hand buried deep in his trousers pocket. She looked back at Reed and rose on tiptoe to place a kiss on his cheek. Carol rested her head on Reed's chest as her gaze swiveled once again to Gideon in the distance.

"There's a boy over there who loves you, Reed. And I think maybe you love him too."

Reed swallowed a lump in his throat. He wrapped his arms around Carol, pulling her closer, but not once did either of their eyes leave Gideon.

"I do love him, Carol. I love him more than I've ever loved anyone in my life."

Carol slipped from Reed's arms and gazed up into his face. Her eyes, moistened by tears, sparkled in the sunlight. She slid her thumb playfully across his chin like she used to do, back when times were better.

"Then go to him," she whispered. "Go to him now. I think maybe I've kept you two apart long enough."

Reed's heart leaped inside him. His knees almost buckled as his pulse suddenly went crazy, pounding inside his head. He could actually feel the longing spilling from him as he stared out at Gideon. Wanting him so. *Craving* him so. It was a struggle to tear his eyes back to Carol. But he had to. She was giving him everything. The least he could do was acknowledge the gift.

His voice cracked when he said, "You'll be all right? You won't do anything… stupid?"

She donned a brave face. "No, Reed. I won't do anything stupid. I'll be fine. You found your boy, now maybe I can find mine." She poked him playfully in the chest. "Besides, I don't want to be married to a man who, when I stoop to having extramarital affairs because he never touches me, will be trying to steal my boyfriends away when I'm not looking."

"I suppose I might at that."

"You always were a slut."

Reed grinned. "I didn't think you knew."

Once again, Carol rose on tiptoe. She pressed her lips to his ear. "Go to him, Reed. Go to him now. He looks very sad over there all by himself. I think he needs you as much as you need him."

"G-God, I hope so," Reed stuttered. He slid his hand along the softness of her arm. "Thank you, Carol."

She nodded, her eyes no longer bright with tears. But caring. Understanding. "Go," she said again.

With a look of gratitude, Reed eased himself gently from Carol's embrace and headed slowly across the lawn on rubbery legs. The noisy party going on behind him was suddenly a distant murmur. He barely heard it. He could hear only his own pulse sluicing through his head, and his own heart hammering hopefully—terrifyingly—inside his chest.

"Good luck," Carol called softly behind him, and Reed's heart hammered all the louder.

GIDEON CAUGHT movement at the corner of his eye and turned just in time to see Reed stumble to a stop ten feet away. Behind Reed, off at the edge of the milling crowd, he spotted Carol watching them both.

With a sinking feeling, he turned back to Reed. He struggled to find his voice. "So you decided to come after all."

"I told you I would," Reed said.

"Yes," Gideon answered. "You said you'd come for Arthur."

Reed frowned. "That was a lie. I don't know why I said it."

"You didn't come for Arthur?"

"No."

Gideon's eyes slipped from Reed's face. Not sure where else to look, he gazed down at his own hands. "When I didn't see you, I thought maybe you'd changed your mind and stayed away."

Reed pointed back across the lawn. "I was hiding behind that tree."

Gideon tipped his head, his eyes slipping reluctantly to Reed's face. "Why were you hiding?"

Reed didn't answer.

Gideon clenched his fists at his side. He was suddenly either really mad or really confused. He couldn't decide which. Every muscle in his body seemed to be knotting up. He tried to backtrack in the conversation. "So fuck the tree, then. I still don't understand. If you didn't come for Arthur, why did you come?"

Reed took one step forward, then stumbled to a stop again, as if uncertain of his welcome. His fingers clutched his tie like a man dangling off a cliff by a rope. "I came for you," he said softly.

A silence settled between the two.

"Be careful with your tie," Gideon said. "You're getting it all wrinkled. It's gonna look like a goat chewed on it." His words sloughed away when he saw a tear slide down Reed's cheek. Then another. Reed's eyes were so bright, so *hurt*, Gideon couldn't tear his own eyes away from their pain.

"Why are you crying?" Gideon stammered. Then, "Wait. Did you say you came for me?"

Reed nodded, jarring another tear loose. "I'm so sorry, Gideon. I've screwed everything up."

If Reed expected Gideon to placate him, he was about to be sorely disappointed. Gideon was in no mood to placate. Not one little bit. "Yes. You did," Gideon said, his words icy. Accusing. "And you broke my heart in the process."

Reed rushed forward so unexpectedly, Gideon took a step back. Still, Reed stopped two feet away, apparently not quite brave enough to close the gap completely. This close, Gideon could see a new fall of tears moistening Reed's cheeks. Reed bent and set his cocktail glass in the grass to free his hands. Standing straight again, he stared deep into Gideon's eyes. Reed's words were so quietly uttered they barely traveled the distance between them. Gideon had to lean forward to hear.

"Yours wasn't the only heart I broke," Reed said.

Gideon's gaze slid from Reed's face and settled on the woman watching them. She looked pretty standing there in the sunlight, the skirt of her dress billowing about her trim legs in the wind whipping up the canyon wall. She seemed so attentive to what was happening between Reed and himself, Gideon couldn't quite bring himself to hate her.

"What about Carol?" he asked.

Reed glanced back at Carol, but only for a second. His gaze quickly returned to Gideon. "She doesn't need me anymore."

"Since when?"

"Since today."

"Then why is she here?"

A trace of a smile twisted Reed's mouth. "Arthur hired her to cater the wedding."

"Well, that's awkward." Gideon had been shooting for funny, but somehow it didn't come out funny. It came out making him sound more confused than he already was. He wiped his hand through the air like clearing a blackboard. "But when you said mine wasn't the only heart you broke, you meant Carol's, right?"

"No, Gideon. I meant my own."

Gideon's hands fell to his sides. "Oh."

At long last, Gideon watched Reed take the final two steps toward him. When Gideon didn't draw away, Reed reached out and plucked the cocktail glass from Gideon's hand. In the same motion, with his eyes never leaving Gideon's face, Reed slung the glass into the canyon where they heard it smash against the rocks thirty feel below.

"Your wife will have to pay for that," Gideon said.

"Fuck her," Reed answered.

This time it was Gideon's mouth that almost twisted into a smile. "I hope not. Fucking her is how you got yourself in so much trouble to begin with."

With Gideon's hands now free, Reed edged closer and slipped his own hands around them. At Reed's touch, their first real touch in days, a flood of memories washed over Gideon—beautiful memories.

He squeezed his eyes shut, trying to keep them out. Those memories had tortured him enough. More than enough.

"I—I'd almost forgotten the way your hands feel," he breathed in spite of himself, his eyes still tightly closed.

"Have you forgotten this?" Reed asked in the same breathless voice, and just as Gideon opened his eyes, Reed leaned forward and laid his lips to Gideon's mouth.

This time Gideon did pull back. He tore himself free, anger flashing across his face. He could feel it there, the anger, like two spots of fire burning on his cheeks. And he could see Reed's instant reaction to it. The muscles in his jaws clenched, he seemed to pull in upon himself. Reed's mouth became a tight slit, and once again tears rose in his eyes.

"Baby," Reed pleaded, his voice tight with emotion.

Gideon turned to flee, but Reed grabbed him by the arm. He wasn't gentle. He tugged Gideon back into his arms, trapping him in an embrace Gideon didn't see coming.

Suddenly so tired he could barely stand up, Gideon dropped his head to Reed's chest and muttered words into Reed's snow-white tux. "I can't do this anymore, Reed. I don't have it in me. Let me go. Please."

But Reed did not let him go. In fact, Reed's arms tightened around him, trapping him more securely in a desperate embrace. Gideon could hear—and almost feel—Reed's heart thudding in his ear. When Reed's fingertips brushed the nape of Gideon's neck, resting there, capturing him, holding him close, Gideon finally let the tears spill from his eyes.

"I love you so much," Reed whispered, his lips in Gideon's hair. "I'm so sorry I hurt you."

Gideon struggled to breathe. He was afraid to open his eyes, so he pressed his face against Reed's chest, burying it there, hiding in the darkness behind his eyelids. But even with his eyes squeezed shut, Reed's sweet scent tore through him, recalling a thousand memories, a million moments. Their past. What they had been building toward. And how it had all so suddenly come crashing down around them because of Reed's selfishness. Or maybe Reed's goodness in wanting to protect his ex-wife. Gideon still didn't understand how he truly felt about it all. Or whom he blamed.

But he understood what it had done to him. He understood that perfectly well.

He gathered enough strength to push himself from Reed's arms. He stepped back, furiously wiping the tears from his eyes, straightening the front of his tux and the orchid on his lapel. When he had pulled himself halfway together, he once again stared over Reed's shoulder to the woman watching them from a distance. He thought he saw a smile on her face—a smile directed at *him*—but he wasn't sure.

Returning his gaze to Reed, he said, "I'm telling myself I should make this harder for you."

"Please don't. It's hard enough already."

"How do I know you won't take her back again?"

As if knowing where Gideon's eyes had traveled—knowing and understanding why they had—Reed spoke softly, his words a caress that touched Gideon's heart. "She's all right now, Gideon. She doesn't need me anymore. She's letting me go."

They were words Gideon desperately wanted to believe. Still watching Carol, Gideon saw her lift her hand as her eyes burrowed into his own. A bashful greeting. A blessing, maybe. And before Gideon could react, before Gideon could do a thing, Carol turned and walked away. Gideon watched until she disappeared in the crowd. Only then did he lift his eyes to Reed still standing eagerly before him.

"She's really letting you go?" Gideon asked.

Reed nodded. "We even have her blessing."

"And she won't hurt herself anymore?"

"No. She won't hurt herself anymore." Reed took a deep breath, as if steeling his nerves. "But it's not Carol I'm worried about now. It's you. I'm so sorry I hurt you the way I did. I never should have done that."

Gideon tried not to pout. To fight it, he looked stern instead. "No, Reed. You shouldn't have."

"Can you ever forgive me?"

Reed's eyes began to fill with tears again. Gideon stood speechless, watching them. He found himself even more speechless when, without warning, Reed lowered himself to his knees before him.

Gazing up into Gideon's face through flooded eyes, Reed took his hands. He kissed first one palm, then the other. Closing his streaming eyes and resting his forehead against Gideon's stomach, Reed whispered, "Please, Gideon. Take me back. I promised you once I'd never hurt you, and I broke that promise. I'm so sorry. This time the promise will hold. I swear it will. This time I will truly never hurt you again. Please trust me enough to let me prove it to you."

Gideon's fingers slid through Reed's sun-warmed hair. A shudder trammeled through him at the feel of it in his hands. The shudder was so intense, for a second Gideon thought it was another earthquake.

"Do you really still love me?" Gideon quietly asked. For the first time in a long while he heard hope in his own voice. He felt happiness returning to his poor shattered heart. His hands were shaking with the wonder of what was happening.

Reed nodded against Gideon's belly. His broad strong hands clutched Gideon's back, keeping him close, holding him near. "I never stopped loving you," he gasped, fighting back a sob. "I never stopped for a minute."

Gideon's tears were falling freely now. He tugged at Reed, trying to pull him to his feet. "Get up. Did you ever try to get grass stains out of a white tuxedo?"

Still kneeling, Reed gazed up at him, his eyes red, his face smeared with tears. "Please be my lover again. Please, Gideon. Please take me back."

Gideon laid his hands to Reed's cheeks. He brushed his thumbs over the lips he remembered so well. When Reed kissed each one as it slid past, Gideon almost smiled.

His voice was nearly gone, but Gideon managed to nod. Once. Then he muttered, "All right."

And with that, Gideon finally succeeded in yanking Reed to his feet. They fell into each other's arms, and their lips came together as if homing in on invisible beacons.

Before Gideon could really settle into the kiss, before he could actually come to terms with what had just happened, he stiffened in Reed's arms.

He glanced at his wristwatch over Reed's shoulder. "Oh no. It's time."

A second later, the band nipped Billy Joel in the bud and instantly struck up the dulcet tones of the old Joe Cocker song "You Are So Beautiful," rendered by two trombones, a fiddle, one keyboard, an annoying set of drums, a guitar that could have used tuning, two clarinets, and a singer in skintight pants.

"Holy crap!" Gideon and Reed cried in unison. "That's the prelude to the 'Wedding March.' It's starting. We're supposed to be with Arthur!"

Gideon gasped. "He's going to kill us!"

Still dripping with tears and snot and with grass stains on Reed's poor knees and his tie wrinkled, but laughing too, since they were so damned happy, they took off running hand in hand across the lawn.

Chapter 16

CLOMPING ACROSS the Belladonna Arms's front porch, Reed, with Gideon in tow, crashed through the front door into the lobby. There they found Arthur encased in his humongous wedding gown, Tom in full wedding regalia as well, ten young men in white tuxedos, a few assorted flunkies, about a dozen cats, and one of the bartenders from out on the lawn who had somehow lost his clothes and was now clad in nothing but a snow-white top hat and a jockstrap. He was cradling a wicker basket of posies.

Arthur saw them staring at the damn near naked bartender. "What? He's a flower boy now," he explained. "I realized suddenly we didn't have one."

"But why doesn't he have any clothes on?" Gideon asked. "Not that I'm complaining."

Reed elbowed him in the ribs, making him grunt.

Arthur studied the almost naked flower boy as if these questions had never occurred to him before. "Because that's the way I found him."

"But wasn't he a bartender?"

Arthur's mouth turned down. He considered the question with a disappointed expression on his face. "Yes. Yes, he was. In hindsight it might have been a mistake to open the complimentary bar so early. It doesn't say much for his work ethic either, does it? Or his morals. Being a bartender. Drinking up all the booze. Ending up without his clothes." He turned his eyes back to the young man in question. Seemingly oblivious to all the attention, the mostly naked bartender hiccuped, then sniffed at the basket of flowers dangling from one hand, while with his other hand he adjusted his dick inside the jockstrap. It seemed to be a healthy specimen. The bulge was considerable.

Arthur sighed like a man on a hunger strike staring at a tray of donuts. He guiltily glanced at Tom glowering his way and made a big show of clearing his throat. He brushed back the crisp white veil, which hung around his head like a great cumulous cloud, and took a closer look at Gideon and Reed standing there hand in hand in front of him.

Quite possibly hoping to change the subject, he fussed, "You two! Why are your tuxedos such a mess? And you!" he railed, nailing Reed with a glare. "Why does your tie look like a goat chewed on it?"

"Told ya," Gideon whispered, snuggling closer to Reed and shrinking under Arthur's malevolent scowl.

Arthur ignored the interruption. He kept staring at Reed, growing unhappier by the minute. "What in heaven's name have you been doing? Why are your knees green? Why are your eyes red? Why do your lips look puffy? Why is your hair standing on end?" He stomped his foot somewhere down under the mass of white fabric billowing out around him, shaking the building and jarring a few more leaves loose from the plastic ficus in the corner. His anger suddenly encompassed the entire lobby and pretty much all of the western seaboard. "And why are you both so *late*?"

Reed hooked Gideon's arm and dragged him close. He tried not to gloat, but he was so happy it was impossible not to. "Because we just made up. Gideon and I are lovers again. And my, you look lovely, Arthur. Simply lovely. I've never seen a lovelier bride than you. Ever."

A blush rose to Arthur's cheeks as he batted his lashes and cast a virginal glance down at his feet, which were presumably shuffling bashfully somewhere under a mountain of petticoats and white tulle. "Oh gosh, honey. Do you really think so?"

Reed smiled maniacally, like the sleaziest sycophant in the world, even though, to be truthful, he thought Arthur looked a little like a toad swelled up after sitting in a bucket of water overnight, then stuck upright in a humongous mound of Marshmallow Fluff.

Eyes narrowed as if he was about to start yelling again, Arthur froze as Reed's words seemed to suddenly sink in. His eyes popped open wide and slid from Reed to Gideon, then back again. "Did you say you're back together?"

Arthur's big round face softened behind the layers and layers of pancake, rouge, lipstick, glitter, three-inch-long sequined eyelashes, and a disposable Gloria Swanson mole, which he had glued to his right cheek. Tears welled up, and two of his three chins puckered accordingly. He patted his bosom, which was even more voluptuous than usual, and before anybody could breathe a sigh of relief that Arthur was no longer teetering on the brink of a massive snit, he reached out and dragged Gideon and Reed into a bone-crushing hug. He hoisted them off the floor and squeezed them until they didn't have an ounce of oxygen left in them. When their lungs had completely collapsed, he set them back on their feet like a couple of deflated balloon animals, limp and lifeless, barely able to stand.

"Are you *really* back together?" Arthur asked, eyeing them suspiciously. "Or are you just trying to weasel me out of being mad at you?"

To answer the first question, Gideon and Reed nodded their heads up and down like those little dolls with the springy necks that bob around in the back windows of cars. Then they shook their heads sideways to answer the second question.

"Honest?" Arthur asked, still looking skeptical.

Gideon and Reed nodded and bobbed some more.

"And you're really together again? I mean, for good this time?"

"We really are."

"Truly?"

"Truly."

Satisfied, Arthur turned to Tom, suddenly all business. "You owe me twenty bucks."

Tom, who was decked out in a baby-blue tux, the biggest splash of color in the wedding party, rolled his eyes, then dutifully pulled twenty bucks from his wallet and handed it over. Arthur snatched the twenty-dollar bill out of Tom's hand and stuffed it down between his tits, where Reed suspected it would never be seen again. That out of the way, Arthur snatched Gideon and Reed back into his arms, catching them by surprise, and whispered in their ears. "I *told* Tom hiring Carol would get you two lovebirds back together. But nooooo, he didn't believe me, so we made a little wager. Now I'm twenty bucks richer. That'll teach him to try to outsmart Arthur Moss when it comes to matters of love or money. Of course, after today I'll own half his deli too. God, I love community property. A queen's best friend, don't you know. But then Tom comes out ahead too. He gets half of the Arms and the benefit of all the tricks of the marriage bed I plan on sharing with my honey over the next thirty years. And trust me, sweeties, I've got some whoppers." Arthur shot them an obscene wink.

Reed tried not to cringe. Gideon looked intrigued. Tom just shook his head and stared at his watch.

For the first time, Arthur appeared to notice the dozen or more cats milling around behind him.

"What's with all the cats?" he screamed. "Why are they here?"

Tom looked guilty. "You dragged the tail end of your dress through a dish of cat food when you were coming out of the apartment. I guess they still smell it on you."

"Well shoo them away!" Arthur screamed again. "Call the pest control man! Get a gun! Set some traps!"

Tom looked uncertain. "Uh, sure, honey. I'll get right on it." He bent over and flicked his fingers, trying to steer the herd of cats up the stairs with little or no success. The cats were so enamored of Arthur's tuna-smelling train, they couldn't be budged.

Arthur, trusting Tom to handle the problem, smacked his hands together like a gunshot, and everybody in the lobby jumped. He started spouting orders like a longshoreman. "Wedding party, line up ahead of me! Two by two, just like we practiced! Now, dammit! Let's get this show on the road!"

A dozen boysmaids in white tuxedos scattered hastily to pair up and find their proper places, bumping into each other like Keystone Kops, giggling, muttering congratulations to Gideon and Reed, simpering in their spiffy outfits, wishing they had another drink, and surreptitiously eying the flower boy, who still had his hand down his jockey strap.

"Tom!" Arthur barked. "Why are you messing with those cats? And what the hell are you doing here anyway? You're not supposed to see the bride before the wedding! Get out of here! You should be waiting at the altar!" Poor Tom whooped once in terror, then scurried out the door like an abused puppy.

"You there!" Arthur screeched after reassuring himself everyone was in their proper position. "Signal the musicians!"

Reed watched as the peon who had apparently been assigned this task, scuttled out onto the front porch and shot a thumbs-up to the old guys parked on the gazebo, instruments in hand. Half of them were ogling the singer with the tight pants, who was still immersed in a spirited version of "You Are So Beautiful." Strangely, he sounded exactly like Ethel Merman on crystal meth channeling Lady Gaga on psychedelic mushrooms. Reed suspected that, like the flower boy and most of the guests, the singer had taken full advantage of the open bar. Still, he took the hint when the signal was given and stepped aside to let the band take over. The "Wedding March" swelled out over the crowd, and all heads turned expectantly, awaiting the entrance of the bride.

Hearing his cue, Arthur fluffed his gown around him, shook out his massive veil until it settled softly over his face like a curtain of snow, then adjusted his tits one more time.

"Bouquet!" he suddenly bellowed, making everybody jump *again*.

Some unnamed flunky groveled up to him with the bride's bouquet, apologizing profusely.

Arthur snatched it out of his hand, and screamed, "Flower Boy! *You* there, with the big dick! You go first! Stop playing with yourself and don't forget to strew the daisies! Lightly! Lightly! You're not chucking cantaloupes!"

The mostly naked flower boy shot off a salute, straightened his top hat, gave his dick a final adjustment, and took off at a snail's pace through the front door and down the red carpet, sprinkling daisies in his wake and cleaving a path for the procession through three hundred drunken, ogling wedding guests.

Reed and Gideon were the last of the twelve bridesboys, so consequently they would stroll the red carpet behind the other ten and directly ahead of the bride. They clutched hands and tried to ignore Arthur mumbling and sniffling and sobbing with joy behind them.

Arthur and his many attendants slow-marched down the red carpet through the gaping hordes. Each and every one of the guests was sucking on a cocktail and looking cheerfully bleary-eyed. By the time Gideon and Reed reached any particular spot in the processional, they would find the applause just beginning to dissipate from the enthusiastic greeting the mostly naked flower boy had received when he and his dick strolled along scattering daisies ahead of them.

"I'm so happy for you boys!" Arthur hissed from behind.

Gideon and Reed both wheeled and lit up with smiles in return.

Reed hissed back, "Thanks for hiring my ex and getting her business up and running. Now she doesn't need me anymore. She even gave us her blessing! You had that planned, didn't you?"

Arthur blushed beneath his veil. "Of course I had it planned. Nobody understands love like your Auntie Arthur. And honey, just so you know. She never *did* need you." He peeked out from under his veil, laying gentle eyes on Gideon's beaming face. "But I knew someone who did."

At that, it was Gideon's turn to blush.

"Thank you, Arthur," Gideon and Reed muttered in unison, and turning back, they tried to compose themselves, get back in step with the rest of the boysmaids, and do Arthur right on this very special day. They owed him a lot, after all. Hell, Reed thought, they owed him everything.

Once again facing forward and soft-stepping along the wedding route to the tempo of the music, nodding now and then to a familiar face in the crowd, Reed took a beat to lean in and whisper for Gideon's ears alone. "I love you so much."

He was rewarded by Gideon's fingers tightening their hold on his hand. Peeking sideways, Reed saw a tear sliding down Gideon's freckled cheek. Reed reached over gently and brushed it away.

With the mostly naked flower boy out of their line of sight, the crowd began making appreciative murmurings at their first sight of the bride. Arthur's gown was truly a wonder. It poufed out around him for yards in every direction. The snow-white train, aglitter with sequins, dragged along behind him for twenty feet. The opaque veil, billowing about his head in the afternoon breeze, trailed along even farther. Luckily the veil was clamped securely to Arthur's head with a band of stainless steel, rather like one of those claw machines at the arcade clutching the head of a teddy bear it had snagged from a pile of prizes.

Gleaming white in the sunlight, Arthur resembled nothing less than a magnificent glacier gliding majestically across the lawn.

Scampering along in his wake came the cats. More than a dozen of them. Meowing and purring and sniffing excitedly at Arthur's train. Occasionally a cat or two would pounce directly onto the end of the veil and Arthur's head would jerk backward, his momentum momentarily stymied. But soon the cat would leap off, and Arthur would pull himself together and proceed relentlessly down the red carpet, as unstoppable as time.

Still, the cats were a great hit. Comments began to skitter through the crowd. "Oh my, would you look at that?" "However did he train them to follow along like that?" "What a lovely addition to the wedding. Pussycats! How cute!"

Reed snickered to himself while Gideon pointed to the singer on the gazebo bandstand, over by the lip of the canyon, who had the microphone up to his lips and was now humming along to the "Wedding March." He was clearly so caught up in the romance of the moment, he had all but fallen apart with emotion. Tears were streaming down his face. Not to mention the fact that he showed a rather impressive boner poking down the front of his tight white pant leg. Reed suspected he either really liked the song, or he had popped a couple of Viagras between cocktails.

In the crowd, Reed spotted Pete and Sylvia. Pete was beaming happily, a broad handsome smile plastered to his face. Reed quickly figured out why. The baby was nowhere in sight. And since little Artie wasn't hanging off Pete's chest, kicking like a mule, Pete's nuts weren't being pulverized. It was enough to make *any* man happy.

Looking beautiful in her shimmering silver gown, Sylvia stood proudly at Pete's side, blowing them both a kiss. Reed shot her a wink in return while Gideon gave her a merry finger-waggle of greeting. By the pure bliss registering on Sylvia's face, Reed knew she was aware that he and Gideon were back together. He fully expected to find bags of celebratory Toll House cookies on their doorknobs before the day was through.

Arthur sucked in air behind them like a bellows. "Oh my God!" he cried. "Look how handsome he is!"

Reed stared up ahead to where Arthur was pointing, and sure enough, there was Tom in his baby-blue tuxedo that matched the spray of forget-me-nots in Arthur's hands. Tom stood tall and proud, watching with love-filled eyes as his bride approached. He wore a heart-stopping smile on his face that made him the sexiest man present. Reed had to admit Tom was the handsomest groom he had ever seen.

Reed squeezed Gideon's hand and they edged closer to each other. Their hands still clasped, Gideon leaned in and rested his head on Reed's shoulder as they strolled along. Reed's heart swelled up like a puffer fish when Gideon breathed a romantic sigh.

Beside Tom, standing beneath the arch of the altar, stood the preacher. He had a sickly expression on his face like he'd eaten a rotten pistachio nut. He seemed to be inordinately confused by the herd of cats trailing along behind the bride, as if wondering why, since they were clearly now part of the ceremony, they hadn't shown up for the rehearsal. Reed suspected the half-naked flower boy hadn't calmed the preacher down much either.

Reaching the altar, the twelve bridesboys peeled off to either side of the red carpet. They stood hand in hand with their partners, which was only proper since they were all lovers anyway. Lester and Dan. Roger and Stanley. Charlie and Bruce. (Bruce had foresworn his cowboy hat for the occasion.) Barney and Ramon (whose pink hair caught the sunlight like a wad of cotton candy.) Shiloh and Ben.

And last but not least, Gideon and Reed.

Reed shot a wink at Shiloh when he saw him patting his heart at the sight of Reed and Gideon standing so happily side by side.

"Are you two together again?" Shiloh whispered over the music and the caterwauling of the cats and the wheezing and sniffling of Arthur, awash in happy tears.

Gideon and Reed both sang out, "Yes." Then quickly hushed themselves because the sobbing bride was now stepping up to the altar. Her six hundred yards of taffeta, or whatever the hell it was, mushroomed out around her in great, rolling folds of white. Reed half-expected to see a pod of dolphins breaching in the spume.

Suddenly standing face-to-face with the biggest drag queen *ever*, the preacher dropped his Bible. He snatched it off the ground, cleared his throat for an interminable length of time like he was trying to cough up a sock, and finally gave the bride a nervous smile.

"Dearly beloved…," he began in a shaky voice. "We are gathered here in the sight of God and… and…." Here he slid his glasses to the end of his nose and gazed out across the crowd to survey all the drunken wedding guests and the assorted drag queens and the nearly naked flower boy and the wedding singer with the boner, and finally finished up with a mesmerized "And *others*."

After that, the reverend seemed to find his footing. Clearly a man who liked to hear himself talk, he assumed a pious manner that didn't fool anybody. He yammered on and on, looking more sanctimonious as time rolled by. By now more cats had joined the throng, mewing and yowling and sniffing at Arthur's train while Arthur hissed under his breath for them to "Beat it! Scat! Shoo!"

Reed had leaned down to lay his mouth to Gideon's ear and was whispering to him all the things he would do to Gideon's naked body the minute they got upstairs to the apartment. Gideon giggled and blushed and laid his hands across his crotch trying to hide the fact that he was suddenly in the same state of arousal as the wedding singer on the stage.

A sudden jarring of the earth beneath their feet made everyone freeze, including the preacher and the cats. Silence fell over the crowd until Arthur squealed, "Eek!" That seemed to break the spell. Three hundred heads swiveled one way or another, each of them trying to gauge what the seismic gods had in store for them this time. But apparently the gods were feeling benevolent today. The teeny earthquake quieted as quickly as it came. The ground settled to stillness beneath their feet. Three hundred inebriated souls breathed a sigh of relief, and the cats began pawing at Arthur's train, once again delirious with the smell of tuna.

Coughing up another sock, or quite possibly a boot this time, the preacher finally snagged the raveling end of whatever he had been trying to say before and recommenced his pious jabbering. It took him about a week, but he finally got to the good stuff. The "I dos."

"Thomas Allen Berger, do you take Arthur Remus Moss to be your lawfully wedded partner?"

A few scattered heads in the crowd turned to their neighbors and snickered, "Remus? Did he say *Remus*?" Meanwhile Tom, standing straight and tall before the altar, blushed very sweetly and said, "I do indeed, sir. Proudly."

Reed and Gideon grinned when they heard Arthur pat his bosom and gasp under his breath, "Oh my!"

The preacher stared at Tom as if to say, "Are you crazy?" but he quickly pulled himself together and faced Arthur instead. "Arthur Remus Moss, do you take Thomas Allen Berger to be your lawfully wedded partner?"

"Try to stop me!" Arthur bellowed, startling the preacher so that he dropped his Bible again and almost fell over backward. Flinging his veil over his head, Arthur snatched Tom off the altar and dragged him into his arms.

The preacher sputtered in surprise, "Uh, I guess you can kiss the bride."

"No shit," Tom cried, his diction rather marred by the fact that Arthur's tongue was already down his throat.

Reed leaned in to Gideon and said, "We're supposed to be kissing too!"

"Oh yeah!" Gideon giggled and flung himself into Reed's arms. They were followed quickly by the other ten boysmaids who suddenly realized this was their cue to kiss as well. The flower boy in his jockstrap and top hat, apparently feeling left out, vaulted onto the gazebo stage and swept the wedding singer into his arms while the band struck up an up-tempo reprise of the "Wedding March." The flower boy's naked butt flashed for the crowd below, and the wedding singer's two hands laid claim to it without any hesitation at all.

A rousing cheer rose from the guests, and with Gideon in his arms, and their kiss going on and on and on, Reed peered over Gideon's shoulders to Carol standing at the steam tables, her hands cupped beneath her chin and tears streaming down her face. Watching Gideon. Watching Reed. Watching the bride and groom. Carol always was a sap for weddings.

When she saw Reed watching her back, she blew a tearful kiss his way. Reed raised his hand, briefly acknowledging the kiss, then closed his eyes and settled back into Gideon's arms. He had never been so happy in his life.

Mother Nature, apparently, was a little less pleased. In fact, she chose that moment to lodge a serious complaint.

The lawn beneath the kissing wedding party and the three hundred drunken wedding guests and the cats and the waiting staff and the band and the preacher and the caterer and a few passersby on the street who had stopped to watch the show—suddenly gave a tilt to the left. A *big* tilt.

The preacher jumped out of the way as Arthur and Tom fell sideways into the arch of plastic morning glories, instantly splintering the altar into kindling. Guests tumbled from their chairs. Cats scattered. The massive white pavilion swayed alarmingly. The mostly naked flower boy and the wedding singer with the boner were tipped from the gazebo stage, each screaming "Wooh-ooh-ooh-ooh!" like Goofy as they disappeared over the side of the canyon. An octet of aging musicians tumbled off the stage in the opposite direction and landed in the grass, their instruments flying everywhere, two pairs of false teeth and a hearing aid soared through the air along with them. A piccolo sailed in a magnificent arc across a score of heads and landed upright in the wedding cake like Excalibur impaled in stone. Needless to say, the music stopped.

Clinging to each other, Reed and Gideon managed to stay upright, while many around them didn't. There was laughter, whoops of terror, and considerable cursing going on as people crashed into each other and tipped over backward off their chairs. Many managed to keep their drinks from spilling even while they themselves were being flung back and forth like ragdolls and doing somersaults across the lawn. This showed considerable dexterity and also came in handy, since the drinks were sorely needed immediately after.

The earth gave a second jolt and the limbs of the tall eucalyptus trees at the corners of the Belladonna Arms thrashed across the sky. Arthur and Tom, who had reclaimed their feet after the first spill, were now knocked down again. They rolled across the already shattered altar, this time bowling over the preacher, who went flying out onto the grass as if shot from a cannon. Tom was buried instantly in the folds of Arthur's gown as if swallowed by an avalanche. With his heels in the air and his billowing skirts up around his ears, Arthur tried to untangle himself from the mass of morning glories. He let out an earsplitting scream of terror when Tom landed on him with an "*Oomph!*"

A long arm in a baby-blue sleeve with a very attractive cuff link at the wrist slipped free of the mountain of taffeta and patted Arthur's chubby cheek. Still buried in mounds of fabric, Tom's heavenly baritone muttered soothing words while the mayhem continued on around them.

"Don't be afraid, Mrs. Berger. You're safe with me."

Arthur's head popped out of a satin snowdrift and his mouth made a perfect O as he slapped his hands to his cheeks and flapped the tears from his eyes with his three-inch-long sequined eyelashes.

"Oh, Tommy," he cooed above the caterwauling crowd, "You called me Mrs. Berger!"

Digging desperately through the folds and clumps and sweeping drifts of his voluminous wedding gown, Arthur tried to unearth the missing parts of his groom. When he finally found them all and was pleased to see they were still connected, he plucked Tom in his entirety from the rolling waves of snowy fabric. Arthur gathered his groom into his arms and dragged Tom over him like a blanket. Two seconds later they were smooching in the rubble.

Gideon and Reed smiled down at them. And as quickly as it began, the earthquake stopped. Heads everywhere popped up to see what would happen next, but nothing did. The shaking had ended. Silence settled over the mess left behind. The earth lay still. Mother Nature went back to sleep.

Arthur broke Tom's kiss long enough to stick his head up like a gopher and peer across the crowd of wedding guests who were busily trying to pick themselves off the ground. He swiveled his head around, surveying the damage. His eyes landed first on the food.

"Thank God!" he cried. "The wedding cake's still standing!"

Arthur looked momentarily confused when one of the musicians plucked a piccolo out of the top tier of the cake, but since the cake didn't collapse, Arthur remained pleased.

He turned to Tom and asked innocently, "The wedding went pretty well, don't you think?"

"Slick as snot," Tom grinned. Most of his face was covered with Arthur's cherry-red lipstick. One of Arthur's glittery eyelashes was stuck to his chin and he had a plastic morning glory dangling over his left ear.

Tom shot his bride a wink and pulled him into his arms. Laughing like hyenas, they lost themselves in another kiss.

Reed gazed down at Gideon, still wrapped tightly in his arms. "Hi," he said softly.

Gideon snuggled closer, pressing his face to Reed's welcoming chest. "Hi back."

"Tell me you love me," Reed said.

Gideon didn't hesitate. "I love you."

"Lots?"

"Lots."

Reed tightened his embrace. Laying his lips to Gideon's hair, he breathed in Gideon's scent. As far as he was concerned, it was the best smell in the world. "I love you too," he whispered, his voice going all shuddery with emotion. "I love you more than anything else in the whole wide world." Then he lifted his head and with a surprised expression, said, "Holy cow. Would you look at that?"

Gideon turned to see what Reed was talking about, and there at the edge of the lawn beside the empty gazebo, they spotted the wedding singer. He was climbing up out of the canyon with twigs in his hair and a sappy, drunken grin on his face. His white pants were a mess, his shirt was torn, but on the plus side, his erection was gone. At the last moment, he turned and tugged the mostly naked flower boy out of the canyon as well.

They stood for a moment, inspecting the ruins before them. Then, as if deciding they had more important priorities to consider, they slipped back into each other's arms as if nothing had happened.

"That's the spirit," Reed said, eying them with pride. Just as quickly, he muttered, "My turn," and pulled Gideon into a kiss.

Beside them, Arthur and Tom giggled and cooed from somewhere deep inside the mountainous folds of Arthur's wedding gown. God knows what they were doing under there.

Clearly concerned by that very question, and also looking a bit bedraggled around the edges, the minister muttered, "Fuck it. I need a drink." Without further ado, he tossed his Bible aside and headed for the open bar, which by a massive stroke of good fortune, was still in operation.

Not surprisingly at all, a goodly number of wedding guests brushed the grass off their clothes and trailed merrily along behind him.

Epilogue

Two Weeks Later

AFTER THE 6.8 jolt that had surprised the hell out of Arthur's wedding guests, knocked a three-hundred-pound drag queen off her five-inch heels, and caused the bill for Arthur's open bar, which was already exorbitant, to soar even higher, the earth settled down for a while. Apparently the tectonic plates buried deep beneath the earth's crust had been relieved of enough pressure to offer Southern Californians at least a few years of peace and quiet.

Most of the shaking that ensued *after* the wedding was epicentered in either Reed's or Gideon's bed.

It was a Sunday morning. Both Gideon and Reed had the day off. They were lying naked in each other's arms in a puddle of sunlight with both Punkin and Hitler purring contentedly at their feet. The sweat was drying from their skin as a cool breeze wafted through the open window above their heads. Their heartbeats were hammering down to a slightly more sustainable rhythm after their recent orgasms, which were doozies. Somehow Gideon's and Reed's orgasms were *always* doozies.

Reed's breath was still coming in fits and starts. He could barely talk. "I should keep cardiac paddles on my nightstand."

Gideon spit up a giggle, then burrowed close to Reed's side, his nose in Reed's armpit. It was one of his favorite places to be. Reed knew this because Gideon had told him so a hundred times.

"You smell heavenly," Gideon muttered.

Reed's arms tightened around him, and Gideon sighed in bliss.

"I have news," Reed said softly, his voice still fragile from spent testosterone and the explosive expenditure of several thousand calories.

Gideon peeked up at his face. "Good news or bad news?"

"Good news."

Gideon twiddled the ginger swath of hair surrounding Reed's belly button. "Let's hear it, then."

"Arthur and Tom are coming back from their honeymoon in a couple of days."

Rather than simply twiddling the hair around Reed's belly button, Gideon slid down farther in the bed and pressed his lips to it instead. Much more fun. "We knew that already, didn't we?"

"Yes," Reed said, his broad hand holding Gideon's face against his stomach. Gideon loved it when he did that. "But there's more."

Gideon's tongue slid into Reed's navel. He was pretty sure he tasted come down in the fuzzy depths. He had no idea if it was his come or Reed's, and frankly he didn't much care. "So tell me," he said. "What is it?"

He joined his hands across Reed's belly now, interlocking his fingers and resting his chin on them so he could stare up at Reed's face.

"It's about the flower boy," Reed said with a teeny grin as he peered into Gideon's eyes. He slid a thumb along the gentle slope of Gideon's nose and smiled at Gideon's look of confusion.

"What flower boy? You mean the almost naked one at the wedding?"

"Yes. And the wedding singer with the boner."

Gideon slid his hands upward to cup Reed's furry pecs, and without his hands there to support his head, he rested it on Reed's belly instead. That was his plan all along, of course, because he loved the way Reed's belly hair tickled his chin.

"What about them, then," he asked. "The flower boy and the wedding singer. Don't tell me they're an item."

Reed's fingertip had abandoned Gideon's nose and was now dragging a tender swipe across Gideon's bottom lip, which looked red and puffy from recent activities.

"They're more than an item. They've fallen in love."

Gideon sighed. It was a happy sigh. A romantic sigh. "You mean like us?"

Reed's eyes warmed, just as Gideon knew they would. "Exactly like us," Reed smiled.

Gideon smiled right back. "That's lovely." Then in a dreamier voice, he said, "Love pollen."

"Yep. Love pollen. It's struck again. And there's more."

"There is?"

"Yes. They want to move into the Belladonna Arms."

Gideon's smile broadened. "That's lovely too. Imagine introducing your lover to people. Hi, this is Half-Naked Flower Boy. I met him tumbling down a cliff with a hard-on in an earthquake during a gay wedding."

Reed laughed. "There's *still* more. Do you want to hear it?"

Gideon dipped his tongue in Reed's belly button again. "I'm trembling with anticipation."

"Arthur doesn't have any vacancies."

Gideon's smile died on the spot. "Oh no. Poor guys. What are they going to do?"

Reed cleared his throat and fluffed up the pillow behind his head so he could get a better view of Gideon's face. "It's not what they're going to do. It's what we're going to do for them. I hope."

"Why? What are we going to do for them?"

"Move in together."

Gideon rose up on his elbows, his eyes as big as fried eggs. "What did you say?"

Reed sat up all the way, wiggled to the head of the bed, and pulled Gideon up along with him. He shifted Gideon around until Gideon was nestled comfortably against his chest and tucked neatly inside his arms. He pressed his mouth to Gideon's ear. "I said we're going to move in together and give them one of our apartments. What do you think?"

"What do I think?"

"Yes. What do you think?"

"Are we ready?"

Reed shrugged. "I know I am."

"You really want us to live together?"

"I do indeed."

"You're ready for that kind of commitment?"

"I've never been readier. I love you, Gideon."

Gideon's voice was breathless. He sounded a little stunned, like someone had just banged him on the head with a rock. "I love you too."

"Then live with me. Please. Our rent will be cut in half."

Gideon frowned. "That's not very romantic."

"I was kidding."

"Oh."

"Still, I'm not *averse* to paying less rent."

Gideon thought about it, but not for long. "Neither am I."

Silence reigned for about three seconds. "Is it legal?" Gideon asked.

"What? Paying less rent?"

Gideon's smile returned but it had a sarcastic little bend in it this time. "No. Is it legal for two redheaded guys to live together as lovers? You know how you never see a baby pigeon? Well, I've never seen two gingers living together as lovers."

"Then we'll be the first."

"You think?"

"No. I'm sure there are others. Now stop stalling. What's your answer?"

Gideon chewed on his lip, but not for long. "My answer's yes."

"Thanks heavens! That's what I already told him."

"Who? Arthur? You already told him yes?"

"Sure. Why not?"

"Well, you might have run it by me first."

"Why? I just did."

"Oh yeah." Gideon paused, then cast Reed a worried glance. "What is Carol going to say?"

"She's rooting for us 100 percent."

"Did she say that?"

"Yes. I already told her too."

"So basically I'm the last person you decided to mention it to."

"Pretty much. Although I haven't wired the governor yet."

"Wiseass."

Gideon's eyes began to mist. Reed thought that was a good sign. At least he hoped it was. He cleared his throat. "There's one more thing."

The misting stopped. "And what pray tell is that?"

"We have to be out by tomorrow."

"You're kidding." Gideon thought about this latest piece of news a little longer. Maybe *five* seconds. "Well, okay. I guess it's doable. Neither one of us has that much stuff. Say, what are their names? The flower boy and the wedding singer?"

Reed shrugged and nuzzled his lips into the tender spot behind Gideon's ear. That was one of *his* favorite places to be. "No idea. Does it matter?"

Still a little shell-shocked, Gideon nestled down against Reed's chest, listening quietly, as he always did, for the gentle thudding of Reed's heart. He stroked Reed's warm thigh, enjoying the way the blond hair there bristled against his palm.

"Reed?"

"Hmm?"

"Are you as happy as I am?"

"Happier."

Gideon tilted his face up for a kiss and Reed instantly obliged. Five minutes later the kiss had morphed into more energetic pursuits.

WITH THE humans at it again, how was a cat to sleep?

Punkin and Hitler, growling deep in their throats, leaped from the bed. Tails high, grumbling, they stalked from the room.

JOHN INMAN is a Lambda Literary Award finalist and the author of over thirty novels, everything from outrageous comedies to tales of ghosts and monsters and heart-stopping romances. He has been writing fiction since he was old enough to hold a pencil. He and his partner live in beautiful San Diego, California, and together, they share a passion for theater, books, hiking, and biking along the trails and canyons of San Diego or, if the mood strikes, simply kicking back with a beer and a movie.

John's advice for anyone who wishes to be a writer? "Set time aside to write every day and do it. Don't be afraid to share what you've written. Feedback is important. When a rejection slip comes in, just tear it up and try again. Keep mailing stuff out. Keep writing and rewriting and then rewrite one more time. Every minute of the struggle is worth it in the end, so don't give up. Ever. Remember that publishers are a lot like lovers. Sometimes you have to look a long time to find the one that's right for you."

Email: john492@att.net
Facebook: www.facebook.com/john.inman.79
Website: www.johninmanauthor.com

Serenading
Stanley

THE BELLADONNA ARMS
JOHN INMAN

A Belladonna Arms Novel

Welcome to the Belladonna Arms, a rundown little apartment building perched atop a hill in downtown San Diego, home to the city's lost and lovelorn. Shy archaeology student Stanley Sternbaum has just moved in and fills his time quietly observing his eccentric neighbors, avoiding his hellion mother, and trying his best to go unnoticed… which proves to be a problem when it comes to fellow tenant Roger Jane. Smitten, the hunky nurse with beautiful green eyes does everything in his power to woo Stanley, but Stanley has always lived a quiet life, too withdrawn from the world to take a chance on love. Especially with someone as beautiful as Roger Jane.

While Roger tries to batter down Stanley's defenses, Stanley turns to his new neighbors to learn about love: Ramon, who's not afraid to give his heart to the wrong man; Sylvia, the trans who just wants to be a woman, and the secret admirer who loves her just the way she is; Arthur, the aging drag queen who loves them all, expecting nothing in return—and Roger, who has been hurt once before but is still willing to risk his heart on Stanley, if Stanley will only look past his own insecurities and let him in.

www.dreamspinnerpress.com

Work In
Progress

JOHN INMAN

A Belladonna Arms Novel

Dumped by his lover, Harlie Rose ducks for cover in the Belladonna Arms, a seedy apartment building perched high on a hill in downtown San Diego. What he doesn't know is that the Belladonna Arms has a reputation for romance—and Harlie is about to become its next victim.

Finding a job at a deli up the street, Harlie meets Milan, a gorgeous but cranky baker. Unaware that Milan is suffering the effects of a broken heart just as Harlie is, the two men circle around each other, manning the barricades, both unwilling to open themselves up to love yet again.

But even the most stubborn heart can be conquered.

With his new friends to back him up—Sylvia, on the verge of her final surgery to become a woman, Arthur, the aging drag queen who is about to discover a romance of his own, and Stanley and Roger, the handsome young couple in 5C who lead by example, Harlie soon learns that at the Belladonna Arms, love is always just around the corner waiting to pounce. Whether you want it to or not.

But tragedy also drops in now and then.

www.dreamspinnerpress.com

Coming
Back

JOHN INMAN

A Belladonna Arms Novel

Barney Teegarden knows what it's like to be alone. He knows what it's like to have a romantic heart, yet no love in his life to unleash the romance on. With the help of a friend, he acquires a lease in a seedy apartment building perched high on a hill in downtown San Diego. The Belladonna Arms is not only filled with the quirkiest cast of characters imaginable, it is also famous for sprinkling love dust on even the loneliest of the lovelorn.

At the Arms, Barney finds friendship, acceptance, and an adopted family that lightens his lonely life. Hell, he even finds a cat. But still true love eludes him.

When his drag queen landlord, Arthur, takes it into his head to rescue a homeless former tenant, he enlists Barney's help. It is Barney who shows this lost soul how to trust again—and in return Barney discovers love for the first time in his life.

It's funny how even the hardest battles can be fought and won with laughter, hugs, friends, plus a little faith in the goodness of others. All it takes to begin the healing is the simple act of coming back.

www.dreamspinnerpress.com

Ben and Shiloh

THE BELLADONNA ARMS
JOHN INMAN

A Belladonna Arms Novel

Shiloh Smart is alone and looking for a fresh start. Convinced he's finished with love forever, he signs a lease at the Belladonna Arms, a tacky, run-down apartment building situated high on a hill in downtown San Diego.

Determined to turn his back on romance, Shiloh works hard at carving out a life for himself where love doesn't stand a chance and staying single is all that matters.

Then his drag queen landlord's nephew, Ben Moss, moves in. Thanks to a rumor Ben has heard since childhood of a fifty-year-old crime and a fortune in stolen money, he sets out to find the loot supposedly hidden decades ago in his uncle's apartment building.

The minute Ben spots a kilted Shiloh toddling off to work at the Scottish restaurant up the street where he waits tables, he falls hard and fast for the aloof young redhead. Even a hidden treasure can't compete in Ben's eyes with the beautiful waiter with the fiery copper hair.

But even while he diligently works to break down Shiloh's defenses, Ben doesn't give up his quest for buried treasure. Soon, as their friendship deepens, the two young men join forces in a search for the stolen cash.

As the treasure hunt gathers steam and all the tenants get involved, Ben and Shiloh come to realize the greatest treasure isn't buried in the Belladonna Arms at all. It's buried far deeper—in each other's hearts!

www.dreamspinnerpress.com

LAUGH
CRY
Repeat

JOHN INMAN

Wyeth Becker is a quiet man. Staid, serious, calm. A librarian. When he meets preschool teacher Deeze Long, he discovers joy for the first time in his life. With joy comes laughter, excitement, and a new way to look at the world through the eyes of the kindest, most loving man he has ever met.

When tragedy strikes and Deeze loses his joy, it is Wyeth who helps him find it again. It is Wyeth, the man who never truly understood happiness, who pays that gift back. Giving all he can of himself to the man who changed his life. Restoring in Deeze what he now so desperately needs.

But the road of their relationship doesn't end there. The joys and sorrows of life are never-ending. As they set out to weather the highs and lows together, Wyeth and Deeze hang on to the one thing that makes all the tears and laughter worthwhile.

Love.

For only through love can life be truly savored at all.

www.dreamspinnerpress.com